Lord Ballingto... nearby chair an... curve of his Steinway. ~~Positioning the~~ carefully on its gleaming surface he bends his Frannie across the instrument.

'Don't move,' he whispers in her ear. 'Don't *move*.' Taking hold of her camiknickers he pulls them to her knees. 'Half-mast, I think. Perfect.'

He stands well back, momentarily hypnotised by the view of his wife, and Frannie, who knows better than to make any movement other than a suggestive little wriggle, whose flesh is aglow with a fire matched only by the fires of lust which course through her belly – Frannie *waits*.

Frannie, Lady Ballington, is off again
on her adventures, bound
for another instalment of her erotic
odyssey around the world . . .

FRANNIE RIDES AGAIN!
Lady Ballington – Her memoirs

ANON

Futura

For my friend Berth Milton
In hopes that he may learn something from it!

A Futura Book

Copyright 1989 James Hallums

First published in Great Britain in 1990
by Futura Publications, a Division of
Macdonald & Co (Publishers) Ltd
London & Sydney

ISBN 0 7088 4769 2

Printed and bound in Great Britain by
Collins, Glasgow

Futura Publications
A Division of
Macdonald & Co (Publishers) Ltd
Orbit House
1 New Fetter Lane
London EC4A 1AR
A member of Maxwell Macmillan Pergamon Publishing Corporation

'There is a tide in the affairs of women,
Which, taken at the flood, leads – God knows where.'

LORD BYRON

'The wren goes to 't, and the small gilded fly
Does lecher in my sight.
Let copulation thrive.'

King Lear, Shakespeare.

1

LADY BE BAD

THE SHEEREST OF SILK STOCKING BY Christian Dior exquisitely encases legs long and slender; beneath a loose, sharply pleated, cream chiffon skirt from Diane Von Furstenberg, skimpy, yellow Yves Saint Laurent knickers in fine mousseline cosset the sweetest of pussies, its fleshy outer lips topped by a delicate fuzz of soft, light brown pubic hair; a white, Coco Chanel blouse, the top three buttons alluringly undone, exposes the lacework of a frivolous, buttercup bra from New York's Sonia Rykiel whose matching suspender set keeps the stockings neatly in place; beneath this expensive, self-indulgent collection reposes the perfectly moulded, unblemished, well-handled, twenty-four-year-old, creamy-white body of Frannie Jones, Lady Ballington.

Frannie, supremely comfortable, reclines amongst silk cushions on an eighteenth century chaise longue in the elegant drawing room of Stratton Castle, her husband's ancestral home. She is barefoot. Her trim and shapely ankles are crossed, snugly indenting a cushion at the backless end of the chaise longue, silk against silk. Full, gleaming blonde hair framing a beautifully sensuous face cascades over slender shoulders. Large, opaquely green eyes, eyes which have looked upon more things sexual than are even *known* to the average female, smile lazily with pleasures remembered. The captivating little dimple beside softly erotic, eminently kissable lips puckers as the tip of her tongue adds a patina of saliva to mildly pink lipstick.

Her fine-boned right hand, possessed of a perverse will of its own, begins to slide, infinitely slowly, across her right knee and up to her thigh. Her palm begins to press warmly into the firm, yielding flesh, the tips of immaculate, green-painted nails trail lightly against stocking with the barest persceptible hiss. As her hand moves higher the Diane Von Furstenberg chiffon rides with it until suspenders, stocking tops and upper thighs are invitingly exposed. Palm and thigh mingle hotly, relishing the mutual contact. The yellow mousseline-pampered crotch is tantalisingly revealed as the hand wilfully moves on, as, with a sudden hunger, fingertips greedily insinuate themselves beneath the hem of the panties and find the welcoming nub of clitoris and the Heaven which lies beyond.

Her Ladyship gasps with a sharp intake of breath as the tips of her index and second finger discover the warm, damp comfort of her pussy.

In her other hand Lady Ballington holds a book which her eyes devour avidly, lasciviously, the words of which are responsible for her growing masturbatory urge. The title of that book is *Frannie* . . .

God, I've done *that* again, the so-called onanistic sin. And why not? It was splendid, spoiling myself in that way as I flicked through the pages of my first novel. I had almost forgotten how *horny* it is. Matter of fact, I have just made a beginning on my second book, to be called *Frannie Rides Again*! but Victor, Lord Ballington my dear husband, expects me to entertain today upon his return from the hunt, so I am taking the day off.

2

Bloody *hell*, I got *so* worked up there! I hope the new book will be good enough to turn the same trick as well – at least a dozen times over. No, I do not believe that it is conceited of me to be so turned-on by my own words. They are, after all, absolutely true, it *is* a diary, albeit in novel form, and why on earth should one not get pleasure from one's own diary?

I hear the echoing ring of many hooves as horses approach the stables. My husband and his friends are returning. It is time for me to rearrange my clothes and go down to meet them, to put my literary self away.

Until tomorrow.

2

A LITTLE TENDERNESS

AT FIFTY-TWO, LORD BALLINGTON reminded Frannie more than ever of the dashing Clark Gable in his prime. Straight black hair with only the merest flicker of grey at the temples sat comfortably on a face whose features were generous, ever ready to break into a broad smile, sometimes mocking, sometimes cynical. There was little trace of a lifetime's sexual excess etched into the aesthetic features which were his blood-right.

Victor Ballington, who had made Frannie his bride when she was a demure and mouth-watering, but far from innocent, seventeen, was immensely rich. The Wiltshire castle was just one, albeit the most lived-in, of a collection of properties which rivalled in number his string of racehorses. There was the Scottish manor, the Irish lodge, the Alpine ski lodge, the New York penthouse, the French chateau, the recently acquired villa in Marbella – the list was almost endless. Lord Ballington was at least as rich as the Duke of Westminster, though he regretted that his wealth could not match that of the Sultan of Brunei.

Attending to his vast money empire took up a great deal of his time, but that was not his only interest in life. He filled his extensive leisure hours with the gentlemanly pursuits of racing, hunting, shooting, fishing his own rivers, music – he was an accomplished pianist – tennis, snooker and golf, which he played off a respectable six. He was also, openly and unhypocritically, a connoisseur of all things sexual – the ultimate hedonist.

In his 'Blue Room', as he inevitably called it, he boasted perhaps one of the most comprehensive collections of erotica in the world and in his extensive travels he wasted no opportunity to add to it. As a twenty-third birthday present treat, and with her delighted cooperation, Frannie had been packed off on a three month erotic adventure. He had supplied her with a handbag cleverly disguising the latest in video technology and she had been successful in filming several of her encounters for their later mutual enjoyment. These videos, unexceptional in quality but explosive in content, Victor prized most highly. One cassette, however, was locked away in a secret place – the shocking episode in which Frannie nearly became the unwitting victim of a 'snuff' movie (in which the female victim is repeatedly raped and finally murdered on camera). Frannie herself, rescued from death in the nick of time by Gregory, her bodyguard, had never seen this film and Victor never intended to *let* her view it – although he occasionally watched it himself in secret, finding that it induced in him a weird and uniquely frightening thrill.

The latest proud addition to his collection was a leather-bound copy of his wife's recently published book of her adventures, simply entitled *Frannie*. Amused, even a touch jealous that Lady Ballington had succeeded in getting her words into print – he had himself been working for more than a year on a novel of highly erotic content without progressing nearly as far as he would have liked. Lord Ballington adored reading about his wife's 'dirty deeds' and revelled in having the details verbally embellished when they were alone together in sensual mood. ('You wrote,' he would comment, for instance, 'That this man had a big cock. But how about his balls? You mention nothing about the size of his *balls*. How were they, say, compared to *mine*?')

Despite what many might think an excessive indulgence in whims and fancies of the flesh, and in spite of their twenty-eight year age difference, Frannie and Victor were ideal for each other. They enjoyed a special kind of love, a love which few apart from themselves and perhaps the myopic Matilda, Frannie's personal maid, understood or cared to understand. It was based on a high regard for each other, a healthy appreciation of money and the pleasures it could bring them, and an unfailing honesty between the two of them. They had no such thing as a single personal secret.

Dinner at Stratton was frequently served with formality even when there were no guests. At such time Matilda, to the manor born but like so many of her contemporaries utterly potless, would usually dine with them.

Candles flickered in the two sixteenth century silver candelabra which neatly divided the oblong Sheraton dining table. Fractured light danced over the three perfectly groomed diners: the plumpish Matilda in black velvet and pearls, hair out of its habitual bun but her appearance marred by the heavy bi-focals without which she could hardly see what was on her plate; Lord and Lady Ballington, fully fourteen feet apart at either end of the table, he in mauve smoking jacket and a floppy, hand-tied bow, she stunning in silver lamé which clung sensuously to her curves like the scales of a fish, milky breasts spilling provocatively from her décolletage.

A servant topped up the sparkling Waterford crystal glasses with a Beaune of exceptional vintage and Lord Ballington raised his high. His voice was deep and resonant. 'Well, my lovelies, what shall we drink to tonight?'

Frannie peered at him down the length of the table, her head tilted to get a clear view of him past the candles, a wicked little smile hovering around her lips. 'I think you ought to know that I've been feeling exceptionally horny today!' she breathed.

Matilda chuckled as Victor replied, matter-of-factly, 'Nothing unusual about that. But it's hardly an answer to my question.'

'No. But it's, well, it's a sort of a start,' said Frannie.

Ballington's glass still hovered aloft. 'Well, finish then.' There was no trace of impatience in his voice.

Frannie pursed her lips prettily. 'I think,' she said, 'that we should drink to my *next* adventure into sexual fantasy land.'

Victor Ballington cocked his head to one side, an amused smile beginning to crease his face. 'We *should*?' he exclaimed. 'This is, of course, news to me, but I'll go along with that.' He drew his glass towards his lips. 'To my darling Frannie and the continuation of her erotic travels –' he paused '– whenever that may be.'

Matilda drank with them, her eyes sliding from one end of the table to the other. 'Oh, dear,' she whispered.

'I thought that perhaps tomorrow would not be too soon,' said Frannie, casually.

'Oh *dear*,' mouthed Matilda, louder.

Victor studied Frannie over the rim of his glass, took another appreciative sip. 'This is very *good*, you know,' he said. 'Very good indeed. I had feared it might be corked, like the last one.' He pursed his lips. 'Eager as you seem to be, my darling – and who could blame you? – I fear tomorrow is going to be just a *touch* too soon.'

'Oh – why?' Frannie's raised eyebrow suggested the beginning of impatience.

'Always so bloody impractical – one of the things I love about you.' He inspected the wine in the candle-light. 'Colour's absolutely superb as well.'

'*What*? Impractical? *Me*?' Frannie downed half a glass in one go.

'Yes, *you*.' The Ballington gaze strayed briefly to her décolletage. 'You'll be requiring the Lear Jet, I presume?'

'Naturally. What *other* way is there to travel?'

Matilda, who was in unholy terror of aeroplanes and had to be almost dragged aboard for every flight, groaned. '*Boats*, for instance? Do we have to fly, do we *really* have to? If we *must* cross oceans can't we go by sea, for God's sake?'

Apart from a brief, amused twitch of the lips from Lord Ballington, this little protest went ignored. 'There's the crew,' he said. 'They have to be organised. The Lear's been on the ground for a while, they're not expecting duty. They could be anywhere.'

'I'm sure they won't be that difficult to find.'

'Maybe not. Then there's Gregory. I won't allow you to go without Gregory, you know that.'

'You won't *allow* me to go?' Frannie tossed her head, causing ripples through her cascade of hair. 'I wouldn't *dream* of going without him.'

'Precisely. Well, you seem to forget he's on holiday.'

'Oh. Can't we get him back?'

'I'm sure we can, he's only in Italy somewhere. But it'll take a couple of days. Bound to.'

Frannie drained her glass and Charles, the butler, appeared out of nowhere to replenish it, then, the soul of discretion, faded once more into the shadows. 'I refuse to go *any*where without Gregory.'

Indeed, she considered the good and massive Gregory, ex-SAS man of advanced pugilistic talents, the loyal and devoted Gregory whose personal disapproval of his mistress's excesses he tried unsuccessfully to keep to himself, totally indispensable.

8

Equipped with a pocket bleeper which was activated by a simple turn of an emerald in one of Frannie's rings, during her past sexual escapades he had always been close enough to rush to the rescue if things began to go wrong.

'I should think three days minimum.' Victor paused. 'Of course, a week would be far more sensible.'

'*Sensible*? But why? *Can't* we make it three days?'

'You've really got the hots, haven't you? I'll see what can be done.' He returned his attention to the roast suckling pig. Then, as he savoured it with great gusto, he remarked, 'You *do* intend taking your video equipment?'

Frannie's fork paused midway between plate and suggestively smiling mouth. 'But of course, Victor. It's half the fun – then all the fun over again when we watch the films together.' Licking the succulent meat suggestively off her fork she said, 'You truly have the most exquisitely dirty mind, my Lord.'

Victor Ballington laughed aloud, the sound echoing in the lofty dining hall.

'Do we *absolutely* have to *fly*?' Matilda protested. '*Couldn't* we go by boat and *car*?'

Victor laughed some more, Frannie joining in. Matilda's genuine resentment, her fear of flying, was nothing if not comical.

Later, as he watched the fire flame briefly over a *crêpe suzette*, Victor said, 'Naturally, you must expect to be punished for this.'

The breath caught in Frannie's throat. 'Punished, Victor?' she whispered. 'Whatever can you mean?'

'Girls need a good spanking when they entertain dirty thoughts and intentions.' He cast a questioning eye on Matilda. 'What say you, Matilda?'

Matilda peered at him over the top of her bi-focals, seeing nothing but a blur, her apprehension of imminent flights vanishing as she realised that one of those domestic scenes which she always found *so* entertaining was about to be enacted. 'I'll say,' she commented with great enthusiasm.

'But first some music.' Victor sliced at his *crêpe*. 'After the pudding, that is. We shall retire to the music room and I'll play a little whilst contemplating my shamelessly debauched wife's fate.'

Frannie's eyes widened fractionally as she affected nervousness. 'No, *please* Victor! *Please*, no punishment! *Darling*?' she begged, clearly meaning quite the reverse.

The music room was housed in one of the original old towers of Stratton Castle. Square, built from York stone, the room rose loftily to a heavy-beamed ceiling, its past austerity buried in the trappings of modern comfort: double glazing sealed the narrow, fluted windows, automatically regulated acclimatisation kept the temperature at a steady 68 fahrenheit in deference to the needs of the perfectly tuned Steinway grand piano. At odds with the style, yet managing to complement the Englishness of the tower, Persian rugs were spread over the uneven flagstones and Middle-Eastern tapestries festooned the walls. The furniture was delicate, near-priceless, eighteenth century and French. Having performed there during private parties, singers of such diverse talents as Shirley Bassey, Placido Domingo and Elton John had nothing but praise for the remarkable accoustics.

Lord Ballington took his place with exaggerated care on the piano stool while Frannie and Matilda perched side by side on a Louis XV sofa and sipped coffee and Tia Maria. Sitting very upright at the piano, Ballington flexed his long, white, tapering fingers – appendages which were strangely at variance with the stockiness of his build, yet perfectly in accord with the aestheticism of his nature - and began to run them up and down the keyboard, delightfully reproducing the subtle variations of a Chopin nocturne.

10

Frannie, who could not even bang a drum, usually listened with attentive pleasure to her husband's playing. This evening her mind was not on it, her thoughts elsewhere, as delicious, tingling anticipation invaded her psyche. Matilda, meanwhile, smiled a secret and wicked smile while she savoured her liqueur, her pebble-glassed eyes darting from her mistress to her master and back again, her imagination dwelling unchastely on lustful games yet to be played.

Chopin tailed off in mid-phrase. Victor turned suggestively to Frannie, his expression alive with sexual innuendo, his eyes lingering on her silver lamé dress whose skirt was hitched fetchingly to mid-thigh. 'Not *quite* the mood, friend Chopin,' he said. He glanced briefly at the keyboard as he repositioned his hands, then back at Frannie as he began to sing, accompanying himself with quite a different piece of music. His deep voice was pleasantly in tune.

'She may get weary . . .' he sang, then carried on with a light descant as he spoke pointedly to Frannie.

'Of course, you *have* got weary, my darling, isn't it *so*? You've got so weary you want to run off and get *screwed*.'

'No. Yes. No . . .' stammered Frannie. It was beginning. Now it was *beginning*.

Victor continued briefly with the song. 'She may get weary . . .' He returned to the descant. 'Matilda – perhaps you'd better help her off with her dress – *now*!'

'Oh.' Small, from Frannie. Argument clearly not being a part of this particular scenario, Frannie obediently turned her back on Matilda and plump, eager fingers made short work of the zipper whilst Victor carried on with his fractured song.

'She may get weary . . .' He paused. 'And you may get wearier still *after* your punishment.'

Frannie standing, Matilda easing the tight lamé over her equally tight haunches, slipping it down to her spiky, silver evening shoes, Frannie stepping delicately out of the pile of dress, waiting like that, uncertain. Naked to her waist, her superb, pink-tipped breasts hanging free and firm, the nipples already erect, a snowy-white lace and organdie slip from Bonni Keller at mid-thigh, Frannie looks and feels exquisitely vulnerable.

The final notes echoed and died in the rafters. Swinging his legs slowly away from the piano until he faced the sofa, Victor held out his arms and beckoned. 'You, my dear, over here. Matilda – fetch me a paperback copy of my wife's smutty little book, would you? I've devised a somewhat unique castigation!'

Frannie, weak at the dimpled knees, ambling to him, taking his hands, feeling the direction of their insistent pull, obedient, sinking to the carpet, folding herself over his lap. He is already hard, she feels this hardness digging at her belly as her hands fall discordantly on the keyboard, and remain there. She watches her reflection in the gleaming lacquer of the raised piano lid, the word 'Steinway' cutting across her forehead, then the image of Matilda handing her husband the book.

'Hike the *slip* up for me, Matilda,' said Victor throatily, as he tested the flexibility of the paperback with both hands. Matilda willingly, eagerly, obliged, sliding the material all the way up into the small of Frannie's back.

'Oh, *cami*-knickers, how nice,' commented Victor. The right hand holding the book aloft like a paddle, he hooked finger and thumb of the left through the crotch of the silky material and pulled it taut and high until a thin strip of material bit hard into the crease of Frannie's behind, fully exposing her tight, quivering buttocks.

'You wrote this filth, this *porn*,' Victor muttered gloatingly. 'Now be *punished* by your work!' He brought *Frannie* down in a broad, sweeping arc smack onto its authoress's cringing left buttock. It thwacked into her flesh with the sound of a meaty handclap.

Not just Frannie's bottom but her whole body jumped beneath the assault. Her jaw clenched, her toes curled, her arms and legs went rigid, fingers clawing at the piano keys produced more discord.

Yet this is not *pain*, this is a hot, penetrating sting which has time for just half a throb before the book bites into the same place again, then again – and again – the tormented flesh getting hot, blushing scarlet.

Frannie's eyes are tightly closed, she makes little mewing sounds which are a cross between hurt and ecstasy. Over and over, now the right buttock, a concentrated beating, Victor grunting a little with the effort, executing a *thorough* job, his straining penis digging into Frannie's belly as Matilda licks her lips, fingers straying to her velvet-covered crotch as the heat of her abused and glowing behind spreads right through Frannie and her sexual juices ooze.

A dramatic pause. The tool of punishment hovering on high. The sound of Victor's slow, heavy breathing in chorus with pants from Matilda as her fingers go to work, and pleasure/pain sighs from Frannie. Then the last, powerful, assault on each half of Frannie's behind, carefully spaced, her pounded flesh quivering, her feet jerking upwards and back off the floor both times.

With lecherous interest the master of the household surveyed the results of the beating. 'A thoroughly disciplined, well-trounced bum,' he breathed in satisfaction as Frannie's feet met the floor and her hands slid off the piano keys, her arms hanging lifeless. He spared a moment's glance at the book; the cover of Frannie's 'explosive journey of erotic discovery' was creased and wrinkled but remained untorn. 'And a nicely battered book.' He tossed the paperback carelessly on top of the grand piano. 'No permanent damage to either.'

Matilda's fingers were still busy through her dress, her two pairs of eyes drooling over the sight of her mistress's enflamed rear end. 'You may administer a little comfort if you wish,' muttered Victor. 'With your mouth.'

Matilda needs no further bidding. She sinks to her knees behind Frannie, grasps her around her waist, leans forward and begins planting avaricious kisses on the abused flesh, licking it, marvelling at its heat as Victor reaches down and slips off her glasses. Tempted beyond resistance, Matilda nips a little tuck of buttock between her teeth and *sucks* on it. Frannie *yells*, her head jerks up and back, her eyes open wide and she *yells* again. Such castigated flesh is in no condition to receive a powerful lovebite, it feels exactly as if a hot knife is being jabbed into her.

'That'll *do*, Matilda.' Lord Ballington reproves. As a man of highly-seasoned sexual tastes, who is well aware of the value of dragging out each pleasure to certain limits and no further, he realises that this behaviour should come to an end. Besides, he finds that his play-sadism, his voyeurism, has induced in him an overwhelming need which he does not wish to contain further.

'You may leave us now, Matilda.'

'*Leave*?' Matilda is crestfallen. The hors d'oeuvres have been delicious, now she hears that she is to miss the main course.

'You heard correctly. I wish to be alone with my wife.'

'But . . .'

'*A plus tard*, if you *don't* mind.' There brooks no further argument and Matilda sadly takes her aroused and needful pussy through the door and away, to do with what she will.

Gently, easily, Victor lifts Frannie up. Picking up a cushion from a nearby chair, he takes it, and her, to the graceful, concave curve of his Steinway. Positioning the cushion carefully on its gleaming surface he bends his wife forwards and across the instrument. 'Don't move,' he whispers in her ear. 'Don't *move*.' Taking hold of her cami-knickers he pulls them to her knees. 'Half-mast, I think. Perfect.'

He stands well back, momentarily hypnotised by the view, and Frannie, who knows better than to make any movement other than a suggestive little wriggle, whose flesh is aglow with a fire matched only by the fires of lust which course through her belly – Frannie *waits*.

Victor feels the need to be naked. His eyes dwell in hungry greed on the bawdy sight of Lady Ballington's lusciously exposed flanks, the patchily scarlet bottom in lewd contrast to the milky white of the surrounding skin. They never stray from this as he strips of his jacket, his bow, his shirt, his shoes, his socks and, lastly, his evening trousers and underpants together. Then he stands there for long moments slowly caressing an old and valued friend, an erect and throbbing penis which is as proud, as big, as hard and as strong an organ as any man could wish to be endowed with. A cock with a growing and terrible need.

Frannie dares to steal a glance over her shoulder and the primitive sight of her rampant lord causes her nostrils to flare as she sucks in her breath.

He plays his hand soothingly over her *derrière*, then curiously prods and touches the small mauve and purple patch where Matilda's teeth have so recently inflicted damage. Stooping, he briefly kisses the wound before straightening and grasping her buttocks. He squeezes, he grunts. He can contain himself no more.

Frannie is impaled. In one smooth, determined movement, Victor plunges himself to the hilt. For the moment he subdues the basic urge to lunge wildly in and out of her until orgasm, but he knows that this can be no controlled and drawn-out copulation. He contains himself there, buried in her, hips thrust forward, his weight on the balls of his feet – there is no movement except for a slight tremble at the knees.

Filled with a heat which is even more compelling than the burning of her bottom, Frannie is also aware that this coupling will be brief and close to violence in its intensity. She is about to be *banged* and, tense with anticipation, she watches as her impatient breath clouds the varnish of the piano where her cheek is pressed against its lacquered surface.

An unplanned contraction of Frannie's vaginal muscles and Victor's lust finally erupts out of control. His upper body engulfs her back, his hands clasp hers into tight balls on the piano top. Drawing almost completely out of her, no pause to tease the entrance with his glans, he *thrusts* in with a great, shuddering heave, pulls out, plunges again, faster, ever faster, bestial grunts escaping his throat as Frannie gasps, climaxes, squeals, comes *again*, and then he shouts, raising his head to the raftered roof, every muscle taut as he floods into her and the noise of the shout hits a sympathetic string on the piano. It rings, reverberates, dies as the tension in Lord Ballington begins to drain away and as Lady Ballington lets loose a choking sob as final evidence of unadulterated pleasure.

His mouth is touching her ear. As his heartbeat starts to slacken and his breathing begins to slow, Victor Ballington whispers, '*Now* you can leave, my lady. Go. Search the world and *see* if *anyone* can fuck you better than *that*!'

3

THE SWINDLING SODOMITE

'GREGORY WILL BE HERE TONIGHT. THE aircrew are all located and under orders and the Lear's being thoroughly checked from top to tail.' Lord Ballington neatly pocketed a difficult pink, replaced it on its spot then managed to fluff an easy red. 'Damn!' He turned from the table. 'You can count on leaving some time tomorrow.'

Frannie made short work of the red, her designer jeans stretched tantalisingly taut as she bent over the table. But she miscued on the blue, leaving her very capable husband the chance of the final red and the possibility of clearing the table, in which he succeeded with speedy and silent proficiency.

'Thirty-five break and game to me by seven, given your forty start,' he commented in satisfaction.

'Your eyes are older and therefore more experienced than mine,' Frannie said with a grin as she slotted away her cue.

'In all things, my pet.' Victor, not about to perform any chore which could just as well be done by a servant, left his cue lying on the table. 'I want to talk to you about your travels. Something occurred to me this morning which could give you some extra interest and motivation.'

'You don't believe sex is enough?' Frannie com-

17

mented, managing to sound demure.

'Well, just in *case* it should pall.' Victor took her elbow. 'Let's go up to my study.'

Victor's study was at the very top of a tower of exact proportions to that of the music room, only differing in that he had sliced it through the middle. A wide spiral staircase led from games room to study and, as with the music room tower, the original window slits had been proportionately widened. On the red leather top of his spindly-legged desk, taken from a book thick with such cards, lay a visiting card embossed with elegant silver print. He handed this to Frannie.

'Mean anything to you?' he asked.

'CLOVIS CARTER-SMITH', it read, 'CARTER-OSBORNE INTERNATIONAL SECURITIES' and, beneath this in smaller print, 'London, Geneva, Paris.' She glanced at Victor. 'Wasn't there some sort of a financial scandal? Recently – in the last few months or so?'

'I'll say. Good, you've been paying proper attention to current affairs. Maybe you recall me having a very definite grumble about him?'

'The *swindler*, of course. You lost a bit of money, didn't you?'

'Just a little. A hundred and fifty thousand pounds to be precise. Unlike me. Well, he had begun to move a bit in my circles, we played a couple of games of golf together. He's gross, in a way, yet possessed of a certain amount of charm. I suppose I fell for it. Anyhow, what I lost is of practically no importance. It's the thought of the thousands of little people which bugs me.'

Lady Ballington arched an eyebrow. 'Since when did you care about the little man?'

'Don't be so cynical, dear – it ill-becomes you. Yes, I *do* in my way. I help where I can, you know that. The Carter-Osborne bubble burst massively, over a quarter of a billion pounds worth of it and most of it small investors' money – life savings, retirement nest-eggs, that sort of thing. A trail of misery caused by one man. Patently unfair.'

Frannie looked again at the card. 'London, Geneva, Paris, what . . .' she began and he cut her short.

'Front offices. All subscribers funds were invested in, to say the least, dodgy, and at worst even non-existent, stocks and shares. In worthless paper companies of friend Carter-Smith's own creation, offering attractive, minimum fourteen percent, interest rates, *naturally*. All of it chanelled into dummy off-shore companies, mere shells littering the beaches of the world's tax-havens – the Bahamas, Panama, Gibraltar, the British Virgin Islands – you name it.'

'He vanished, right?'

'Four, five months ago. The pending investigation of Carter-Osborne International was needlessly telegraphed and by the time the fraud squad moved in their bird had flown taking all his eggs with him.'

Frannie flopped back in the big old armchair which was Victor's favourite, her legs outstretched, arms on the rests on a level with her face. She appeared vulnerable amongst all that heavy, nutty-brown leather. 'So what exactly do you want me to do?' she asked.

'Find him, of course.'

'*Find* him?'

Frannie looked at Victor as if he had lost his mind.

'You might just succeed where Interpol and the rest have so far failed. You're not cluttered up with departmental procedure, nor will you be looking for any pay-offs.' He leant carefully back on his desk, his hands behind him, frankly admiring his wife as he considered his words. 'Two hundred and fifty million pounds is a largish lump of money. He can't have got through more than a few million, twenty at the very most. All his bank accounts are of course wiped clean, the known ones, that is. The only way to trace that money is to unravel perhaps the most complicated web of off-shore companies ever put together by one man. Put together and then hopelessly, deliberately, tangled. And that is impossible without the man himself.'

'I'm *hardly* a detective, darling.'

'You're free, you're fully mobile, you can travel wherever in the world you damn well please at the drop of a hat – which will hardly interfere with your projected sexual adventures. On the contrary, I should imagine. Moreover, you rub shoulders with the very rich, the elite, you have carte blanche into almost any society. You're young, you're beautiful and –' a smile twisted his lips '– you are infinitely desirable.'

Reaching across his desk he opened a drawer and took out a photograph. He studied it for a couple of seconds then went over to Frannie and perched himself on the arm of the chair. He handed her the photograph. 'That's him. In the middle.'

There were three people. A massive man with an unruly shock of grey hair was flanked by a peroxided woman and a smaller, but still large man with a droopy moustache. Carter-Smith was wearing a baggy suit and a smile which looked smeared on. Everything about him was big, his nose, his ears, even his teeth, and the hands which were hooked possessively around the shoulders of his companions were meaty, with closely trimmed nails.

Frannie grimaced. 'Who are the other two?'

'His wife, who is safely ensconced in her own little flat in Peckham and swears she knows nothing. I believe her and so, apparently, do the police – just *look* at her! And his so-called business manager who has also flown the coop.' He paused. 'Our man, as all men, has his weaknesses. Two of them. A love of the lavish life-style which he might find difficult to accommodate while on the run and, ah . . .' he trailed the side of a finger down Frannie's velvet-smooth cheek '. . . a *penchant* for beautiful young females whom he takes great delight in buggering.' The finger played amongst loose tresses. 'Especially blondes. *Most* especially blondes!'

Frannie snorted, slapped the photo face down on the chair arm. 'Well, thanks a *lot*. He's hardly my *type* Victor!'

'I should hope not. However, in the remote possibility that you should get close enough to the man to tempt him with your bottom, then we'll have a chance at him, won't we?'

'Perhaps. But I wouldn't even know where to start.'

Almost absently, Victor's hand strayed into the open neck of Frannie's white cotton shirt, finding a bare breast. He rolled the nipple gently between the sides of index and second finger knuckles as he spoke. 'But *I* would.'

'Then tell me. And *stop* that!' She pulled the hand firmly away.

'But . . .'

'I can't *possibly* listen and let you do that at the same time. You *know* what will happen.'

Victor stood up and reluctantly shoved his hands deep into the pockets of his Harris Tweed jacket. 'Very well.' He grinned fleetingly. 'Pity. Anyhow, it's my idea that you start your travels down in Marbella. In any case I've a couple of million quidsworth of villa on the beach there which has never played host to either of us since I bought it, and that's over a year ago.'

'No objection – I could do with a bit of a tan.'

He looked at her in reproof. 'You know very well I like you *white!*' He complained.

'Just a touch of sun, darling. It's good for my skin.'

'I somehow doubt that. But, all right, if you must, you must. There's a jet-set sort of place there, if you remember. Called Puerto Banùs.'

'Oh, yes. Garish, a bit grubby. Full of fugitives from British justice and other undesirables.'

'Neatly understated. Also some of the biggest privately-owned luxury yachts in the world. Kashoggi's "Nabila" before it went to Trump. The Saudi royals. Oil and movie moguls, those sort of people. Carter-Smith had one there. Not supertanker size, but a hundred and ten feet of ocean-going comfort. I was aboard her once in Cannes before she went to Spain. Clovis confided in me that there was no way she could be traced to him as owner – we were talking tax shelters and so forth. She might still be in Banus. For all I know Clovis is hiding aboard.'

'Sounds like a long shot.' Frannie thought for a second. 'What's it called?'

'It . . .? Oh, I see. "The Golden Hind".'

She spluttered. 'The *Golden Hind*? You're *kidding*! That's a touch more than gauche, isn't it?'

'And so is the man.'

'And you expect me to let him sodomise me?'

'I wouldn't want him to have the pleasure. Find him, if you can. Locate him and wherever he might be I'll send Gregory the appropriate help to get him aboard the Lear and back to retribution.'

Frannie tilted her head back and laughed. 'It's absurd, of course. The whole idea. But suppose I *do* catch this man. What's in it for me?' Struggling out of her leather cocoon she took the two paces which separated her from her husband and dropping her hands on his shoulders she stared up into his eyes. 'Well?'

'You are a mercenary little bitch, do you know that?' He kept his hands resolutely in his pockets as she teasingly pressed her denim groin at him.

'*Nobody* does *nothing* for *nothing*,' she breathed.

22

Lord Ballington was mightily amused. 'Very well,' he responded, slowly. 'Trap Mr Clovis Carter-Smith and I'll present you with a pair of strapping young negros, all sex and muscle, just like the two I hired for your twenty-third birthday surprise. To do with as you will – totally under your command for one entire night.' His voice dropped almost to a whisper, his lips brushed the top of her hair. 'Do we have a deal?'

'A deal?' Frannie nodded slowly, her eyes dancing green laughter. 'Yes, that sounds *more* than fair enough.'

Pulling fractionally away from him she flattened her hand, fingers downwards, over the crotch of his corduroys. She squeezed gently, eliciting immediate response. 'There's just one proviso, though,' she went on, holding one of the most important parts of the Ballington inheritance most firmly, thrilling at its challenging reaction.

'Which is?'

'If, and when, I get my reward, *this*' – another, *hard* squeeze – 'joins the party.'

'You have my most solemn promise, my lady.' He glanced down at himself.

'It's, ah, it's in a *partying* mood right now.'

'You bet.' Frannie sank to her knees. She began to ease his zipper down.

'You *bet!*'

4

OTHELLO

THE WEATHER ON THE COSTA DEL SOL WAS as perfect as early spring in that part of the world can be. The Lear jet sank over the Sierra Nevada then nosed its way over a calm, sparkling Mediterranean before banking into its touchdown path to the Malaga runway.

Frannie, a seasoned world traveller, was supremely unimpressed with the vista of yellow beaches ribboning into the distance; her seat-belt warning sign was ignored as she flipped over the pages of *Vogue* magazine. By her side, firmly strapped in, hands so tight on the edges of her armrests that the knuckles showed white, Matilda – sweated. Landings and take-offs were to her nothing less than journeys through hell, the 'bit in between', as she referred to the flight, just tolerable if her nerves were well shored up with champagne, or whisky, or gin, or indeed anything alcoholic which had a repressive effect on her neural system. But any pre- or in-flight panacea simply dissolved as the engines roared into life for take-off or ominously changed their note in preparation for touch-down – and there was nothing that Frannie, or anyone else, could do about it.

Across the aisle, Gregory mashed out his cigarette, rested a sympathetic eye on the near-catatonic Matilda, then watched without expression as limpid blue sky swooped down to meet aquamarine sea and the Lear lined itself up with the runway. Thoughts which were not a part of his brief intruded on him. Keenly aware of the elegant, cream-suited, cross-legged shape of his mistress, sophisticated, sweet-smelling, so close that he could reach out and touch her and yet a million miles away – he wondered what possessed her, one of life's winners with the world at her feet, to go off in search of wild, erotic adventures which, the last time, had nearly led to her death. To Gregory's logical, unimaginative, uninspired brain her ladyship remained an enigma which he was incapable of solving.

As Frannie looked up from the magazine he happened to glance in her direction. Momentarily, green and grey eyes locked.

Frannie raised an eyebrow. '*Thinking* again, Gregory?' she said. 'I wouldn't, if I were you.'

The villa typified what a couple of million pounds or so could buy in the continually expanding resort area of Marbella. Small compared to the magnificent mansion and splendid acres that sort of money would secure in the heart of the English countryside, it was marginally larger than two million pounds-worth of Belgravia townhouse.

The chauffeur-driven Mercedes 500 purred sedately through electronically-operated gates and whispered to a halt in front of wooden, porticoed doors on a drive big enough to accommodate perhaps ten such vehicles.

Matilda sat immobile as the chauffeur opened her door. Laughing, Frannie took firm hold of her arm. 'Come on, darling,' she said. 'We've been on the *ground* for at least an hour and a half!'

The house stood in acre and a half of land three kilometres to the west of the nearest village. The grounds sloped down to a fenced-off cliff overlooking a fairly secluded stretch of beach. The garden was simple, most of it neatly tended, undulating lawns playing host to an oblong swimming pool, an ornamental pond and a small copse of pine trees. The villa was solidly and expensively built on rustic lines and featured a cavernous drawing room with a heavy-beamed ceiling and enormous sliding glass doors which offered panoramic views of the garden and the Mediterranean beyond.

Frannie, who had seen the place only briefly when Victor bought it, unfurnished, from the previous owner, immediately embarked on a swift tour of inspection. She rather liked what she saw, approving of her husband's decorator's taste (except for his choice of books in the mezzanine library) and she decided to add some personal, feminine touches whilst she was there.

A resident Spanish couple looked after the property, not an awesome task considering that for most of the time it was empty apart from themselves. A gardener-cum-handyman was employed full time during the day.

It was now four o'clock of a particularly beautiful afternoon and the temperature was well into the seventies. Wandering down past the pool to the fence overlooking the beach, Frannie paused, momentarily startled. The handful of people sun-bathing on the sand, alone or in pairs, were all naked and, for the most part, evenly tanned. Once her surprise had given way to interested amusement, Frannie, who on a visit to an official nude beach had quickly decided that the average bare body should stay covered up, was impressed to see that these sun-worshippers all appeared to be youthful and not one of them was in any way gross.

Still wearing her cream Givenchy travelling suit, Frannie suddenly became aware of the sun beginning to burn through the padded shoulders of the jacket. Stripping it off she carelessly dropped it at her feet. She kicked off her shoes and padded through an unlocked gate to the wooden steps which led down to the beach.

As she made her way down the steps she felt the sun bite warmly through her silk blouse. A pleasant breeze disturbed her hair, carrying with it the fresh, salty tang of the sea. She closed her eyes and flared her nostrils, savouring the contrast between this and the still wintry Wiltshire countryside which she had left so recently.

A perverse temptation began to take hold of her.

Opening her eyes, she observed that the nearest sunbathers, at least a hundred yards away, were a couple of boys in their late teens. They were lying on their stomachs, laughing together, engrossed in each other, backs and behinds an even, nutty brown. Probably gay, thought Frannie – well, all the better. Quickly, she stripped off her clothes, hesitating only momentarily at the last garment, her flimsy lace mini-briefs. A swift raise of each knee, a point of the toe, and these joined the untidy pile at her feet.

Naked, feeling deliciously naughty, she stretched, luxuriating in the special feeling of warm sun on bare skin. Then, as gleamingly white as her neighbours were brown, she began to walk slowly towards the sea, the hot sand not quite burning her feet and trickling delightfully between her toes.

The water was icy; she tested it gingerly then pulled back as if stung. But the sun slid balmy, caressing hands all over her and she stood quite still for long moments, eyes closed, head tilted, hair cascading down her naked back.

After a while she became aware of someone approaching and of sudden, stifled laughter. She opened her eyes and saw a couple strolling hand in hand in her direction, a few yards from the water. They were very brown and his penis swung confidently. Both of them seemed to have been looking at her backside, at once she realised that there might be more than one reason why.

'Hello,' said the man, with a broad grin.

'Oh, er, hi,' Frannie responded, feeling, unusually for her, somewhat awkward.

The two didn't make as if to stop but, as they drew level with her, the man commented gleefully in passing, almost as if he were daring himself to say the words, 'You really *could* do with plenty of sun, you know. Especially on that poor, abused bum of yours!' The girl unsuccessfully smothered a giggle.

'Oh,' mouthed Frannie, dismayed. Of course, she had forgotten when she so impetuously undressed that her backside was still a faded red framed with several straight edges from Victor's beating of three days previously. Not to mention that purplish mark on one cheek which, to the experienced eye, could be nothing other than a love-bite. Her hands strayed to her buttocks as the girl's giggles, mingled with the man's laughter, drifted away. She watched them for a while with mixed feelings.

Finally, she smiled.

'What the hell,' mouthed Frannie to herself. 'Let's start to get it brown.' She eased herself down onto her belly, feet close to the lapping sea, magnificent body hugging the upward slope of the beach, head cradled in her crossed arms.

Her gaze fell on the two boys who were now enthusiastically rubbing oil into each other's rear ends. 'What the hell,' she repeated, with a grin, and covertly continued to watch them.

'We'll eat in, try out Maria's cooking and then have a wander around that marina place.' Frannie, a fluffy white towel wrapped around her and tucked above her breasts, her hair turbaned in another, was perched on a vanity chair in front of her dressing table. Her face was smothered in a thick layer of moisturising cream.

Matilda smoothed more cream into her mistress's bare shoulders which the sun had kissed a light shade

28

of pink. 'Where that financier person's boat's supposed to be, yes, let's,' she said, then, in the same breath, 'you should watch this Spanish sun, it's stronger than you imagine.'

'I have to get pink before I turn brown. Mmmmm!'

'Nice, no?' Matilda's thumbs circled towards the nape of Frannie's elegant neck. 'Victor will be less than delighted.'

'Who knows *when* I'll be seeing Victor again. I'll probably be deathly white again by then. Anyway I only want a light tan.' As she tweezered an errant eyebrow hair she jerked one elbow high causing the towel to unwrap itself and fall from her body. Matilda's gaze dropped to Frannie's blushing breasts.

'As a matter of fact, I tend to agree with his lordship,' she remarked. 'Look at you – you're all blotchy.'

'Not for long.' Frannie's eyes smiled lazily through a mask of Lancôme. 'That'll do for my shoulders.' She pursed her lips and cocked her head on one side. 'My tits could do with a bit of soothing, don't you agree?'

Matilda, ever-anxious for the pleasure of laying hands – or lips – on Frannie's most desirable parts, squeezed cream into eager palms and slid them smoothly down and over the classic sweep of Frannie's breasts, cupping them with almost reverent tenderness from below. She began spoiling them with slow, experienced, circular movements, kneading like dough. Frannie drew in a deep, sensuous breath. She closed her eyes. As her legs parted slightly she felt the towel creep across a thigh then slide to the floor. 'I feel wanton, Matilda,' she breathed. 'I feel suddenly very *wanton.*'

'I'm pleased.' Matilda leant her comfortable belly into Frannie's bare back and she played with her nipples in a way which had nothing to do with easing sunburn, her buxom bosom quivering as she did so, a perfect cushion for Frannie's be-turbaned head.

Frannie sighed. 'I don't know what's got into me. It must be the sun,' she murmured.

'Ha!' exclaimed Matilda. 'Something to do with it, there's more to it than that.' She added a touch more cream to her palms. As one reclaimed a breast and the other moved confidently to the tight abdomen below, she continued, her voice a husky caress. 'There's a . . . *tension* within you. Perhaps you haven't realised it, but I see the signs. You're a little afraid – am I right?'

Frannie shook her head. She frowned as she looked at the reflection of Matilda's eyes. Vague, fractured hazel, it seemed that they studied her from two angles at once. 'I *am*? *Me*?' She watched Matilda's expert hands at work, doing arousing things to her. 'Perhaps you *are* right. I am, I'm a little tense.'

'Hardly surprising. Who knows *what* may happen to you? Anything and everything – consider the last time.'

'That had its supreme moments.' Frannie's voice had dropped to a hoarse whisper, her eyelids drooped, she was only fractionally with the conversation, the rest of her was beginning to float to a sexual high.

'And its danger.' Matilda was stooping across Frannie's shoulder, reaching. The fingers of one hand had found silky pubic hair. 'Don't forget the *danger*.'

Unexpectedly, almost fiercely, Frannie grabbed Matilda's fingers and thrust them insistently deep into her bush. 'I want you to get *rid* of it,' she muttered. 'Get *rid* of my tension.'

'Like *this*?' Matilda's fingertips, with Frannie pushing down on her knuckles, found the already damp opening, slid inside and warm thigh flesh tightened around her hand. 'Or do you need something *more*?'

Frannie's mind raced ahead of her body. Inventive, dirty, as always in moments like this. 'I need a f . . .' she mumbled. 'Fetch my bag – you know which one.'

Reluctantly, Matilda's hands withdrew from her favourite places. Frannie, tense indeed, revelling in her wickedness, her vivid imagination already savouring what she was about to have done to her, watched as her maid, her friend, her lover, now her slave, fetched a small square bag. She set it down on the dressing table, opened it. Innards churning, impatience mirrored in a trembling hand, Frannie rummaged through it.

She sighed. 'Here,' she said. 'Othello.' She held it with lascivious affection, one hand wrapped around its shaft, the other clasping its bulging rubber testicles – an enormous, black dildo, beautifully moulded, attached to it a criss-cross of thin velvet straps. She offered it to Matilda. '*Do* me.'

Matilda had been this route before. It brought out the butch in her. Understanding exactly what was required of her, as impatient to be giving it as her mistress was to receive it, she fumbled at her clothes and within seconds she was naked. Frannie's eyes feasted on the luscious Rubens curves, the big fat tits and thick black pubic thatch as Matilda strapped on the dildo, her impatient fingers clumsying at the straps and buckles.

The monstrous artificial phallus now in place, she slipped her hands under Frannie's armpits, grasped her around the breasts, brought her to her feet like that, then turned her to face the bed.

'On your bed. On your *knees*.' It is a rare moment of dominance for Matilda, her voice guttural as excitement constricts her throat. Frannie coaxed by insistent hands at her buttocks, indenting the blue silk counterpane as she does as she is ordered, her face a creamy-white mask beneath the towel-turban, her pink skin tingling, glowing from the sun, from her shower, from Matilda's administrations, offers herself blatantly, legs akimbo, patchy pink and red bottom with its telling little bruise raised high.

Tongue wetting her lips, Frannie stares in fascination under the length of her body, past dangling breasts to her downy mound, watching the thick black phallus as

Matilda's fist wraps around it like the hand of a man. She positions it, prods tentatively, finds the way and slides it up, up, into hot wetness, all the way up until Frannie, who can now see only the artificial balls, expels every breath of air in her body with a shuddering gasp.

Frannie is *filled* with this unfeeling rubber which has somehow become one with Matilda, flesh of her flesh, transmitting Matilda's extreme urgency as she withdraws the instrument to the very tip and *shoves* it all the way back in, fleshy thighs slapping against the backs of Frannie's legs while one hand hungrily grasps a breast, two fingers of the other finding the clitoris, working her mistress up in every way she knows how, fat tits flattening on her back, the nipples sliding up and down as Matilda starts to pump like a machine, her entire body building into a powerful, obsessed, rocking, *fucking* action, the reflexive tightening and slackening of her buttocks making them quiver and shake around the thin strap which divides them, more flesh bulging and wobbling around the webbing at her waist.

Frannie is transported. On another planet of dreams where chubby maids screw their mistresses with dildos called Othello and all the enthusiasm of giant, black studs. Rigid, her eyes clamped shut, the orgasm beginning to build, she sways solidly, blissfully back to meet each thrust with a challenge of her own, mewling, fingers screwing the counterpane into tight knots as if they by themselves are capable of screaming out her need.

Orgasm. The cleverly designed extension behind the rubber testicles has teased Matilda's clitoris and inner lips unbearably, working her to the point of no return as surely as she has been teasing Frannie and she comes with a sudden, massive heave which is so powerful it is as if she has shot semen through the dildo – a breathless climax which coincides perfectly with Frannie's own. Frannie shouts, once. Matilda groans, heavy, drawn-out, trembling. She allows her weight to sag into Frannie's back and they collapse together across the bed, panting, slippery with perspiration, Matilda's arms cradling Frannie as if she were in need of protection.

After a while Frannie reaches her hand between her legs, finds the rubber balls. 'The tension's gone,' she mutters, languidly. 'You can take that thing out of me, if you like!'

5

MESSING ABOUT IN BOATS

IT WAS APPROACHING EASTER AND PUERTO JOSE BANUS was beginning to bustle. A cabin cruiser which had been bought with the house was berthed there. The Ballingtons' had never laid eyes on this, but with ownership came the right of access of a private car to the marina.

The white Mercedes 500, with Gregory at the wheel, swept through the electronic entrance to the port with Frannie and Matilda resplendent in the back. Gregory, despite his objections, was uniformed in grey with a matching peaked cap and white gloves. Puerto Banùs being accustomed to style, albeit for the most part contrived and artificial, the slowly cruising Merc elicited only the occasional stare as it nosed through the crowds of early evening strollers.

Gregory found them a parking space in the middle of the port, in front of the open air tables of Da Paulos café, a popular rendezvous. It amused Frannie to wait until Gregory opened her door before she stepped out. She was wearing one of her favourite Sarah Percival evening dresses, a slinky explosion of tiny coloured sequins, each one hand-sewn, and an unnecessary white sable wrap to protect her shoulders from the warm air, guessing that in what was reputed to be one of Europe's showplaces she was unlikely to feel overdressed. Matilda, glowing with inner satisfaction from her recent lesbian coupling with her mistress, was clothed simply but expensively in a fine velvet gown of dark blue which partially disguised her plumpness. Hair down, cleverly coiffed, glasses tucked away in her bag, she carefully clung to Frannie's arm, stumbling only once as they made their way to a table.

The mis-matched pair attracted a certain amount of guarded attention – Frannie as dazzling an example of female pulchritude to be encountered anywhere, and her slightly unlikely companion who was utterly outshone and yet not unattractive in her own chubby way. Meanwhile, the supremely unimpressionable Gregory put his seat into recline, tilted his cap over his eyes and went to sleep – a useful trick which he seemed to be able to perform at the drop of a hat.

It was only just dark. A dull pink glow in the west faded away in the time it took for a waiter to take their order and fetch it, but the port itself, a huge collection of boutiques, bars, shops, restaurants and nightclubs, not to mention more than a billion dollars-worth of private yachts, was a confusion of light and colour.

Frannie, in contemplative mood, shushing Matilda when she started to speak, settled back to absorb the atmosphere. Like a fairground, it was vibrant with a life entirely of its own. Noise intruded from a myriad of directions, yet somehow managed not to deafen. Strains of different pieces of popular music rose and fell on the gentle breeze, and Sade from the café speakers clashed with Bob Dylan from the restaurant next door. Laughter abounded. Voices were animated and noisy. Others murmured close by, and snatches of conversation were torn from the passing crowds. A parrot squawked on an overhead balcony, a pair of canaries somewhere nearby responded with warbled song. Cars drifted by with muted engines, the racket of a two-stroke motorcycle briefly intruded. From far away, or perhaps not so far, could be heard the plaintive voice of a flamenco singer. And in the background, played a soft symphony of creaking boats shifting in their moorings, the muted rattling of hawsers, lazy sounds from a regiment of resting vessels.

Fleetingly, Frannie recalled the traumas of an unwanted but irresistible love affair which had snared her on the Marbella leg of her first erotic adventure. She was suddenly glad that she and her movie-star lover had never visited this place together and that it held no wistful memories for her.

'Penny for them?' Matilda's voice broke rudely into her thoughts, she started to shut her up again, then changed her mind.

'Oh, nothing really. Drifting.' Frannie smiled. 'How does it strike you?'

'I'm not sure. Hang on.' Matilda hunted in her bag.

'It *helps* if you can *see*, Matilda.'

'You're right.' Matilda threaded on her spectacles and slowly glanced around. She pursed her lips. 'I don't know. A bit, *exaggerated*, some of these people, aren't they?' Her gaze swept over the multinational crowd, hovering over a table of Arabs drinking Chivas Regal, alighted on a pair of expensive young blondes who, eyes covertly on the Arabs, might have been whores, settled briefly on three men whose conversation, loud, London, not pleasant, Frannie had caught grating snatches of. 'My God!' Matilda exclaimed. 'I don't believe I've ever seen so much *gold* on *men* in my life!' One of them grinned at her. She looked hurriedly, huffily, away. 'Well, *really*!'

Frannie laughed. 'They call glasses *gafas* in Spanish. You're not so bad in your *gafas* after all, Matilda!' She drained her whisky sour, picked up the bill and, without looking at it, handed it to Matilda. 'Pop inside and pay this, there's a dear. Let's go for a stroll.'

Standing, Matilda started to take off her glasses.

'Keep them *on*, twit!' said Frannie. 'You want to break your neck in the cause of vanity?'

'Well, we could wait for the waiter.'

'I'm getting *rest*less, Matilda.'

'Right.'

As they became a part of the endless bustle, Frannie noticed how ubiquitous was the English language. They could have been in some up-market Blackpool marina, except that when they found their way to the most westerly pier it was crammed with massive yachts flying the flags of a multitude of nations. This was where Frannie hoped that the crassly named 'Golden Hind' would be moored.

Arm in arm, Frannie and Matilda strolled past flags as varied as Panama, Guernsey, Sweden, Australia, Hong Kong and Egypt until they reached the control tower, where the largest of these super-expensive toys was berthed. This was 'Shaf', a sleek, two hundred foot mini-liner reputed to have been a gift from a massively wealthy Saudi-Arabian sheikh to a member of the Saudi royal family.

No 'Golden Hind'.

On the way back they paused to admire a schooner, no potentate's plaything but a beautifully crafted wooden sailing ship, more than a hundred immaculate feet of her. She ws flying a South African flag and a cheerful voice hailed them in the same accent.

'Want to come aboard?' He was a rough and ready character in cut-off jeans and a torn shirt, walnut brown, with a friend leaning comfortably on a mop nearby. Clearly crew.

Frannie smiled. '*They've* got some nerve,' she whispered to Matilda, then called out in good humour 'Thanks very much, but *no*.'

'Suit yourself, sweetheart. Your loss!'

37

Undaunted, she ventured, 'But perhaps you can help me?'

'*I'll* say I can.' Amused, pale blue eyes swept up and down the Sarah Percival creation, stripping it right off her. Frannie managed to ignore this.

'Seriously,' she said. 'I'm looking for a boat called the 'Golden Hind'. Has it been here, do you know?'

'Hell of a dumb name for her. Matter of fact, she *was* here, just a couple of berths away. Left, oh, two, three weeks ago.'

'Oh. You wouldn't happen to know where she went?'

''Fraid not.' He looked at his companion. 'Do you, Tom?' They exchanged a few garbled words, then the man looked back at her. 'Young Davy, he might know. He was working on her engines. You'll find him . . .' a strong, lean arm waved towards the centre of the port '. . . somewhere over there. Pier five or six. Cabin cruiser name of 'Saucy Girl'."

'Well, thanks very much. I'll ask him.' The two women began to move away.

'*Sure* you won't come aboard, now?'

'Don't be *silly*!' Frannie treated him to the most saccherine of smiles.

'I should be so fucking lucky,' the man grumbled, but to himself.

The gangplank of the 'Saucy Girl' was up, there was clearly noone at home. Electing to explore the port from end to end, Frannie and Matilda went bar-hopping, finding the general atmosphere one of friendliness and easy camaraderie. They felt, however, that over it all there lay a veneer of false bonhomie: it was as if everyone was thoroughly determined to have a whale of a time, come what may.

When this unnatural gaiety began to pall Frannie dragged Matilda along to have a last look at the 'Saucy Girl'. She lay dark and silent between two other unoccupied boats, in mute contrast to the light and laughter of the shore front.

'We'll lunch here tomorrow,' Frannie decided. 'Let's go and find Gregory and get ourselves home to bed.' Yawning, she hung an affectionate arm around Matilda's ample waist and squeezed. 'It's been rather a long day.'

The villa being where it was and the day dawning gloriously, the morning was for nothing but beach. Frannie had Gregory bring loungers and towels and a refrigerated box of drinks and she and Matilda parked at the edge of a sea which was so calm it barely lapped at the sand. She waited until Gregory had departed before shrugging naked out of her beach robe but Matilda, dressed in a summery frock, refused to take off anything; at first she even niggled at Frannie's behaviour.

'The gardener or the servants might see,' she complained.

Frannie grunted. 'So what – they can't *look* me away!'

'*Gregory* might see.'

'Gregory has seen me before – in far more compromising situations than this.' Rebuffed, Matilda retreated into silence for a while then, her face covered with a handkerchief, she mumbled, 'You'll get burnt. You came close to it yesterday.' The cotton rose and fell with her words.

'*Do* be quiet – what are you, my maid or my mother?' Frannie rolled onto her stomach and Matilda, eyeing her from under the edge of the handkerchief, saw that the night's rest had contrived to make the pink of yesterday's exposure and the red of her wounded buttocks merge into almost the same shade. The bruise from Matilda's teeth had faded somewhat, too.

Frannie wriggled happily as the morning sun bit into her behind. 'Why don't you fix us a couple of Bloody

Marys?' she suggested. 'You'll find all the gear in the box.'

Until midday they had the sand to themselves, then people began to arrive and shed their clothes; the same ones as the previous day, parking in much the same places. Frannie noted this in idle curiosity; even Mediterranean beach life seemed to have set behaviour patterns.

By one thirty she had had enough. She slipped on her robe then used her ingenious emerald ring for the first time that trip, twisting the stone in a clockwise direction to activate Gregory's pocket bleeper. Forewarned, Gregory did not come charging (as he was wont to do) down the steps like an enraged bull elephant about to pulverise whoever was overstepping the limits with his mistress. Barefoot, in shorts, shirt hanging loose, he descended slowly and heavily, throwing a long look of undisguised disdain at the two naked boys lying, face up, who had just arrived.

Frannie's little party gathered together its possessions and moved up the beach. As they drew near to the boys one of them smiled; Frannie smiled back briefly, openly studying their masculine attributes and finding them somewhat lacking for her taste; Matilda looked the other way in flustered embarrassment; Gregory made his opinion perfectly clear with a loud and contemptuous grunt.

At the house, Matilda suddenly felt unwell. Frannie, convinced that Matilda should have removed her clothes and not fried with them on, was chauffeured off to Puerto Banùs for a lunch by herself.

Content with her own company she sat in the sun at Antonio's restaurant and enjoyed a seafood salad, then she wandered down the pier to where the 'Saucy Girl' was moored. As she approached it she saw that the gangplank was down; there was no visible sign of life but a dull thumping from within announced that it was occupied.

Frannie stood opposite the stern and shouted. There was a muffled verbal response, the banging stopped and, in seconds, a head and shoulders appeared in the open hatch doors of the wheelhouse. A muscular young man emerged, all six feet three of him. When he caught sight of Frannie, he became suddenly very still and Frannie, in the act of taking a step forward, froze momentarily, too.

They stared at each other with undisguised curiosity.

Frannie found herself looking at somebody who might easily have been a film star playing the part of a mechanic. His overall was open to the waist exposing a bulging brown chest with a thick mat of black hair. His pleasant smile was immobile, framing gleaming white teeth and the green eyes which surveyed Frannie, much the colour of her own, were surrounded with laugh lines. He had unruly black hair, his hands were grimy, grease smudged one cheek and smeared his neck and chest. In Frannie's eyes none of this detracted in the least from his powerful sexuality.

He saw a vision of loveliness. A sensational, unbelievably voluptuous young lady in a yellow muslin dress which emphasised every tempting curve. An expensive vision, tastefully suggesting money yet managing not to shout it. A dream of perfection and yet real, standing there in the appetising flesh, assessing him as he was her.

Frannie broke the silence. 'Are you Davy?' she asked, barely loudly enough for him to hear.

He managed to restrain himself from ogling her shamelessly. 'Yes. Davy Jones, they call me.' He had an unmistakeable Welsh accent.

Her face relaxed into a smile. Wholly intrigued by this man, she almost stumbled over her words. 'That's,

41

that's odd – my name's Jones, too.' Her single name, which she had kept Lady Frannie Jones Ballington.

'Mine's *not*, actually' – the word *actually* was lilted into four syllables – 'the real one's unpronounceable to anybody but a Welshman, do you see.' As he spoke, Davy produced a rag which he used to wipe his hands. 'What can I do for you, Miss Jones?'

'Frannie,' she said. 'And it's not Miss Jones, it's La . . .' she corrected herself. '. . . it's Mrs.'

'I see. Well, Mrs Jones, may I say it, you have to be the loveliest thing I've ever set eyes upon.'

'Thanks.' It was a compliment from a man who might have been a mechanic in Stratton village's one garage, yet it was produced with such sincerity that she cared about it.

'Will you be coming aboard, then?'

There was the briefest of pauses, a tiny silence as their eyes played with each other.

'Yes. All right. Just for a moment. Thanks.' Frannie took hold of the heavy wires which secured the gangplank and awkwardly pulled herself up, her spiky high heels almost doubling under her. Davy's grease-soiled hand stretched forward in assistance, the brief contact charged with a feeling which seemed to make her arm tingle.

As she stepped down onto the deck and Davy broke his grip, he said, 'You won't mind taking your shoes off, will you?'

She obliged, supporting herself with one hand on the rail, folding her legs back in turn at the knee and slipping her shoes off with the other, intensely aware of this hunk of a man who watched her in fascination.

'Have a seat, won't you?' Frannie eased herself into one of the cane chairs which stood around a matching table on the small deck.

'Drink?'

'No thanks, I just had lunch.'

42

Removing a pale green cushion from another chair, Davy propped it against the table before sitting down on bare cane. 'Wouldn't want to get it dirty,' he offered. 'She's not mine, you see, more's the pity. Now, what can I do for you?'

With difficulty Frannie held in check her outward signs of interest in him. 'I understand you might have some information about a boat?'

'Which one?'

'Silly name. The "Golden Hind".' As Frannie spoke she crossed her legs. His eyes slid briefly to her knees and the exposed flesh above her stocking.

'There was some engine work I couldn't tackle, couldn't be done here anyway. She's left. Gone to Gib.'

'Gibraltar?'

'Right.'

'That isn't too far away, is it?'

'An hour, if you take the road.' Making an effort to keep his eyes on her face, he was marginally losing the battle. 'Sure you won't have a drink?'

'Just a beer, then.'

'Right.' She watched his back disappear as he dropped down into the galley; his shoulders were so broad he had to turn sideways to get through the hatch doors. Pursing her lips she allowed herself a speculative smile.

Understanding her libido perhaps more than most women of her age, Frannie had come to happy terms with it. The initial shock of a raw sexual attraction beginning to subside, she settled back in her chair and allowed herself to enjoy the warm excitement of anticipation.

She was going to have this Welshman.

As he emerged, two tins of lager in one hand and glasses in the other, she studied him with barely disguised prurient interest. The sleeves of his overalls were rolled to the elbows exposing powerfully muscled forearms. His hips were as trim as his shoulders were wide and he carried himself with an effortless grace which seemed to belie his station in life.

He stripped the ring-pulls from the cans with a certain air of authority and, as he filled a glass, he watched her levelly at the same time. Handing it to her, he said, 'You have sensational eyes, Frannie Jones.'

'I do?' She liked the lyrical way he said that, was pleased with his self-confidence. Well, if *he* was going to have *her* instead of the other way around, that might be all the better.

He poured a long draft of beer down his throat. Still standing, he said, 'Why are you looking for the "Golden Hind"?'

'An, ah, friend of mine might be abroad.' She started to open her bag, then realised that the photo of Carter-Smith was back at the villa, on her dressing table. 'I have a picture, but not with me. Clovis Carter-Smith. Did you ever hear of him?'

'Can't say it rings any bells. But now and again I saw people on board who weren't crew.'

'A big man? Grey hair?'

'Maybe. I'd need to see the picture. Is he lost then?' David sat down heavily. His eyes had not drifted away from her for one second since he brought the beers.

'In a manner of speaking.' She glanced around the deck, his image remaining, clouding her perspective. Changing the subject she asked, 'Do you live here?'

'For a while. Until I've finished what needs to be done, do you see. Then I move to the next one.' He paused. 'I get my jobs through the tower. The owners aren't here. I don't even know who they are.' He paused again, in his eyes more than mere amusement. 'I have her entirely to myself,' he said, the intimation quite clear.

Frannie's next breath hovered for a moment in the back of her throat as she experienced a familiar knot of excitement tie itself in the pit of her belly. 'How nice, ' she managed.

'It's all right. Funny life, but I enjoy it.'

'Got a girlfriend?'

'No one in particular. No one remotely like you. By God, it's beautiful you are. Do you mind?' Without waiting for approval he reached out and gentled her cheek with a knuckle. 'Sorry about the grease.'

'Don't be.' Swallowing, feigning an awkwardness which she did not feel, Frannie fumbled with her handbag, picked it up from the table, stood. This was perhaps going just a little *too* fast. In the eyes of a man no self-respecting girl allowed instant sex, however much she might crave it. Especially in the eyes of a young man like this – what was he, twenty-two? He must at least appreciate the conquest.

She kept her emotions in check. 'Are you here all day?'

'You're leaving?' Regret.

'I have a couple of things I really must attend to. Then I thought I might bring you that photograph.' She watched him stand, uncoiling himself with an easy strength. 'Will you be here?'

'If you're coming back, I'll be here, Mrs Jones.' A message was flashing between their eyes as if their brains were linked by telephone wires. 'I'll be here.'

'Later, then.' Slipping into her shoes, she took hold of the gangplank wires. As she pulled herself up on it she half expected to feel the pressure of his touch on her behind, was pleased when it didn't happen; that sort of macho brashness didn't endear her to a man. As she carefully crossed the swaying strip of wood and metal he leapt from rail to quayside, offered both his hands to help her down.

They stood like that, the grubby bear of a mechanic with the laughing green eyes and slender, sophisticated, super-rich Frannie, fingers entwined, searching each other's faces, the telephone wires continuing to sing, until Frannie gently drew herself away.

A few paces down the quay she turned and capriciously blew him a little kiss. 'I won't be very long,' she said, just loudly enough for him to hear.

'Feeling any better?' Frannie called gaily, popping her head around Matilda's half-open door.

Dressed, Matilda was comatose on the bed. 'A bit,' she said. 'I took a couple of aspirin, had a snooze.' She frowned at the happily grinning Frannie. 'What's got into you? You look as if you've won the pools.'

'What on *earth* do *I* need to win the *pools* for?' Tossing her head she ran a hand through her hair. '*Much* better, my sweet – I'm about to get *laid*!'

Matilda's expression remained inscrutably blank. 'Is *that* all? Anybody nice?'

'*Very*, yes. Hunky. Strong, young, virile – I hope, gorgeous. He's got these smashing eyes, this . . .'

A groan from Matilda as she let fly with a pillow and it hit the wall by Frannie's head. 'Well, go and get *on* with it, for Christ's sake. Don't torment *me*!'

Frannie laughed. 'I'm going. I'm *going*. Tell you all about it later. Better – we'll watch the video together if it comes out!'

Her initial shouts were greeted by silence and at first Frannie thought he had left but then Davy's smiling, tousled head appeared in the hatchway doors.

This time she took her shoes off on the quay, handing them through the window of the Mercedes to Gregory who took them stoically between finger and thumb, face unreadable.

Davy wiped his palms down the front of his overalls before helping her aboard; they were greasier than ever, there was a fresh smudge on his forehead.

'I would have cleaned up a bit,' he said, as Frannie dropped her video-concealing bag on the table, sat down and opened it. From a false compartment above the camera she took the photograph of Carter-Smith. 'But I somehow didn't expect you to come back, do you see?' he went on. His eyes fell on the Mercedes. 'Did you come in *that*?'

'What?' Franny followed his glance. 'Oh, *that*.' So used to luxury travel, unless she had a deliberate reason to do so she seldom considered other people's reactions. 'Well, yes. That's Gregory. He sort of chauffeurs me around.'

'Does he, by God? Worse ways to travel, I suppose.'

'Don't let it worry you, Davy. It doesn't make a scrap of difference.' To what, she left unsaid, but she assumed the allusion was obvious. 'Here.' She handed him the photograph and he sat down with it, careful once again to remove the cushion. 'That's the man, in the middle.'

'Oh.' He nodded slowly. 'Yes, I've seen him.'

'You *have*?' Somehow, she hadn't been expecting that.

'Once or twice. On the boat, in a bar as well. The other man, too.' He handed the photo back. 'Good news, then?'

'Yes, yes it is. Perhaps he's not far away, then, if he's still on the boat.'

'Not too far, no. Tell me, I get the feeling this is more, like, than a missing friend. Am I right?'

'Perhaps.' Raising an eyebrow she dared a hand on his knee. 'I'm ex*trem*ely grateful.'

'You really are, aren't you?' he said, as she squeezed then removed the hand. There was a tacky smudge on her thumb which she rubbed against her forefinger.

'Sorry about the dirt.' He shrugged. 'As I said, I didn't expect you back.'

'But you didn't tell me why not.'

'It's obvious, isn't it? You, me . . .' he nodded towards the Mercedes. 'Two worlds apart, isn't it?'

'In some things,' she breathed. 'But I doubt in all. Davy.' There, it was way out in the open. A heavy silence. Mutual desire lay thick and tangible in the salty air. He reached confidently for her hand.

'We'd better go below then, isn't it?' Davy said with a quiet authority which sent a delicious shiver down her spine.

Gregory watched balefully as his mistress and the mechanic vanished from the deck. He tried to convince himself that this meeting was entirely innocent, that she was buying the boat or something, yet all the signs were there for him to see. It may have been more than eighteen months since he had acted for her ladyship in the capacity of minder, but he recognised those signs, all right. With a deeply discontented sigh, he turned on the radio, put his seat into recline and sank back into the hand-tooled leather.

In the small cabin in the prow of the boat, which held little more than the master's triangular double bed, Frannie was already in Davy's arms. Leaning herself hungrily into him, her head tilted back as lips and tongues merged, oblivious to the grease, the slightly tangy smell of his sweat, she tasted him with a passion which had her on her toes so that their bodies could clsash in roughly the right places. Surprised at her voracity, enflamed by it, he dug his fingers into her buttocks and pulled her into him, streaking the yellow muslin with grease. Breathless at the power and need of his hardness she flattened her palms against his iron-banded chest and pushed herself slowly down through his encircling arms, her tongue trailing wetly to his navel. He watched her, his breath beginning to force itself out in little gasps.

Frannie on her knees at this Welsh mechanic's feet, unzipping the overall all the way down, delighted to find beneath it a thick black mat of shiny pubic hair which is unencumbered by underpants. The huge bulge of his erect penis trapped between denim and thigh, she eases her slim fingers in there, finds its throbbing warmth, brings it slowly up, around and out, enthralled by its masculine potency, in that attitude of prayer which is the closest she ever gets to religion. Both hands reverently encircling the object of her beatitude she puts it deep inside her mouth, while from high above her Davy moans as if in pain, his hips jerk forward and he freezes like that, unable, unwanting, to move.

Her eyes drooping, not quite closed, she gives herself to a pleasure which, while it is as different for her as it is for him, is mutually self-consuming. Her hands, predators of his flesh, slide to his knees, slip to the back of his thighs, crawl up over knotted muscle to find his tense buttocks, gripping them, using them for leverage as her wet lips slide up and down his shaft. Restless, they feel their way around to his tight belly where they push, her lips relinquishing their prize as he is insisted down onto the bed. He lies back propped on his elbows, his erect cock in the centre of his vision, as she slides off his sneakers, pulls the overalls over his feet and he is naked.

Wearing tights, aware that their erotic effect lacks the succulence of suspenders and stockings, she, naturally – she is *Frannie* after all – has ways of making them salacious. Her muslin outfit is in three pieces. Showing him her teeth, wetting them, she unzips the side of the skirt, lets it fall, steps out of it. The matching loose top and blouse come just to the top of the tights, where the white of panties shows through the finest of light grey nylon. She hooks her thumbs into the waistband and with one wriggled movement hauls knickers and tights down almost to her knees, and there she lets them hang as green nails trail up the inside of a thigh, the middle one lightly brushing her lewdly displayed pubic mound. Her other hand slips under her hair, wraps itself around the back of her neck and she cocks her head suggestively, pin-up queen bawdily on offer.

It is too much for the Welshman. Growling through clenched teeth he rolls forward from his elbows, leans, grabs her wrist in steely grip and pulls Frannie over and into him with one clumsy, lurching snatch. He rolls her onto her back on the bed, scrabbles his hands to the back of her thighs and, opening them as far as the encircling tights will allow buries his head between her legs and his tongue deep in her bush. But this lasts only seconds, time for Frannie to open her lips and drag in one ecstatic gasp before he clambers up her body in fumbling impatience, tries to force himself between legs which won't open wide enough, reaches down and back across his own, rips tights and pants to one shin as Frannie, eager to help, lifts her knee. He tears the nylon off a foot and plunges himself so hard into her that his balls slap the underside of her buttocks.

It is all over in furious seconds. A frenzied, obsessed coupling, Davy lunging widly in and out of Frannie, Frannie's crotch jerking hungrily up to meet each lusty invasion as she whimpers a string of little orgasms and he goes rigid, weight on his arms, back arched, his sperm flooding into her in one, two, three, four great gushes and he holds himself like that for long, shuddering moments as Frannie's vaginal walls go through a series of contractions, milking the last drops from him and bringing her to yet another, wailed climax.

There is a long, sweaty silence as they lie side by side and then Frannie, awkward because she's not up to the effort of getting up, languidly works off the rest of her clothes. No erotic display is intended but when she is naked she is pleased to see that Davy's penis is stirring again. It rolls over his thigh as he stares at her and, as it rises, except for its commendable size, Frannie is reminded for some strange reason of the index finger of a choirmaster, his palm down before his face, lifting as he prepares his boys for the first note of a song. Stifling a giggle, which brings an amused smile to Davy's face, she reaches for this lively tool, runs a finger and thumb in gentle contemplation from glans to base, thus helping it back to fully erect glory.

'There is nothing, but nothing, in this world . . .' She murmurs and rolls over on top of him.

This time their lovemaking was more or less under control, intense but lasting. He was good, he was very good, Frannie was delighted to discover, then of course a young man who looked like *him*, living in the environment of a jet-set marina, must have the girls queuing up – he was surely screwing his balls off.

No doubt I could teach him a thing or two, she thought, riding him, sitting upright, her knees splayed, facing him, looking down at his massive, hairy chest and lasciviously admiring the thickness of the base of his cock as she worked herself up and down on it. *But I think I'll just take him the way he comes*.

Later, as they shared a cigarette, the only time that Frannie liked to indulge a little in the weed being after sex, he remarked, 'You're in quite some mess, isn't it?'

She glanced down at herself. His grease was evident in light, grubby patches on her breasts, her belly, her thighs. Where she could not see, dirty finger marks had added themselves to the pink and red of her bottom. 'It's very nice,' she drawled comfortably. 'Sexy.' She rolled over onto her stomach.

'Perhaps, but what will *Mr* Jones think?'

'*Mr* Jones? – Yes, well that's *another* story.'

Sitting, he took a final draw at the cigarette, stubbed it out. 'Grease marks on your behind, too.' He touched it. 'Someone been tanning it besides the sun, then?'

She wriggled. 'Never you mind, Davy bach.'

'Oh. Speaking Welsh now, is it?' His eyes were fixed on Matilda's almost faded bruise. 'You, you're quite some girlie now, isn't it?'

'You might say that, I suppose. Yes. Quite some girlie.'

She had stretched her hands above her head, the fingertips touching. He reached out curiously for the emerald ring. 'Are you *very* rich, then?'

'*Very*, yes.'

'Oh.' His fingers played with the emerald. It moved.

A shrill bleep from Gregory's top pocket awoke him from a light snooze. He was out of the car before the second one sounded.

Frannie became aware of rushing, clumping feet somewhere overhead. Davy began to notice as he was saying, 'How come this stone is loose, then?'

'Oh, my God, you haven't . . . ?' Which was as far as Frannie got before the door was smashed wide open and into the cabin wall by a size fourteen boot with such violence that a hinge was torn off and Gregory erupted onto the scene.

Before Frannie, momentarily paralysed, could interfere, seventeen stone of solid, forty-five year old, SAS-trained Gregory had plucked fourteen stone of fit, muscular, twenty-two year old Davy from the bed as if he were no heavier than a pillow and delivered a sledgehammer blow to the Welshman's solar plexus.

Davy's eyes bulged in shock and pain. He doubled over and collapsed on the deck at Gregory's feet as Frannie's frantically screamed, 'No, it's a *mistake!*' came just in time to prevent Gregory's raised and lethal boot from landing a K.O. kick to the side of the Welshman's head.

A questioning grunt from Gregory as Frannie shouted again, unnecessarily, 'No!' and then mumbled, 'Shit, oh *shit*,' as she rolled off the bed and reached for the stricken Davy.

Gregory's eyes rolled from her to him, lingering a moment on each of them, missing nothing, not the crumpled bed linen, nor the clothes strewn about, nor the torn tights, nor the smears of grease over his mistress's flesh.

'Good God, I'm so *sorry*, Davy,' Frannie breathed, a hand on his shoulder as, clutching himself he gagged and fought for breath. 'It was a mistake, a dreadful mistake.' Her eyes found Gregory's, which narrowed although the rest of his face remained impassive. 'It was a mis*take*, Gregory.'

'*Was* it, Lady Ballington?' he responded tonelessly. His gaze once again roamed over the bed, her, the Welshman. 'Perhaps. Perhaps *not*.' Taking a deep breath as if trying to bring some inner seething under control, he spun around and strode from the cabin.

6

FOR GETTING – FORGIVING

'YOU SHOULDN'T REPROACH YOURSELF, GREGORY.'

'Reproach? You did say *reproach*, my lady?'

'Well, just on the off chance you might have the *slightest* pang of regret, it's quite all right. You did what you have to do.'

'Very *well*, so I hear,' Matilda put in admiringly.

It was early evening. Frannie and Matilda were sitting together on the veranda overlooking the pool, Gregory hovering nearby in an attitude which suggested he had something better to do.

'Do shut up, Matilda,' said Frannie. She frowned at Gregory. 'Perhaps we should initiate some sort of a system. How about *three* bleeps before you're sure I'm in trouble?'

'Suppose you don't *manage* to signal three times?' Gregory folded his arms across his chest. 'What then?'

As she considered this, Frannie blinked several times. 'Yes. I, I *see* what you mean.'

'With respect, Lady Ballington. I'm employed by 'is lordship to make sure that nothing . . . *untoward* 'appens to you. If you remember, there *was* Amsterdam. Worse, Los Angeles. If I 'adn't . . . '

'Yes. *Thank* you. You don't have to remi . . . ' Frannie interrupted, was herself cut off.

54

' . . . you would quite probably 'ave been *dead*.'

'Yes. All *right*, Gregory.'

'The smallest bleep, I'm on my way. That's what I'm paid for.'

Frannie sighed. Her eyes flickered over the pool, the pine copse, the blue of the Mediterranean beyond, her mind somewhere else. 'That's the way it has to be, I don't see what else. In that case, if there *should* ever be a mistake again like this afternoon's . . . ' She paused, then finished in an irritable rush. 'I'd be grateful if you'd refrain from acting so bloody self-righteous!'

A jaw muscle twitched. Apart from that Gregory's expression remained inscrutable. '*Yes*, my lady.' He unfolded his arms. 'Will that be all, then?'

'For the moment, yes. I won't be needing you later, we'll be staying home.'

Gregory nodded and walked away wordlessly. Watching his back disappear through the veranda doors, Matilda said. 'He's a bit upset. Perhaps there was no need to tell him off?'

'Phooey. He's not upset, he's revelling in it. Anyway it was all so . . . shit, it was embarrassing!'

'*You*? Em*barr*assed?'

'In more ways than one.' She took a sip of whisky sour then said, brightly, 'Anyway, let's skip it. Life isn't all roses!'

'Really?' Matilda studied her briefly. Her mistress. Her enigma. 'And the boy, this Davy of yours – you're sure he'll be all right?'

'Apart from wounded pride, I think so. Thank God Gregory managed to miss his ribs. Smashed the wind out of him. Badly bruised his stomach, no doubt. Hopefully, that's all.' She contemplated her nails, buffed them against her blouse.

'You took your special bag. Have you got everything on film?'

'Hardly the time to ask, is it? I assume the wretched thing came out. I haven't checked it and frankly I'm not in the mood.'

'Ooops. Sorry.'

'You know, I really ought to do something for Davy. To make up for things.'

'Why? He *had* you, didn't he?'

'Matilda, you are *some* . . . ' She shook her head in despair, whatever she thought Matilda was, left unsaid. Then she smiled. '*I* know. I've just had a *great* idea.' She called for Gregory who reappeared moments later.

'Gregory,' she said, animatedly. 'That little card which gets us through the gate at Puerto Banús?' He nodded. 'It corresponds to some sort of a *boat* in there. Does it say on it which one?'

He slipped a bulging wallet from his back pocket, located the pass. 'No, there's just a number.'

'There ought to be papers somewhere.' She bit her lip. 'I know. If you go in the house and wave that under Paco's nose and say *papeles* and, er, *barco*, I'm sure he'll get the message. Would you mind awfully?'

'I'll see what I can do.'

Within minutes Gregory was back, clasping a clear plastic wallet containing some papers. Taking it, she slipped them out, unfolding them one at a time and glancing briefly through them. Then, one immaculately tweezered eyebrow slightly raised, she pursed her lips. Replacing the papers, she put them very carefully on the table before her.

'Thank you *so* much, Gregory,' she said. 'That ought to do very nicely.' As her eyes fell on Matilda she smiled an elated, but secret little smile. 'Very nicely indeed!'

Wearing jeans and a thin, pale burgundy sweater that belied its Donna Karan label Frannie walked briskly along the quay towards the 'Saucy Girl'. She was apprehensive this late, fine morning. Meeting a lover again after a first sexual encounter being in any case a moment for unwanted intrusion of the nerves, she found that that natural timidity was mightily exacerbated by the fact that the man in question had been pole-axed by her minder – while utterly in the buff, what was more.

There was no one home. Disappointed, she stood across from the prow, running her eyes over the clean lines of the boat as events from the previous afternoon crowded her mind.

Lost in thought, she took little notice of the engine of the mini, two-stroke motorcycle which Davy parked behind her, was unaware of his presence until a melodious Welsh voice said, 'On your own then today, Frannie? No hired assassin with you, is it?'

'Oh.' Frannie flinched. Well, she deserved some sort of a remark like that. She turned a rueful face on him as he took hold of a mooring line and, muscles rippling beneath an overstretched T-shirt, leant his weight back on it to heave the boat a little closer to the dock. She noticed that he winced as if in pain as he did this. Grunting, he spanned the narrow gap over the water with an awkward, strung-out pace and swung himself aboard. Without looking at her he began to lower the gangplank.

'How do you feel?' she ventured.

'As well as can be expected, I suppose.' Still he didn't glance at her. 'I'd dearly like the chance to get a poke back at the bastard, though. Do me a power of good, shouldn't wonder.'

Frannie ignored that. 'Seriously, are you all right?'

The gangplank was down. For the first time his eyes met hers. Unreadable, they were anything but smiling. 'Nothing that won't go away in a day or so. I've been worse done to. Well then . . .' he seemed reluctant. 'Are you coming aboard, or no?'

'I'd like to, yes.'

'Come on then, woman.' *Woman*? She thought, as she accepted the help of an ungreasy hand. Nobody had *ever* called her 'woman' before. It was a bald contrast to 'my lady'.

Safely across, she leant back against the rail, staring at him. The awkwardness of the initial encounter dealt with, nerves in retreat, she allowed herself a brief exploration of other emotions finding that, happily, her carnal desire for him had not evaporated with his emasculation beneath Gregory's fist. 'I'm so terribly sorry for what happened,' she said.

'You told me at least fifty times yesterday.' A touch of feeling finally crept into his voice. 'Okay, it wasn't your fault, I understand that. Why don't you sit down, then?'

She did, unslinging her shoulder bag and dropping it on the table. Inside was her gift to him, but she hesitated to produce it, uncertain how fierce his pride might be. She had heard somewhere that the Welsh were renowned for it.

He was wearing faded but clean cut-off jeans and when he sat he left the cushion in its place. He studied her and the longer he did so the more his expression softened at the edges. Finally he said, with the hint of a smile, 'You're just as beautiful – despite what I now know about you.'

She frowned. 'Meaning?'

'You don't exactly fall blindly into sex, do you? I'd say there's some pretty hard calculation gone into the having of a gorilla in the background, isn't it then?'

What else but frankness? 'Yes. Yes, there is. Gregory is paid to protect me.'

'Ah.' He nodded slowly. 'By you, or by *Mr* Jones? – But I forgot, there *is* no Mr Jones, is there?'

'Why do you say that?'

'Didn't I hear your ape call you *lady* something or other?'

'Ballington. Lady Ballington. My single name was Jones though. I still have it.'

'Lady *Ball*ington, is it? Amusing, in its way, that.'

She blinked. He wasn't going to hit her with sarcasm, was he? *Please* don't do that. 'I never thought about it.'

'*Didn't* you, then?' He shook his head. 'Amazing, this part of the world. Don't think I've ever bumped into such a weird bunch of people in my life.'

'I see. You think *I'm* weird, then?'

His voice softened. 'Sorry, it's just that – hell, let's forget it.' A hand covered hers. 'I think you're sensational. Very, *very* different.'

She reached in her bag. 'I wanted to make up for Gregory.' Pulling out the plastic wallet of ships' papers she handed it to him. 'Here. A little present. The "Saucy Girl". It's yours. Well, it will be once my husband's lawyers have sorted out the details.'

It was as casually offered as a sweater at Christmas time and he gaped at her, stunned, uncomprehending, the wallet loose in his fingers. For the first time she allowed herself to express the delight of her discovery of the previous evening. Her face creased with pleasure, she said, 'One of those extra*ord*inary coincidences of life – you know, the ones which seem to happen all the time? I *knew* we had some sort of a boat here, can you *imagine* my astonishment when I found out last night that it was *this* one?'

With difficulty, he found words. 'You *own* this boat? And you want to *give* it to me?'

'It's the best way I can think of saying I'm sorry.'

A spluttered, astonished laugh. 'This, this is too ridiculous. But *why*?'

'Because I very much want to, Davy.'

Glancing at the wallet, seeing it properly for the first time, he tossed it on the table. 'What do I get if he breaks my neck? The QE2? – No thanks, Frannie.'

'Don't Davy. Please? I was very much afraid you'd react like that. Now just listen to me a moment.' She put a hand on his knee, feeling how warm it was from the sun, leaving it there. 'Believe me, this boat means absolutely nothing to either me or my husband. It was more or less thrown in with a house we bought. It will do you far more good than it'll ever do us.'

'But she must be worth twenty-five, thirty thousand pounds.'

'It doesn't *matter*.' She increased the pressure on his knee. 'Look, I don't mean to be patronising, I don't want to sound boastful, but here's a simple fact. You asked me yesterday was I rich, I said yes. Actually that's a bit of an understatement. My husband is probably the richest man in England.'

Outwardly, he didn't react.

'He spends more on me at one fashion show than the "Saucy Lady" is worth.' Letting go of his knee she picked up the wallet, offered it again. 'Take it, Davy, why don't you? I really, really want you to.'

His eyes on the wallet, he said, 'A boat's a woman, Frannie. I wish you'd at least learn to call her she.' Gingerly, as if he expected them to explode at any second, he took hold of the papers. 'All right, since you insist so eloquently, then I will.'

'Good. Am I now at least forgiven for Gregory?'

'I'll let you know later,' he said, letting the wallet fall back on the table. Standing, he drew her to her feet and into his bulky warmth. 'I'm taking us below first, where we'll get out of these clothes and I'll thank you properly for the boat.'

As the power of his sudden need surged through her she trembled. 'A truly *proper* thank you should take up most of the rest of the day,' she murmured, kissing his chest through the T-shirt. Sliding her hand down to his crotch she found his rising erection as his fingers dug into the softness at the underside of her buttocks.

'At least the rest of the day, isn't it?' he said. 'That is provided your hired killer doesn't get other ideas.'

Tugging at his zip she slid it down, eased her fingers inside, under his pants, and wrapped them around her favourite plaything of the moment.

'No Gregory,' she muttered, squeezing gently. 'There will be absolutely no Gregory.'

7

PUSSYCATS IN PARADISE

IDYLLIC DAYS. SEX, SUNSHINE. GOOD FOOD, BETTER WINE – more sex, more sunshine. Frannie's skin turning the syrupy brown which she found a gratifying change from white, her body pleasured daily, and nightly, by the ever-eager Davy. Perhaps not the riotous start to a sexual romp which it might have been, but a satisfying preparation for unknown wickedness which surely loomed on the horizon.

Almost a week drifted by like that, a languid, luxurious, orgiastic week, Frannie living only for this moment and the next.

A niggling intrusion on this indolence were thoughts of Clovis Carter-Smith, possibly in Gibraltar aboard the 'Golden Hind' and finally Frannie decided it was time to seek him out. Instead of making the short drive along the coastal road she had her lover take her and Matilda there on the 'Saucy Girl'.

They started early. The weather still held, though a thin wedge of purple cloud over the distant Rif mountains in Morocco hinted at imminent change. The swell increased as they approached The Rock but there were no threatening waves and dolphins turned out, as so often, to perform their friendly, graceful, breathtaking tricks around the boat.

Three hours at sea and Gibraltar loomed close, grey and craggy, crowned by a swirling cushion of cloud. As they neared the harbour, many times the size of Puerto Banùs but giving shelter to far fewer and usually less impressive boats, a white yacht, rather grand, nosed out and began a slow turn towards the west. Frannie focused binoculars on it, training them with difficulty because here the swell was beginning to cut up and get choppy.

Finally getting a few seconds hold on the stern, she made out the name. The 'Golden Hind'. 'Damn,' she exclaimed, to no one in particular.

'What's up?' Davy called from behind the wheel.

She slipped the glasses back in their case, left the rail and took them into the wheelhouse, waving them as she did so in the direction of the yacht. 'My man,' she said, 'if he's on board, that is. One step ahead of me.'

Davy studied the boat. 'Going out into the Atlantic. That means either west to America or south to Morocco and Africa.'

'Where the bee sucks, there suck I,' Frannie muttered absently.

'What?'

'Sorry. Nothing. Something from school days. Do you think we can find out where it, where *she's* bound for?'

'The harbour master should know.'

As they slid into calmer waters and Davy throttled down, he said, 'What *is* it about that man on the 'Golden Hind'? Is he really just a long lost friend? If so there's nothing to stop us radioing him.'

'He's a swindler. He owes my husband a great deal of money.'

'So *that's* it. And you've been sent to find him, is it?'

'Something like that, yes.'

'I think I'm beginning to see the light. Gregory.

That's why you have Gregory, no?'

Smiling, she laid a hand on his bicep. 'It's a good idea. But not *quite* accurate, I'm afraid.'

He shook his head. 'Perhaps I'm not *meant* to understand you.'

The harbour master was pleased to help. He told them that the 'Golden Hind' was on route for Casablanca, that there was nobody on board called Carter-Smith but there was a Mr Digby who was big, thick set and with grey hair.

'How far away is Casablanca?' Frannie asked as she and Matilda strolled with Davy through the bustle of Gibraltar's Main Street.

'Boat that size, two days the most,' said Davy.

'Oh, good, then we won't have to fly,' Matilda commented. A wind had sprung up since they berthed and it was getting stronger, beginning to gust down the hilly shopping street, making it cold enough for sweaters.

'You don't seriously think I'm spending two days at sea, do you?' Frannie shivered, pulling herself tighter into Matilda's fleshy side.

'Couldn't we *drive*, then?' said Matilda hopefully. 'It's only sort of . . .' she waved vaguely, 'over there somewhere.'

'We fly. Besides . . . ' Frannie tugged on Matilda's elbow, stopping them, peering into the neon-lit interior of an open-fronted pub. 'Good *grief* . . . ' A thin man of about fifty with a walnutty, wrinkled face and crinkly hair so black it looked dyed, was in the act of rising from a bar stool, grinning in delighted recognition. He was dressed in a grey suede jacket over an open-necked flower print shirt, two heavy gold chains hung around a scraggy neck and a gold Rolex was half-buried in hairs at his wrist.

Frannie suddenly wished she were somewhere else, that this meeting was not about to take place, but it was too late. The man bounced into the street, hand outstretched. 'Well, waddya know, Frannie, right?' he enthused, the voice North American. 'Franny Ballington?'

Frannie had no alternative but to accept the hand. It was dry and leathery. 'Hello,' she said coolly. 'I'm afraid I don't remember your name, but I know you're a long way from California.'

'Goldberg,' he said. 'Bernard Goldberg.' He pumped Frannie's hand for unnecessary seconds, then did the same with Davy and Matilda as she introduced them.

He invited them for a drink, he was the sort of character who would not be refused and as they crowded into the pub with him Franny, resigning herself to his company, asked one of the usual questions. 'What brings you to Europe?'

'Enjoying myself, mainly. Plus a little business.'

Frannie slid her bottom, tightly outlined beneath cream, jersey, Valentino slacks, onto a stool, taking instant dislike to the garish pub with its electronic machines and fake wooden beams. 'Making any movies?' she asked.

'Not over here, no. It's hardly economical. I've been doing some promotion stuff up in Madrid, now I'm taking time off in a little place called Marbella. Thought I'd take a side trip here.'

'*We're* in Marbella,' said Matilda, her interest enlivened by the news that this rather ostentatious man was connected with the film business. 'Davy brought us across for the day on his boat.'

Davy lifted a pint of Bass to his lips. 'Have you made anything famous?' he asked.

As Goldberg's eyes swept over him as if assessing him for star potential, Frannie smiled to herself, realising that the Welshman might be *exactly* the sort of young man who would fit his particular bill. 'I doubt it,' he said. 'My work's rather . . . specialised. I . . . '

'How do you *like* Europe, Bernard?' Frannie interrupted, having no particular wish, at that moment, to have him elaborate on his films.

'It's okay, I guess.' He studied Frannie frankly and she was uncomfortably aware of what must be going through his mind. Memories, salacious memories, were pushing their way into hers, too.

Goldberg was alone, there seemed no alternative but have him join them for lunch where, uncertain how Davy might react to it, Frannie felt obliged to keep steering the conversation away from the exact nature of the Goldberg productions. Afterwards, when they went out into the street, it was to find that heavy, ponderous cloud had blotted out the sun. At the harbour they could see that the sea beyond was getting quite rough, and there being no way Frannie was about to return on the 'Saucy Girl' in that weather she accepted Goldberg's offer of a lift back in his hired car, and she and Matilda parted company with Davy.

On the winding road near San Roque, Matilda said from the back, 'You never did get around to telling us much about your work, Bernard. Do you make documentaries, animal films, something like that?'

Goldberg produced an extraordinary chuckle which seemed to start down by his shoes and shudder its way up through his entire body and even Frannie, easier about this situation now Davy was not present, and beginning to accept Goldberg for what he was, raised a smile.

'Well, you could say that I guess,' he said, as his shoulders ceased to twitch. 'Nature study, right Frannie?'

She raised an eyebrow. 'Nature in the *raw*, rather.'

'What's got into you two?' Matilda protested. 'Tell me the big secret?'

'Mr Goldberg,' Frannie pronounced. 'Makes porn movies!'

'Oh.' Matilda blinked, then pushed the rim of her spectacles tight onto the bridge of her nose. *'Porn?* How very *jolly.'* Her plump cheeks creased into a grin of realisation. 'California, didn't you say. You're not . . . ?'

'The very man,' said Frannie. 'Bernard directed me in my, ah, *starring* role in Los Angeles. The therapy trip.'

'Therapy? What therapy?' Goldberg looked puzzled.

'So it *was*, indeed it was,' murmured Matilda. 'I'd forgotten that.'

Drawing her legs under her, Frannie hooked an arm over the back of her seat and rested her chin on her hand, so that she was looking at both Matilda and Goldberg. 'I was trying to get over a traumatic love affair,' she said. 'The only reason I took the part. Immerse myself in impersonal sex, as it were. Worked like a dream, actually.'

Goldberg shook his head. 'Sometimes I don't get you broads at all. You were but ter*rific.'

Frannie pursed her lips naughtily. She may as well get some mileage out of this rather unappetising person since they were going to be together for a while yet. 'I'm a natural. That's what *you* told me, anyway.'

'Frannie is *not* a *broad.'* Matilda objected. 'She is a lady.'

'Sure she is. *Some* lady, I can tell you.' He paused. 'Boy!'

They drove in silence for a few minutes, part of a continuous stream of traffic which was overloaded with lorries from the docks at Algeciras. Goldberg broke the silence excitedly. 'Heh, what do you *know*, girls? I've got a *copy* of that video with me. The one with *Frannie* in it? Turned out to be one of my best ever. *Pussycats In Paradise.'*

Frannie smothered a laugh. *'Brilliant* title, Bernard,' she managed, with Matilda beginning to splutter in disbelief in the background.

Goldberg failed to see any joke. 'Not bad, is it?' he commented, seriously.

'I've got a great writer works with me. Always comes up with the goods.' He rolled the words over his tongue. '*Pussycats In Paradise*. Great ring to it.'

Matilda was attacked by the giggles while Frannie tried to hold her laughter back and failed. Still not seeing anything funny, Goldberg repeated himself. 'One of the best I ever made.' He paused. 'Ever *see* it, Franny?'

It stopped her laughter. The promised copy had, of course, never arrived at Stratton Castle. She twisted herself back to a normal sitting position. 'No,' she said slowly, realising what the response was going to be. 'No, I haven't, as a matter of fact.'

'*Like* to?'

Of course.

'Well, I, um.' She stared at the container lorry with Dutch number plates which filled the road ahead of them, wondering, dubious, yet intrigued. There was so *much* she had indulged in during the shooting of that video. *So* much. And Goldberg had been right there, on set, directing it every explicit step of the way. Her eyes flickered back to him, dwelt fractionally, slid away as her mouth made up her mind for her. 'I think that, that perhaps I *might*, yes.'

'Well, that's just *great*! No time like tonight. I've got a snazzy little suite in a hotel called Ponty something or other. We can have dinner, take in the action afterwards.'

Doubts lingered. Yes, she wanted to see the film. As a matter of fact, she *very much* wanted to see it. But in the company of this less than salubrious specimen of the human race? The idea of shared sex with him was at the very least disagreeable. His intent was patently clear, the scene already beginning to take shape in her mind. The skinny, brash Bernard Goldberg and her, alone together. The low-lit hotel suite. Booze. Coke – naturally there would be coke. The TV coming rudely to life to expose her in lewd porno action before their eyes. Goldberg unbuttoning his 501 Levis, easing them down over his skinny knees . . . .

'So waddya say?' His eyes on her breasts.

'I, uh . . . ' Inspiration. 'Well, *fine*. But I'm sure Matilda would like to see it *too*, *wouldn't* you dear?'

Matilda smiled happily. 'Not half I wouldn't!'

'That's okay. Afterwards, I lend it to you. I won't need it for a coupla days. Not until I go back to Madrid.'

'Thanks. But what I meant *rather* was that we could all three watch it together.'

'All *three* . . .? Oh.' He was trapped, no way out. He could hardly refuse, not now. Rapid rethink. For sure, he had not failed to notice that the half – blind Matilda was interestingly curvaceous. What the hell, he thought. So maybe they both get turned on. So maybe two'll be better than one. So maybe I'll . . . *this* time maybe I'll . . . What the hell . . .?

Grinning, he fished a cigar from his shirt pocket with a flourish, as if in celebration. 'Okay, it's a deal. Why not?' He said. He bit the end off the cigar. 'To-night we'll have ourselves a little party, girls. A *great* little party.'

Hotel 'Ponty something or other' proved to be Puente Romano, a five star, super-luxury Arab-owned hotel. They dined in the restaurant at a table overlooking lush, semi-tropical gardens with several swimming pools and a meandering stream graced with swans.

Frannie was in a nervously chatty mood, utterly frank, there in any case being little to hide from a man who had directed her in a porno film. She revealed that she was embarked on a second sexual adventure, that she had published a book about her previous one and that she intended penning another about this – assuming, that was, there was enough action to fill it.

By the time she let that remark drop they were on coffee and liqueurs. Goldberg chuckled. '*Enough*?' he exclaimed, his eyes roving over her Christian Lacroix, silk-wrapped torso. 'The way you look, and with your *guts*? Jesus Christ, Frannie, I wanna bet you'll get up to enough games to fill a dozen Kamasutras!'

Frannie smiled. 'You never know.'

'That Davy guy. He's, ah . . .?'

'Naturally.' She decided to be wicked. 'He's *very* good.'

'Nice looking boy. Trouble with these Sylvester Stallone types, you think you've found yourself a new star, then they can't get it up for the camera!'

Matilda grinned. In such a swish environment she was not, of course, wearing her glasses and her impression of Goldberg was an indistinct smudge on the other side of a very blurred table. 'Is *that so*, Bernard?' she ventured. 'Tell us – what do you *do* when that happens?'

'Do? If they can't per*form*, they're out of a job – unless the fluffers get them to function.'

'*Fluffers*?' From Frannie.

'Fluffers, yeah. Horny chicks who aren't in that particular movie. I usually keep one or two off-set to deal with the emergencies.'

Matilda was wholly intrigued. 'How *very int*eresting. Just *how* do they do *that*?' she demanded.

Goldberg shrugged matter-of-factly. 'They give the guy a private exhibition, feel him up, a bit of a blow job, that sort of stuff, then send him back on camera as soon as he's raised a hard-on.'

Matilda blinked several times over her coffee cup, digesting this unusual piece of information. 'Yes, I *see*.'

She managed to keep astonishment from her voice. 'Well, how very amusing.'

'He shrugged. 'It's a job. They get paid for it. I doubt it does much for them.' He scraped back his chair, stood. 'Excuse me just a moment?'

When he returned, a few minutes later, Frannie noticed that Goldberg's eyes were a touch brighter, the pupils somehow sharper. Tell-tale signs. As he sat down he swallowed the remains of a brandy. 'Just had a great line,' he commented. 'One thing you get in this little old town is quality. Expensive as hell, but worth it.' He glanced from Frannie to Matilda. 'Sorry, that's all I brought out with me. But there's plenty back at the suite.'

'That's all right,' Frannie said. 'We don't use coke.'

He looked surprised. 'Oh. *Some* people *don't*, I guess.'

'We don't need it, do we Matilda?'

'What?'

'Coke.'

'Oh. Right. No.' Matilda confirmed, not even sure what she was talking about.

'Different strokes for different folks.' He raised a finger for a waiter. 'Booze is okay though, no? I'm having another brandy. What'll you two have?'

They opted for a Moët Petite Liquorelle champagne liqueur and, as the waiter slid off, Goldberg remarked, 'I just thought of a *great* side-trip for you Frannie, if you ever get to the States again. A *must*.'

'Oh yes?'

'Place called Big River Falls in Southern California. They put on a sex show there weekends which is – believe it or not – but *different*. I never came across anything like it anywhere else. People drive down from LA to catch it.'

Frannie looked suitably blasé. 'Is anything *that* different once you've dipped in the fleshpots of Hamburg and Amsterdam?'

71

'This *is*, I tell you. Let me set the scene. A night club, Paul's Place, big, a raised dance floor in the middle. Tables and chairs around it in tiers – you know, like an arena? Every Saturday night is amateur sex night and I tell you, it's a real gas. There's a big prize for the winning couple based on audience appreciation.' He took a long sip from his fresh brandy, his eyes appearing to intensify, a growing reaction to the mixture of cocaine and spirits.

'A prize for *what* exactly?' Frannie prompted him.

'The best performance. Sex. They're all young, no slobs, one of the secrets of Paul's success. Half a dozen new couples every Saturday, strictly amateur, competing for ten thousand green ones which are covered by the big admission fees. And once you've seen *this*, you don't care *how* much you pay. A couple at a time, dressed in their ordinary Saturday night clothes, they go down there on that floor. There's a bed, get it? A bed, a chair, some cushions, that's all. The lights go down except for spots on them, whatever music they've chosen, whatever turns them on, hits the sound system and they get down to the business of screwing.'

He poured some more brandy into himself as Frannie digested this story and Matilda gaped at his smudge. 'Just like *that*?' said Matilda. 'They, they *screw* in front of all those people?'

'Lots of guys and girls get big kicks out of exhibitionism. More than you might think. Then there's the money – it's a great deal of bread to most of them. I tell you, it's a sen*sat*ional evening, *every* time. Once they get started they really *go* at each other, get my drift, and there's maybe a thousand people getting turned on at once with them. Nothing to do with the usual boring live show with its jaded performers. I mean, this is *wild*! Great place for me, too, I recruit a lot of talent there.'

Her head now agreeably light, Franny opened her evening bag and brought out a little notepad with a gold pencil attached, began writing. 'Paul's Place, wasn't it?' She glanced at Goldberg. 'Whereabouts did you say?'

'Thought it'd grab you. Big River Falls. About seventy miles south of LA. Tell you what, if you're ever there with a stud and you feel like joining the fun, I wanna bet you'll win the ten thou!'

Frannie smiled to herself, failed to comment. She replaced the notepad, pushed a stray lock from her eyes, emptied her glass.

'Why don't we have a nightcap?'

'Aren't you *coming* back with me?'

'Of course.' *And then what?* thought Frannie. Well, anyway, the film. She covered a slight stab of nerves with a little laugh. 'I didn't mean a *final* nightcap.'

As more drinks arrived, Goldberg said, 'You know her pretty well, Matilda. Do you think Frannie would enjoy having it off on stage?' His words were just a little slurred.

Matilda giggled. 'I don't believe . . .' she hiccupped, 'there is any limit . . .' she gulped champagne and ran a tongue over her lips '. . . to her ladyship's versa*til*ity!' she finished, somewhat grandly.

'Well, *really*, Matilda!' Frannie shook her head, frowning, nevertheless amused. 'You're *pissed*, of course.'

'Just a little.' Matilda responded with a toss of her head and an ingenuous grin. 'So when's the porn show?'

Bernard Goldberg set the scene with elaborate care. The three of them on a comfortable sofa, himself in the middle. A big-screened television facing them just a few feet away. Iced drinks, crisps, a little bowl of coke to hand on an occasional table. Low lights, Sinatra warbling in the background, almost exactly as

Frannie had pictured it when Goldberg suggested it on the drive from Gibraltar – except for the welcome, if not totally sober, presence of Matilda.

'Are we all sitting comfortably?' Goldberg drawled. His jacket was off, cravat dispensed with, yellow silk shirt wide open, displaying his gold chains. A half-smoked, unlit cigar jiggled at his lips as he spoke. 'Okay, let us begin, children. An hour or so of good clean fun for the kiddies!'

He pressed a button on the remote control unit in his hand, the TV jerked into life. Another, and three linked crowns appeared on the screen, beneath them the words 'Triple Crown Video'. Slow, pulsing rock music drowned Sinatra, the logo faded away to be replaced by the legend 'A Bernard Goldberg Production', which lingered for several seconds as Goldberg's elbow proudly touched Frannie's ribs. The famous name disappeared, was followed by the flaming red silhouettes of a naked dancing couple superimposed with the credits, and Frannie was startled to find her name at the top of the cast of female actresses – listed just as 'Frannie'.

Then, the blazing title spinning out of infinity to spread itself over the screen – PUSSYCATS IN PARADISE.

EVENING. TIGHT ON A SPRAWLING MANSION.
The illuminated drive is choked with expensive cars.
ZOOMING IN.
Through opened French windows to a spacious lounge filled with dancing figures in fancy dress.
TRACKING ON.
A dancing couple. The devil and a medieval queen with piled-up hair wearing a silver mask.

At first Frannie fails to recognise that this is her and the bony Goldberg elbow insinuates itself once more into her ribs as he freezes the frame. 'That's *you*, Frannie,' he says. 'Remember?'

'Yes.' The word drops hesitantly from Frannie's lips as she also remembers, in lurid detail, what is about to happen to her.

Golberg allows the movie to continue. (Unnecessarily lengthy shots of strangely dressed people dancing, pawing one another intimately, casting heavily suggestive looks all around – but, unhappily, Goldberg is no Fellini and the only atmosphere which is created is that of a film which desperately needs to get moving.)

CUT TO: A DINING ROOM.

A long table heavy with expensive glasses, silverware and cutlery.

The revellers troop gaily in, take their places.

CUT TO: LATER.

Plates piled with food. TIGHT ON various diners.

(Interminable shots of actors and actresses pretending to be exceptionally gluttonous, all-too-evidently false laughter, wine flowing, spilling – it had been real wine, Frannie remembers, but cheap, vinegary – a *Tom Jones*–ish attempt to link the consumption of food and drink with sexual license, not even remotely succeeding.)

Goldberg noisily snorts more cocaine as the action which is the film's *raison d'être* finally begins.

The medieval queen, Frannie, is bent forwards, by her dancing-partner devil, over the table in a space which has been cleared amongst the dirty dishes; and her shoulders are pinned down by a man in a bear suit who is facing her on the other side. The devil lifts the queen's heavy skirts and piles them on her back, to reveal a most un-medieval suspender belt, stockings and see-through Bonni Keller knickers which he slides down her legs as, at the same time, Nell Gwyn, on hands and knees under the table, gives him head.

The drama hots up. The devil is fucking his queen and the bear-man, suit unzipped, has his cock in her mouth whilst Matilda goggles and Frannie-in-the-flesh is transported through the screen and into Queen Frannie herself, feeling it over again, *smelling* it again, getting wet and then suddenly all the vicarious pleasure in this other self is rudely interrupted as she realises that the Golberg hand has crept high under her skirt and is groping for its prize.

'You will *not!*' she protests, shoving the offending appendage from her thigh as Matilda's attention wanders tipsily from the TV.

'Christ! Why the *hell not*?' Grabbing the remote control Goldberg freezes a frame. Nell Gwyn has pushed the bear-man away from Frannie's lips and, lifting her skirts high, has arched her naked hips to the royal mouth, where they remain, inches from the tip of Frannie's tongue.

'I don't *want* to,' Frannie mutters.

'You don't *want* to? You're putting me on. You were *drooling*, your *knees* were tapping together, for fuck's sake!'

'I'm *sorry*, Bernard. Why don't we just watch the film?'

'Yeah, well, that's just *great*. Can't you be normal?'

'Hah!' from Matilda. Then, 'Hah!' again.

Frannie sighs, legs tight together, eyes fixed forward. 'The *film*, Bernard please?'

'Okay. We *watch* the *film!*' The stoned Goldberg is angry. 'You're just about to eat *cunt*, *okay*?' He stabs a button and Queen Frannie's tongue continues on its short journey to Nell Gwyn's pussy as the devil rams his cock into his queen and a cute little girl in a black tailcoat and a velvet tie is prostrated across the table next to Frannie and fucked by the bear-man.

But Goldberg is standing. Mr Producer-Director Bernard Goldberg Esquire has shoved himself unsteadily to his feet and is going through the motions of an exceedingly clumsy striptease.

'Oh, for *God's sake*!' Frannie groans. She picks up the control panel and freezes the picture as her screen self, on her back on the table now, is about to be impaled by a huge Jamaican whose impressive piece of equipment stands in rigid contrast to the unfastened trousers of his white suit.

'Listen – I *want* to be *naked, okay*?' snarls Goldberg, stumbling about as he wrenches striped boxer shorts over his feet – and *is* naked. He glares defiance at Frannie, at the startled Matilda who blinks and says 'Golly!', at the unmoving TV tableau. 'Something *wrong* with having no clothes on?' He looks as if he is about to spit contempt at the screen. 'All of a *sudden*?'

Frannie is irritated but feels little alarm. She notices that he has no erection, wonders at this. In that condition the threat of attempted rape is hardly imminent. Spinning around, he drops heavily back onto the sofa between the two women where his anger abates. 'So why the delay? Let's watch the video,' he mutters.

Frannie presses the release button. The blatantly exposed black man comes to life and lunges into the queen, bringing a gasp to her lips as Nell Gwyn moves away and the devil rides in to her mouth. The on-screen Frannie is immersed in this with all the enthusiasm of enflamed lust, her real self is now merely a curious spectator whose enjoyment is marginally spoilt as she prepares to counter any further initiatives from Goldberg.

The movie-man's eyes are glazed, he seems mesmerised by the screen. Frannie thinks he looks patently ridiculous, pathetic even, as he sits there in his skinny nakedness, wearing only a half-smoked cigar and a pair of diamond-patterned socks.

Frannie's eyes slide over Goldberg, settle briefly on Matilda who is flying on a trip of her own watching her star-mistress being endlessly serviced by six men and two women. Matilda's hand is lost amongst the heavy folds of turquoise velvet on her lap, Frannie realises what it must be doing but supposes that her maid is still sufficiently aware of Goldberg not to make this too obvious.

CUT. LATER.

The medieval queen is unmasked, naked except for garter belt and stockings. The tailcoat girl is now wearing only the velvet bow tie. On their sides facing one another they perform lesbian sixty-nine. The six men, including the devil, the bear and the Jamaican, stand around the table and ogle them, erect members in hand.

Goldberg is getting excitable once more. His hand begins to search out Matilda's amongst the velvet folds, but he touches Frannie only with his eyes which rove from her to the screen to Matilda and then linger lovingly on the screen where all of the men are determinedly masturbating, where the devil's prick, apparently about to erupt, looms over the queen's shoulder. Frannie instinctively flinches away as Goldberg snatches the remote control from her loose fingers.

'*Now!*' he breathes. 'The horniest scene I ever shot. I get *all* these guys to come over you and the chick, Frannie, and they perform like fucking mechanical dreams. First Tony – you remember Tony?' Stupid question, since there he was. Tony, the devil, who later led her into a situation where she was almost killed. Her psyche is being drawn back into the screen despite her wariness of Goldberg, who freezes the picture just as the devil's weapon begins to spurt over her shoulder.

'He starts to shoot,' Goldberg carries on, his voice animated, leaning forward, his glassy eyes shining. 'He starts to let it go and I *shouted* at you, I *made* you tear your mouth away from pussy and open it wide. Watch.'

78

The picture comes back to life, sperm splashes Queen Frannie's shoulder as she twists her head and gaping mouth around and up and catches the second shot full in the face. *'Yeah!'* Goldberg raves. 'What a success. *What* a success. Now, *all* of them, one after the other, *drenching* you two broads. My finest scene. My *finest scene!'* One of his hands is lost with Matilda's deep in the folds of her dress and she, carried away on a sexual cloud of her own, allows it to do what it will there. The fingers of his other hand are wrapped around his organ where they jerk and twitch excitedly. But the Goldberg penis remains stubbornly flaccid.

Frannie is transported to a weird land where Goldberg moans to himself as he unavailingly pumps away at his prick – 'Come on, come *on*, get *up* you *bastard!*' – while on the TV guys heave and grunt and groan as stream after stream of sperm pours over her and the bow-tie girl's naked flesh, and off-screen her maid, Goldberg's fingertips presumably helping, wriggles herself to orgasm while the porn producer still tries frantically, but in vain, to raise an erection.

Goldberg releases himself, replaces his hand with that of Matilda whose fingers curl around his cock without protest. But she is hardly aware of this new development. Her glasses have slipped to the end of her nose, she can no longer see the TV but this does not matter because she is in the throes of orgasm and her eyes are closed.

One final spurt from the bear-man, the queen returns to pussy-eating and Goldberg, cock as limp as a length of pyjama cord, stretches a hand around the back of Frannie's neck and attempts to drag her head down to his waist. No *way* is Frannie about to blow this creature. A loathing mounts within her and she ducks away, stands, reaches for her drink, needing it badly, while on the video the characters disappear into a moonlit garden.

Goldberg emitted a long, pain-filled groan which in other circumstances, would have been heart-rending. He blanked out the screen, then his hands flopped, palms up, to the sofa on either side of him. It flashed through Frannie's mind that he looked like a skinny rag doll. A picture of dejection, he gazed straight ahead at the dead TV as Matilda, recovering, pushed her glasses back on, stared in sudden alarm at him and squeezed herself as tight as she could into the corner of the sofa.

'I've been making movies like that for fifteen years,' Goldberg sobbed. 'And not once in the last seven, the last *seven fucking years*, have I been able to get it up myself. Not *once*! I had hoped that perhaps *tonight*, you two, my horniest stuff ever, that *tonight* . . . .' Glancing down at himself, he sighed deeply. 'Oh, what the hell.' He reached for his bowl of coke, 'What the fucking *hell*.'

Frannie swallowed the rest of her drink, picked up her bag and looked significantly at Matilda. There were no objections from Goldberg as, moments later, they let themselves out. It was almost as if he expected this insult on top of injury.

In the Mercedes, Frannie said to Gregory, 'Drop me off at the "Saucy Girl", please. Then you can take Matilda home.'

Still tipsy, Matilda focused on her watch. 'But it's almost two o'clock.'

'Right,' said Frannie, with a grim little smile. 'It's almost two o'clock. And do I need a *man*!'

8

INTO AFRICA

THE NOVELTY WHICH WAS DAVY the Welsh eventually began to pall. Man as stud animal, muscular, handsome, virile, able to perform with commendable enthusiasm at the drop of a hat – or, more precisely at the drop of his pants – was limited in use, essential though that use might be. On the night of the Goldberg fiasco Davy had responded to Frannie's needs with all the power precision of a well-oiled machine and in the ensuing period there had been no waning in his reliability. But Frannie found that such regular merging of bodies without a corresponding meeting of minds fell woefully short of perfection. Besides, the point, after all, of her sexual foray into the wide, wide world was variety.

Happily indolent with Matilda by the pool the morning after yet another carnal clash with her Welshman, the beach forsaken because of an invasion of Easter sun-seekers, Frannie murmured, 'You know what I'd like to *do* with Davy, Matilda?'

Matilda dragged the floppy brim of a big straw hat down to shade her still pallid cheeks. '*Do* with him?' She chuckled. 'I thought you'd have *done* just about everything in the book by now – plus a few things which aren't!'

'Well, yes, *exactly*,' said Frannie. 'That's just my point.

What I think I'd like is, you know, at Stratton Castle, in one of the courtyards, to have little *cells* built, like monks' cells – oh, say twenty, twenty-five of them. I'd instal Davy in one, every comfort, natch, and fill each of the others with a tasty specimen of masculinity to be visited whenever the whim took me.'

'Good grief.' Matilda squinted into the foggy confusion below her hat brim.

'What you're talking about's a harem!'

'Precisely. Well, the male equivalent of one, just for little me. *What* a thought!'

'Wear yourself out in no time flat.'

'Don't be ridiculous. *Me*? Look at Messalina. And those Arabs had the right idea, you know.'

'Messalina came to a sticky end.'

'But she wasn't an Arab, she was a Roman. Anyway, since Arabs have crept into the conversation, I think that's what we'll do next. Let's off to Africa and the Moors of Morocco.'

Matilda groaned. 'In the remorseless silver bird of prey, no doubt?'

'What else?' Opening her eyes, Frannie grinned surprise at her. 'Well, at least you can finally make a *joke* about flying.'

'Joke? – *Balls*!' exclaimed Matilda.

A heavy mist, rolling in from the Atlantic, cut Casablanca in two. Half of the city was in brilliant sunshine and the other half, sloping down to invisible beaches, was cloaked in swirling grey. From the air the protruding minarets and the towers of the Great Mahjid appeared to float eerily in space.

The airport, well inland to the west of the city, was clear and Frannie's executive jet enjoyed the smoothest of landings which went unappreciated by Matilda who kept her eyes firmly closed throughout.

It was hot, several degrees above the temperature at

Malaga. As soon as her feet met tarmac Frannie found the air bothersomely humid and she soon became irked by a polite but thorough check of all their luggage. It was followed by the seemingly endless scrutiny of their passports, a procedure particularly exhaustive in Morocco, a country with the reputation as one of the most security-conscious in the world.

'What was all *that* about?' asked Matilda as, almost an hour after landing they finally climbed into an oldish but mercifully air-conditioned taxi. 'They even stuck a knife into my new bar of Pears soap!'

'His bloody Nibs,' said Frannie, still irritated.

'His *Nibs*?'

'King Hassan. Victor's pet name for him. I suppose one of the few truly powerful monarchs left in the world. Palace in every city, that sort of thing. Omnipotent. Rather splendid in its way but a lot of people don't seem to agree. There've been a number of assassination attempts over the years, hence his paranoid security.'

They were travelling along a dual carriageway on the approach road to the city and suddenly, high on every lamppost, there appeared a large, head and shoulders colour portrait. 'Elections coming up?' asked Matilda.

Gregory broke his lengthy silence. 'That's him,' he said. 'The king. I was over here for a while with the SAS helping train 'is lot in advanced security procedures. Spreads his picture all over the country – just to make sure you know who the prime target is, like.'

They were swept towards the centre of the city along a wide, impressive boulevard. Here the sun just managed to break through the mist to shine on limp flags, a carefully landscaped profusion of trees and shrubs, neatly proportioned low-rise buildings and interminable pictures of the king. From this viewpoint Casablanca was a bustling, contemporary Arab city. The streets were alive with hoards of robed Arabs on bicycles and horses and carts, and in battered, wheezing, unsafe-looking vans and lorries.

The Hyatt Regency hotel was typical five star splendour with grandiose Arab leanings. Frannie's penthouse suite commanded a panorama of a city still half-cloaked in mist.

Frannie's immediate concern was the 'Golden Hind' and after lunch she and Matilda took a taxi to the harbour. The mist had receded to the ocean, though patches of it still lingered amongst the moored boats and an overhead sun was rapidly drying what was left of a thin coat of damp.

Although she had expected the yacht to be there, the sight of her still startled Frannie. The 'Golden Hind' lay quietly at anchor alongside one of the outer walls with little sign of activity on her decks. They walked up to her and wandered in curiosity from her prow to stern and back again, Frannie making no attempt to disguise her obvious interest. Then they sat together on a small wall for ten minutes, chatting, watching. In all they saw only three people, clearly crew, who moved unhurriedly about their duties. If Clovis Carter-Smith and company were abroad they were staying below decks.

As they finally began to make their way back to their waiting taxi, Frannie remarked, 'Victor will be pleased. There's a tiny piece of his money tied up in that boat. This Clovis character must be around somewhere, I'll have Gregory keep watch.'

'But, surely, once we know he's here all we have to do is tell Interpol or somebody?' said Matilda. 'If he's wanted so badly let them take care of it.'

'That won't do at *all*. I don't even know if there's extradition with Morocco. And even if there is it wouldn't suit Victor. You know him, he'll want his little triumph, to be the man responsible for justice, to take a personal revenge. Victor, after all, is a games player.' She stopped, turned her head in amusement to stare at the elegant yacht. 'For him this is a game, I am an essential part of it. As a matter of fact I've an idea I'm going to get something of a kick out of it.'

As the two of them reached the taxi a lone figure in the stateroom of the 'Golden Hind' lowered his binoculars and thoughtfully rubbed his drooping black moustache. Then, picking up a phone, Christian da Silver, Clovis Carter-Smith's business manager, had himself connected to a number in Marrakech.

9

ARABIAN KNIGHTS

CASABLANCA HELD LITTLE CHARM FOR FRANNIE. The atmosphere of the city failed to grab her and she had long since discovered that five star hotels are much the same the world over. Perhaps the chief culprit was the oppressive humidity. Whatever the reason, were it not for her interest in the person of Clovis Carter-Smith she would have moved on without delay. In her opinion, Casablanca was for old movies.

The wayward financier, however, failed to materialise and, after five days of waiting for a positive report from Gregory, Franny had had enough. They had identified Christian da Silva but there was no sign of his boss at the harbour or in any of the luxury establishments within the city which he might be expected to frequent.

Fatigued and disappointed, Frannie hopped her little entourage to Marrakech where, despite having made a mere twenty minute internal flight, they were subjected to more tiresome checks.

In Marrakesh the *ennui* abruptly came to an end. It was still hot, but the air was as dry and sparkling as freshly opened Dom Perignon. Their taxi carried them towards the city along a straight, poplar-lined road with the Atlas mountains, blue, snow-capped, on the horizon. Between the road and the mountains stretched a vast, green and fertile plain.

Frannie had the driver cruise slowly with all the windows open. The breeze danced in her hair, bringing with it the sweet smells of newly-harvested corn and orange blossom. 'I've just remembered I like this place,' she breathed, a hand squeezing Matilda's knee. 'It's good to be back.'

'Perhaps we can stay on terra firma a little longer this time?' Matilda said hopefully.

'Perhaps.' Frannie smiled, savouring the perfumed air. 'In any case, adventure calls and mysterious Marrakech is just the place for it. It was too damn sticky in Casablanca – how can you fancy anyone in a climate like that?' She blinked, then stared at Matilda in mock amazement. 'Christ, do you realise there's been no one since Davy?'

Gregory, up front with the driver, was unwisely moved to make a gratuitous comment. He slightly turned his head and the words slid flatly out of the corner of his mouth. 'Been all of a week, Lady Ballington,' he said.

Frannie met one unreadable eye with an offended stare. 'I believe you are paid, my dear Gregory,' she said coldly, 'to chauffeur and protect me, not for your ridiculous comments.'

Gregory sighed. 'I *do* beg your pardon, my lady.' But that one inscrutable eye remained on her for several more seconds before he slowly turned to his front. For some reason this encouraged within Frannie the faintest stirrings of discomfort.

Her lips moved soundlessly. 'Damn the man,' she said, to herself. 'Damn the *damn* man!'

The Mamounia hotel was an opulent rendezvous of the international jet-set. A lavish incongruity in a country which was struggling its way out of the Third

World. It greeted Frannie like an old friend who had had a face lift. It had been six years since a brief stay there with Victor but in the interim a reputed ninety million dollars had been spent on it and the refit was sybaritic right down to its gold-plated taps. Frannie took to it with enthusiasm.

She checked into one of the royal suites whose only fault was perhaps an over-zealous indulgence in rich velvet and heavy tapestries. At seven hundred pounds a night it was clearly not overpriced since the other three suites of similar magnificence were occupied.

Frannie's balcony was splendidly appointed. She had a view over acres of garden, walled in like the old city itself, which encompassed massive pools, ancient trees, leafy walks and orange and lemon groves. In the distance stood the snowy Atlas mountains. Frannie dallied awhile alone there, bathed in hot yet friendly sunshine, sipping her way slowly through a hugely iced daiquiri.

Contented, perfectly relaxed for the first time in days, she allowed her thoughts to drift towards sex, to dwell on steamy encounters past, to speculate on what might be in store for her in this enigmatic city of the unexpected. She suddenly realised she was becoming quite randy, the unusual abstinence of a week was taking its toll and the time was ripe for fresh adventure.

In the next door suite, a certain burly, grey-haired gentleman was in no such need. His cravings were being raunchily satisfied by a raven-haired, seventeen-year-old hooker blessed with the kind of perfectly moulded bottom which he constantly lusted after. The two were naked only yards from where Frannie sat indulging her sexual daydreams.

With bare buttocks raised high, the girl crouched on the softness of an astrakhan rug, her slender arms stretched across the bed in front of her, a cheek flatly indenting its woven silk cover. Kneeling behind her, eyes staring diabolically down across his big belly, drinking in every detail, Clovis Carter-Smith energetically buggered her.

Matilda was installed on the other side of Frannie's suite and the communicating door was locked only from Frannie's side. The room, beautifully appointed though it was, was meant for staff or servants. 'We are going shopping, my love,' Frannie announced, having marched in after only the briefest knock.

'Really?' Matilda was hanging dresses in a wardrobe. 'Surely one shops in London or Paris, or New York, not *Morocco*?'

'I didn't quite mean that sort of shopping. We are going to the souk and the kasbah in order to immerse ourselves in the local atmosphere where we shall no doubt make small purchases to please our guide.'

'*Shall* we? Okay. I'll be five minutes.'

Frannie went to Matilda's main door. 'See you in the foyer.'

Vast and richly decorated, the foyer of the Mamounia might have been the entrance chamber to some splendid Eastern palace except that, as usual in things both modern and Moorish it contained certain incongruities. A bank of television sets stood behind the reception desk, tuned into an assortment of European programmes. A video nasty rudely caught Frannie's eye, the sort of human-entrail horror show now banned in many civilised places. Not that anybody seemed to be taking any notice of it or, indeed, of any of the programmes. Frannie sat, thirty feet away, in momentarily appalled fascination, as a ghoulishly grey figure sank bloody fangs into an exposed, beating heart, then her attention was mercifully grabbed by a sight as agreeable to her as the TV action was repugnant.

A massive man, six and a half feet of him, strolled through the ornate entrance hands clasped together behind a broad, powerful expanse of back. White, ankle-length cotton robes and a matching cloak secured with a silver chain flowed around him. On his head he wore a white turban and on his feet open-backed, leather slippers with long, pointed toes which curled slightly upwards at the ends. Around his waist was a broad silver belt, and from below the open shoulder of the cloak a silken sash supported a curving scabbard and knife which rose and fell against one knee as he walked. He was very black: his large-featured, handsomely aristocratic face was clean-shaven.

At first, as he paused at the reception desk, Frannie took this magnificent looking man to be an Arab potentate but then, as he bowed slightly to a couple near the desk, and picked up the woman's bag, she realised that he was nothing more than an employee of the hotel, a part of the elaborate Mamounia stage show.

Watching him, she was reminded that they would need a guide, you didn't go wandering around market places in this country without one unless you wanted to be pestered half to death. Uncrossing her legs, suitably covered to the ankle by filmy layers of the finest paisley muslin, she stood and approached the desk. As she passed the Moroccan giant, he nodded his head politely and offered her a generous, white-toothed smile. It occurred to her just how astonishingly attractive he was.

Her schoolgirl French failed to work, but a receptionist managed a crazy sort of English. He called to the giant in Arabic as he neared the doors with the woman's bag. He would summon a guide from the street.

Watching the man disappear outside, Frannie realised that a familiar emotion was nagging at her. Then, as she watched him return with another man at his side, the emotion surged within her belly: lust, blatant and undeniable. Lady Ballington was experiencing an attack of the galloping hots for this perfect specimum of Arab masculinity.

Serenely composed without, she was churning within, as the object of her incorrigible wantonness introduced her to the other man with a bow and two words. 'Salah, guide,' he said, the voice deeply musical.

The guide was also big, more than six foot, broad-shouldered and wearing an embroidered, light blue jhalabba with a hood, a red fez and sandals. The man's English was fractured but understandable, but Frannie only half listened as she felt herself almost overwhelmed by all this powerful maleness looming above her, the fact that it belonged strictly to the serving classes of absolutely no significance.

The black man walked away, leaving her with Salah, but the lecherous feelings he had aroused within Frannie failed to go with him. Matilda appeared, dressed in a velvet robe with tasselled edges, which did nothing to hide her ample figure from salacious Arab eyes. As the three of them left Matilda noticed Frannie's obvious interest in the black giant. 'Gorgeous,' she commented softly.

On their way through the doors Frannie offered Matilda the sort of twisted smile which revealed inner secrets with a reply which said nothing. 'Not bad.'

They rode to the souk in an open, horse-drawn carriage. The leather seats were worn and patched, the paintwork scarred and faded, yet somehow it retained a captivating charm. Their guide perched above them in front with the driver, turned half sideways to give them a running commentary, Frannie was more interested in the traffic than in what he had to say. They were surrounded by a chaotic sea of movement and sound, an unruly, jostling tide of humanity carried along on foot, horse, bicycle and in motorised transport almost all of which was as old and battered as their carriage. The rules of the road scarcely seemed to exist. The traffic moved chaotically making as much noise as it was capable of. People were dressed in a mixture of ankle-length robes, dowdy jeans, shapeless trousers and sneakers. No one wore shorts except for the occasional tourist who thus managed to look as out of place as a sunbather in Covent Garden.

The souk, a vast, open-air market adjoining one of the walls of the kasbah was vibrant with sound and movement and splashed with faded, dust-engrimed colour. No tourist trap as such, yet neither the place for faint-hearted foreigner to venture without a guide, it was as old as the city which hosted it. More than simply a market, it was a place of entertainment where jugglers and tumblers demonstrated their skills, travelling actors performed in mini-plays, story-tellers expounded ancient myths, wrinkled men charmed sleepy cobras out of wicker baskets, bands of musicians performed and dancers whirled. As Frannie, Matilda and Salah drifted through all this they passed a dentist who was plying his trade from a rickety old table and chair with primitive tools. They saw him wrench out a tooth without anaesthetic watched by a small crowd who, for some reason, found the operation hilariously funny.

Unvirtuous speculations about her black giant faded from Frannie's mind as she let herself flow with the sights, with the sounds, with the rich, heady smells which engulfed her. This was a world of its own, strange, wholly alien and yet unthreatening, a trillion miles from Stratton Castle. She opened herself up to it as widely as she could, probing for the truth which lay beneath its forbidding reality.

After half an hour of wandering around the souk, Salah led them through a crumbling adobe arch and into another seething area of humanity, the kasbah. By now Frannie had warmed to their guide, he was informative, correct, witty and his English, whilst tending towards the absurd, was at least adequate. He followed each whim of the women and answered their questions with no hint of fawning, with dignity even. He was young but well-educated in the theatre of life. He told them that he spoke three other foreign languages and that he had once worked for a spell in Germany.

The open-fronted shops of the kasbah, crowded and squashed into one another like rows of time-worn boxes, offered an enormous range of fare. Whilst still drinking in the atmosphere of the narrow, crowded alleyways, in deference to their guide's apparently genuine enthusiasm and the wishes of Matilda, Frannie pretended an interest in the goods on sale.

They bought some small items which Salah dropped into the hood on his back. Then, having paraded them in front of seemingly endless displays of ceramics, brasswork, copper, basketwear and silks, Salah said, 'You perhaps like see things more different?'

'What different?' Frannie asked.

'You see, no? Yes?'

'All right.' His look lingered and for the first time Frannie was arrested by his eyes. Large, brown and soulful they were like translucent pools. As they flitted from her to Matilda there might have been the merest touch of amusement in them. He led them deeper into the kasbah, finally stopping by a water-seller.

'In here, please come.'

The shop was small and narrow, every inch of wall space covered with uneven shelves containing a crammed miscellany of objects, a great many of them not readily identifiable. The three of them huddled inside; there was barely room to turn around and the wizened, old shopkeeper made matters worse by crowding in on them, adding his dubious smelling breath to air already stale and heavy. In different mood, Frannie would have dived right out of there; but she found herself intrigued. Picking up a small bundle of what appeared to be bark, the size of a slim hairbrush, she sniffed it. It *was* bark, she decided.

'From tree,' said Salah. He poked at it. 'For cleaning teeth,' he explained, eliciting a startled grunt from Matilda. 'Like so.' Taking the bundle from Frannie he stripped a fine string of bark from one edge. Holding it taut he worked it between two front teeth.

'Like dental floss. How *extraordinary*,' Matilda said.

Salah freed the strip from his teeth, let it fall, dropped the little bundle into his hood. 'Two dirham only.' His hand fell on a stubby glass jar with corked neck. 'Here. Something being perhaps more interested.' It was half full of what looked like dead black beetles. He revolved it under their noses, each in turn, his eyes searching theirs for reaction. 'Spanish fly,' he said. 'Very famous. Make you feel you know,' he paused. 'Wanting for it.'

Matilda wrinkled her nose in distaste, not at the sexual implications but at the insects, as Frannie gazed in curious amusement into the jar. 'Odd sort of aphrodisiac,' she said. 'But they're not flies, they're beetles – aren't they?'

'Beetles, sure. Blister beetles. Rare. Genuine Spanish fly. You boil them, make tea, drink.' He shot Matilda a glance that smacked of speculation. 'Ooomph!'

'*Ooomph* is it?' Matilda shied away as Frannie giggled. 'Tea? *Beetles*? It's bloody disgusting!'

Salah remained unruffled. 'Contrary wise it is tasting sweet. You might like to be having some. I get.' The shopkeeper gave him a small plastic bag and, unstoppering the jar, to Frannie's amused, 'Why not?' he tipped a couple of inches inside. 'Rare, therefore a little expensive. Twenty dirham.' He produced a grin, miraculous in the fact that it was wholly innocent and dropped the bag behind him into his hood. 'It is work-ing without question. For sure. The ooomph!'

As Frannie chuckled again he watched her with a bland smile, then scanned the shelves. 'I hope you are not with objections lady,' he said, as he reached for what appeared to be a lump of pale green soap, 'If I now speak of things which are intimate?'

'If you ask me, you already have,' said Matilda.

'Ah. Ah. Well, yes perhaps. This, however, for *secret* places.' Waving the soap or whatever it was, he regarded it with quiet reverence. 'This very special preparation is for application in area of the yoni.'

'Oh. *Is* it?' Frannie gazed dumbly at the stuff. Yoni. A Hindu word, not a Moslem one. But universally under-stood, she supposed.

'You mind I explain?'

'Please *do*.'

'You must rub in a little, not too much, before the sexual intercourse. It is making the the yoni . . .' his eyes wandered quickly down Frannie's body and back to hers in a fashion which belied his hitherto perfectly correct behaviour. '. . . *tighten* lady, you must under-stand. Thereby giving more pleasure to the he.'

'*Really*. Well, well.' Frannie was thoroughly enter-tained. 'Perhaps you'd better drop it in your hat then.'

'Ten dirham only. Cheap.' Wrapping it up in a piece of brown paper he twisted this closed and added it to the collection in his hood.

For the ride back to the hotel Frannie had Salah sit opposite them instead of up with the driver. He seemed to be a slightly changed Moroccan from the man they had departed with, perhaps the merest hint of male arrogance had tinged his confidence, as if having brought up the intimate subject of sex within the claustrophobic confines of a kasbah shop had put him on a level with his temporary employ-ers. Frannie was not offended; it suited a daring plan which was just beginning to take shape in her mind.

The near-springless carriage came to a jolting halt in heavy traffic and the three of them jerked up and down in unison. Changing position to relieve a cramped buttock Frannie said, casually. 'Salah? That, that *black* man who works at the hotel – the one who fetched you for me?'

Salah blinked attention. 'Yes, lady?'

'Does he speak English?'

'No. He speak only Arabic.'

'Oh.' Having decided where she wanted this conversation to lead, Frannie wasn't quite sure how to get it there and relapsed into silence.

A cacophony of hooters and bicycle bells exploded around them as the rush hour hoards became impatient with a policeman on points duty. They lurched forward and, as the noise died down Salah said, enigmatically, 'Jabir.'

'I beg your pardon?'

'The black man, lady. He name Jabir.'

'Oh, I see.' She paused. 'He's *very* black, is he not?'

'Bedouin. From fierce fighting tribe. Big, big man.' A slight smirk advertised that he might have an idea what was going through Frannie's head. '*Strong*.'

'Quite.'

'You have interest in Jabir the Bedouin?'

'Good God, I didn't say that.'

'Then why you ask?'

Matilda, picking up the threads of this conversation, well-versed in the convolutions of her mistress's brain, said severely, 'I believe her ladyship was merely showing polite interest.' She frowned remonstration. 'You are being impertinent, my good man.'

'Please?'

'It doesn't matter,' said Frannie. 'I just thought I'd mention that I found him a particularly *handsome* man. Bedouin, you say?'

'Bedouin.'

'Well.'

They were approaching the Mamounia. 'Are you perhaps free in the morning?' Frannie asked Salah. 'Rather early?'

'I am of course at your service, lady.'

'Excellent. Then you will please hire a car. A modern, *comfortable* car. Have it brought here at nine. My chauffeur will drive.'

The carriage came to a stop in front of the hotel doors and, with a covert assessment of their figures which did not go unnoticed by Frannie, Salah helped them down.

'I'd like to go into the Atlas mountains, have a spot of lunch there.' She straightened her crumpled muslin.

Salah bowed his head. 'Very well. It will be my greatest pleasure.'

'I hope so.' The Bedouin, she noticed had appeared. He loomed large and black in the doorway.

'And, Jabir?' said Salah.

Frannie's eyes were hovering over the Bedouin. 'What *about* him?'

'You want I should say some word for you?'

'I'm sure I can't think *what* you mean.' Smiling wicked innocence, she offered her hand. 'Until the morning, then. Perhaps I'll have a little more to say about, ah, Ja*bir*, tomorrow.'

Frannie and Matilda ascended the marble steps with linked arms. As the doormen held the doors wide for them Salah caught Jabir's eye and nodded in a certain way towards their retreating backs. A look of pure understanding passed between them.

*   *   *

Adjoining the hotel was a casino. The entrance from the Mamounia led through an interior courtyard containing an intricately-tiled fountain. Frannie elected to venture no further afield that evening. She toyed with roulette for a while, spreading chips haphazardly over the table before each roll, winning, then returning her winnings rapidly to the management at blackjack – which she promptly christened 'backjack'.

The casino was only just beginning to fill up when she and Matilda left for an early night. As they crossed the courtyard Frannie failed to notice the large, grey-haired man with a raven-haired young beauty clinging to his arm.

Pausing on the other side of the fountain, Clovis Carter-Smith watched them pass. His walnut eyes dwelt speculatively on Frannie's behind as her clearly-defined buttocks rolled slightly beneath one of her second-skin lamé creations. But his expression was vexed. The unruly, grey eyebrows which matched his hair drew together in an irritated frown as he considered information received less than a week ago from his colleague in Casablanca.

Still frowning, he moved towards the action.

Frannie decided that, however momentarily demeaning it might be, she must speak frankly with Salah. The trouble was that during the morning's drive into the Atlas foothills he sat up front with Gregory and it would have been more than crass not to invite Gregory to lunch with them if she asked Salah. Gregory again! How he irritated her sometimes!

She took her opportunity immediately after lunch, going with Salah to the café's souvenir stall which sat near a bend in the road, its back to a panorama of towering, bluey-brown peaks.

'Jabir? Friend Jabir?' She rolled the name around her tongue slowly as she pretended to examine a piece of sparkling quartz which was still embedded in its rocky shell. The question hovered in the crisp mountain air to be snatched away by a puff of wind.

'Ah,' sighed Salah. 'Jabir, but of course.' He picked up another, smaller, chunk of quartz. 'You see, this example is the more delicate. As I am believing your enquiry might be.'

Enquiry! Well, that was one way of putting it. 'Does he, um, does he have much free time by any chance?'

'Depend on what you want he be doing with it lady.'

'Yes. Quite.' Her eyes strayed from the quartz to the snow-capped mountains on the other side of the huge valley above which they stood. 'Yesterday, the kasbah?' she said, the approach unplanned.

'Please to explain?'

'You took us into a little shop where we bought one or two, *intimate* bits and pieces?'

'Yes?'

'Then you understand the drift of my conversation.' Now for it. 'I wondered if Jabir might perhaps be interested in paying me a private visit? In my suite?'

'Ah. *Ah.*' It was almost a sigh of knowing-this-all-the-time satisfaction. 'Refusing such a request is unlikely as it comes to mind.'

'Good.' Frannie's gaze, not quite properly focused, swept the valley far below her where sheep grazed on the banks of a meandering river. They looked to her like a scene from an impressionist painting. 'Jabir will, of course, be the recipient of a suitable gift.' There it was. *Buying* the man. She shrugged away any distaste at the idea. It would not be the first time men had been bought for her. Victor had hired three black studs for their mutual enjoyment on the night of their sixth wedding anniversary.

'Yes, lady. There will naturally be the question of a gift.' Salah unexpectedly and lightly touched the back of her hand. 'Arranged shall this be.' A pause, the brown, finely tapered fingers still there, Frannie quite motionless. A tiny increase in pressure. 'The Bedouin, he is speaking the Arabic tongue only. Perhaps a translator?' He paused. 'Perhaps it is being some good idea when I am with him together? Such services would not carry a charge.'

One of those electric moments of tingling static passed through her, his meaning was abundantly clear. The implication excited that shamefully degenerate imagination of hers. Frannie's head swivelled slowly until she faced him. His mud-pool eyes danced with lively amusement, there was no trace of the mockery she half expected to encounter. She held his glance fractionally, long enough for tacit understanding. Then, lifting his insinuating hand from hers she let go of it as if dropping a stone. 'Perhaps it is being some good idea, yes,' she said, very deliberately. 'Shall we say then at a half past eight?'

Twenty-five minutes past eight found Lady Ballington seething with an anticipation which played havoc with her nerves. Having briefly entertained thoughts of inviting Matilda to this little party she had changed her mind and sent her off to dinner on her own. Whatever happened it was destined to be a Frannie solo adventure but right now she was wishing that Matilda were there to boost her sagging confidence.

She was dressed with almost schoolgirlish simplicity in pale blue cotton blouse with white buttons, the top three undone, a wide, pleated Valentino skirt which covered her calves and virgin white Reebok sneakers with blue socks. That was all. Frannie wore no underwear. A whim of the moment. Her stage, her scene.

The red velvet curtains in the lounge were open on a dying day. A three-quarter moon, pale and ghostly in the fading light, hung low over the Atlas mountains.

But the bedroom drapes were tightly closed. On a corner table, carefully focused and aimed, sat Frannie's video-bag, needing only the touch of a button to set it filming the action in and around the four-poster bed.

At precisely eight-thirty the bell rang, startling Frannie though she was expecting it. She drained the remains of what had been a healthy shot of neat Glenmorangie malt whisky before admitting her two Arab guests. Seeming as ill-at-ease as she felt, they sat with polite smiles and clearing of throats and then firmly refused the usual socially relaxing drinks; their religion prohibited alcohol.

But Salah had another solution, hardly uniquely Arab. 'Why I not make tea?' he suggested brightly.

Frannie smiled. 'If you like. What with?'

He produced a silver samovar affair, complete with a little paraffin stove, half filling it with water from a pitcher on the sideboard. When he set it down on the carpet, Frannie looked on, somewhat disconcerted at the turn the evening was taking. Squatting cross-legged in front of the teapot Salah produced several little twists of paper from a pocket in his blue jhalabba, opened one, sniffed it noisily and in evident satisfaction then emptied it into the pot and lit the stove. This seemed to be a cue for Jabir to relax Arab style and, with a grunt, he shifted his massive frame from the silk-cushioned sofa and parked it heavily, legs folded, next to Salah. They gabbled a few words of Arabic to one another, then relapsed into silence, both staring at the brewing tea.

'Lady?' said Salah, suddenly. 'Why you not bring the Spanish fly?'

The nasty little black beetles. Frannie took a deep breath. Go with the flow, she said to herself, and stood up. She had almost ditched them, then decided to keep them as a curiosity for Victor.

'Why not?' She fetched the small plastic bag, gave it to Salah and tipped some Glenmorangie into her glass as she watched him open the bag. This was an odd, awkward beginning to what was meant to be an evening of sex. She was a long way from feeling randy. She sipped the whisky as Salah extracted half a dozen of the dead beetles, rolled them around in his palm and inspected them before dropping them into the pot. At least the pure Scottish malt brought a glow to her belly – she had grave misgivings about the beetles. She perched momentarily on the arm of a chair, then decided that perhaps it would be more sociable if she joined them on the carpet. On the other side of the pot with ankles crossed, knees up to her chin, arms wrapping the hem of her skirt tight across her shins she sat and watched.

As a little steam began to whisper from the spout, Jabir produced a crumpled handful of mint leaves from a hidden pocket and dropped it in with the brewing beetles. 'We Arabs, we are always drinking tea,' said Salah. 'Often the mint. Sometimes, things interesting in *other* ways. But using too many of the beetles can be *very* dangerous.'

His eyes were fixed on her now, boring steadily from under the curved lashes. So, she saw, were the black and piercing ones of Jabir. Uncannily it was as if the two had decided at that moment that it was time to concentrate on the real reason for their presence. Their thoughts seemed to reach out to her through a cloud of steam. The moment was almost hypnotic. Her throat constricted.

'Ready. All is ready.' Salah fetched three small, hand-painted cups and filled them whilst Frannie hurriedly downed her whisky. Then she joined them in their aphrodisiac tea-drinking, a ceremony which seemed to have as much to do with suggestive glances as the tea itself which was earthy, minty, and only just palatable. As they downed the liquid they flirted with her without speaking or touching, their eyes and tiny lip movements bringing her out in a sudden rush of goose bumps. She suspected that the fire which was beginning to smoulder in her belly had more to do with neat Scotch than boiled beetles, but she was glad it was finally kindling.

Draining the teacup, Frannie put it on the carpet then wrapped her hands once more around her skirt, holding it tight, covering all but her ankles and feet. Her emotions betrayed only by her unnatural stillness.

The Arabs watched her for long moments, themselves quite still, then Salah said. 'Very well. It is over, the drinking of the tea.' His eyes widened fractionally. 'Now we begin to do to you what it is we are being here for.'

The words, spoken quietly and calmly, had more effect on Frannie than any aphrodisiac could have. *We begin to do to you*. Her hands began to tremble, the inner fires ignited into hot flame. Flinging some straying locks over her shoulder with a toss of her head she let her hands slide up her shins and her knees sag apart. 'Oh,' she said, weakly.

Salah's wide eyes never left hers. 'Be glad,' he murmured, 'that there is other stuff. We were buying this also yesterday. This is, as you remember amazingly well, special for the yoni. The cunt is other word. You will please fetch this?'

Oh. *Oh*. Shock waves sent her to her feet and into the bathroom where the dubious greeny lump lay wrapped in brown paper. The Arabs had not moved when she returned, except that Salah was holding out his hand.

'I thank you.' He unwrapped it, performed the same nose test as he had on the tea. Frannie began to sink to the floor. 'Not to sit,' Salah ordered. 'Come here, please. I prepare you.'

'But . . .'

'What is this but for? You want, or no want?'

'Well . . . ' Frannie shrugged mentally. You were looking for adventure, love, she told herself. Looks

103

like you've found it! She moved close to Salah, looking down on his head. He was still wearing the fez.

'Be taking off your underpants.' He spoke with a detached air, like a doctor, this adding to Frannie's mounting excitement.

'I'm not wearing any.' The words fell from her lips in a pregnant hush.

'Ah. In this case . . . ' he was rubbing the soap-like cake with the tips of his fingers, smearing it greenly on them. 'Your dress. Please to raise it.'

So blatant? Shamefully burning with the heat of this degeneracy she clawed the material up, a few inches at a time, looking no longer on the fez but on Jabir's shining black face as she did so, until the skirt was bunched around her hips and she was brazenly exposed. The Bedouin's eyes narrowed as they feasted on this lewd exhibition of nakedness, hands tensed against his thigh muscles.

Frannie's only slight remaining concession to modesty, her closed thighs, was lost as Salah prised them apart.

Green-tipped fingers touching tentatively between her legs had the impact of an electric cattle prodder, sending shock waves from the nape of her neck to her curling toes. Sagging, grabbing Salah by the shoulder with her free hand, she flung back her head and closed her eyes. They were cool, those darkly wrinkled fingertips, cool and soft with the creamy greenness and they wasted little time dallying on the flesh of her inner thigh. They explored their way to the heart of her sexual self, an index and second finger gentling their way up into her, easing and slipping to the knuckles as her vaginal muscles contracted against them with a welcome which was perhaps enhanced by the mysterious tallow from the kasbah.

Salah revolved his fingers, first one way, then the other, his fez falling to the ground as he swayed under

Frannie's grasping hand. Opening her eyes, looking down across her bunched skirt at what was being done to her, she saw that Jabir had risen to his knees. He was watching the ribald procedure with a rapt expression, his eyes, a breath away from her naked pussy glinted with sheer, goatish lust. Feelings of such lasciviousness took hold of Frannie that she felt she was about to faint.

Interruption. Mournfully sung notes, a male voice in high register, drifted through the open window from a nearby minaret as a muezzin called the faithful to prayer. Hastily muttered words were exchanged between the two Arabs. The fingers were withdrawn and Salah, climbing to his feet, eased Franny back and down onto the sofa. Legs wide, dress still high, she closed her eyes and waited for the next move. She heard a busy rustle of movement and she imagined them to be getting out of their robes. Then silence, no hand touched her.

She opened her eyes to the wholly unexpected sight of the two Arabs kneeling side by side, broad hips high in the air, hands pointed together on the carpet in front of their foreheads. Properly arranged towards Mecca, they were praying! The ludicrousness of this unbelievable switch in activity killed Frannie's ruttishness as quickly as an upended bucket of freezing water. Her legs sprung closed, she scrabbled her dress down over her knees. After watching the Arabs in blank confusion for several seconds as they rocked in their crouched positions mumbling prayers she beat a hasty retreat to the bedroom, closing the door and flopping weakly onto the edge of the bed.

Moments later, it was over. As the final sad, sweet notes faded away across the Mamounia orange groves the door handle turned and Salah appeared, Jabir looming over his shoulder. He approached her with an apologetic shrug. 'The timing was perhaps of the unfortunate,' he said. 'But is a great sin to disobey the muezzin.'

'Quite,' mumbled Frannie. She was lost for words. Jabir, black-skinned face hovering, stared down at her, making her acutely aware that little more than a minute before he had been eagerly watching his companion's fingers invading her most private place, that in the interim, the disrupting prayer had effectively dried up her juices and recent sexual hunger was little more than a memory.

Salah, already proven master of the unsubtle, spoke and shocked response back into her. 'Your eyes must therefore rest upon delights to be yours,' he said. He rattled off a clutch of words and with no change in expression Jabir took hold of the material of his jhalabba and hoisted it to his chest. Frannie found her eyes trapped by the sight of a penis which was as long and thick and black as the dildo she had christened Othello, with the exception that Othello at equal dimensions stood eternally rigid whilst this Bedouin weapon was merely in repose. Her knees trembled and her fingers twisted themselves into the coverlet as her eyes lingered and devoured.

'Is okay, no, lady? Satisfaction?' said Salah.

Shaken out of carnal desire, now jolted right back into it, Franny muttered, 'Okay. Is okay.' Her eyes shifted fractionally as Jabir let the robes fall. They noticed the video-bag. Thoughts tumbling, desire swelling, she left the bed and, taking a brush from the bag as a cover, she activated its camera.

'And why this?' asked a puzzled Salah, 'Before such things as are to be you brush your hair? Is this not for afterwards, no?'

'You pray, I brush.'

'Strange things.' He pointed towards her belly. 'And this, too?' His accompanying grin not simply amusement. 'You brush?'

A familiar, delicious feeling of sinfulness within my lady, a temptation once suggested not to be resisted. She raised an eyebrow. 'Why not?'

Unbuttoning her skirt she let it fall to the floor, stepped out of it. Eyes flickering from Arab face to Arab face she ran the brush slowly, provocativly in curly little upward sweeps through her pubic bush, against its natural lie, making the downy thatch stand out like the hairs of the brush itself. The daring nature of her shameless actions added to a sexual fever which was beginning to make her genitals throb. Degeneracy took unrelenting hold on her. 'If you two Arab bulls would mind now getting naked,' she found herself saying, 'Then perhaps we could fuck?'

Jabir nodded, clutching at himself through the robes. 'Fuck. Fuck.' he expounded happily.

The brush dropped from Frannie's fingers, the tip of the middle one descending on her clitoris, caressing. 'Isn't it lovely,' she breathed, tongue wetting her lips, eyelids drooping, 'how everybody in the world seems to understand that smutty little word!'

Seconds later, they are all three naked, except that Jabir keeps on his turban. Frannie stands near the foot of the bed, right on camera, as the Arabs pay devoted attention to a different kind of worship, rituals she has certainly experienced before but never quite in this way. Tongues, mouths, hands, fingers go busily to work. Salah, on his knees in front of Frannie, licks her pussy then pokes the length of his tongue into her while he clasps her buttocks firmly pulling the cheeks wide apart for Jabir who, kneeling behind her, plays with her breasts as his tongue finds its wet way up her backside. Frannie beginning to writhe, to wriggle, to gasp, sexual fever beginning to rage, head back, neck taut, eyes closing, hands whitely flat, tiny against Jabir's great black ones as he kneeds and massages her breasts and his tongue lubricates her back passage for a certain assault from which she mentally shrinks as she wonders to what enormous dimensions the Bedouin's tool has swollen.

Jabir struggles to his feet. From behind he wraps her in his arms, almost losing her in his hug, the back of her head nestling deep in his bulging pectorals, his palms cupping and covering her tits. He bends at the knees, the tip of his cock sliding from the small of her back to the cleft of her buttocks and, releasing one breast, he helps it, pointing the shaft down, guiding it on its downward slope between them. Then, toolhead warmly snuggled, his hand returns to its breast where it pinches and rolls the nipple between thumb and finger. With legs bent he sways in towards Frannie, then away, the dance of the cobra, the head of his heavy cock sliding up and down her buttock cleft spreading a glistening trail of saliva from her little pink hole to the base of her tingling spine. It is thick she feels – of course it is thick! – but how long Frannie cannot be sure. She surfs on the crest of a carnal wave sandwiched between earthy-smelling Arabs who cocoon her body in lechery, Salah's tongue busy-busy deep in her pussy whose lips are stretched wide by the fingers of both of his hands. She is heaving her hips forward onto Salah's face and then back against the down-sliding purple knob of Jabir's cock each time it probes her anus, the three of them writhing together as if locked in some hypnotic dance.

Jabir breaks this particular spell, releasing Frannie and answering her unspoken question as he moves to the bed to prop his weight on one knee, dissolute eyes dwelling on Salah who continues to eat pussy insatiably. It is big, the Bedouin staff, it is splendidly big as it hangs out over the edge of the bed, swaying proudly there, but it has swollen to perhaps only a third more than its flaccid self and Frannie, at once relieved that she will be able to take it wherever he cares to

108

introduce it, is almost mesmerised by the power which throbs beneath its matt black skin.

Jabir mutters in Arabic to Salah, who at last uncouples his tongue and lifts his head. He grins slackly up at Frannie, his moustache shining with wetness, as he says, 'My friend Jabir, he would much like to be knowing if it meets your approval should he do to you what the Turks did to the captured soldiers of Lawrence?'

Frannie too high on her carnal wave to be dislodged by a bunch of oddball words merely nods. She is coaxed down onto hands and knees on the carpet by Jabir, his hot hand on the back of her neck as he does this. Salah kneels in front of her and this is the first time she has properly laid eyes on *his* cock. It is pleasingly large and held with reverence in a fist just inches from her mouth. She glances over her shoulder at the sound of spitting sees the Bedouin spreading saliva on his tool before beginning to ease it into her cautiously yielding fanny. But there is another needful weapon in front of her, she turns her head, rocking forward with Jabir's push, takes Salah's tool full between her lips and sucks on it avidly like a baby on some oversized, treacle-spread thumb while the Othello-look-alike finds its way deep into her fundament, eliciting but a soupçon of pain at once thrilling and lusciously bearable. A shudder shakes Frannie's sweetly invaded body from top to toe.

Jabir buggers her with devoted enthusiasm, her kneeling form fitting neatly beneath his. The top of his turbanned head rests solidly against Salah's chest as the guide fucks Frannie's mouth with quick, snatched little buttock jerks and the three of them develop a complex copulatory rhythm.

Having had his fill of what the Turks did to the captured soldiers of Lawrence, Jabir unplugs Frannie, draws her face away from Salah's crotch, brings her to her feet, spins her around, tumbles her backwards onto the bed, slides her along the silk counterpane, spreads her knees, lets his weight down onto his elbows, raises his buttocks and thrusts, plunging into her to the thick root of his penis. Holding himself embedded there he rolls them both over so that she lies on top of him and opens her buttocks for Salah as Salah had done for him earlier – but this time a tongue bath is not the intention. Frannie is acutely aware of Salah's cock as it impales the passage just vacated by that of the Bedouin, forcing its rude way up there until the two powerful tools are nestling length against length within her body with only the narrow membrane between anal and vaginal passages to keep them apart. They begin work steadily, pumping like flesh and blood pistons in opposing directions, one up, one down, one in, one out, muscles of thighs and buttocks and backs and loins rigid, trembling as a thoroughly stuffed Frannie tenses and sways between them in this most carnal of rhythms which sends unbearable spasms of lubricious delight coursing from her belly and bowels to the tips of her toes and the fast drying depths of her rasping throat. She is consumed by a succession of orgasms, mewling, moaning, gasping, accompanying each climax with an insane rolling and shaking of her head which is lost in the folds and tresses of tumbling, bouncing hair. Her climactic rapture achieves an intensity which borders on screaming point, then she feels the sudden wet rush of Salah's sperm and she does scream, long and loud, as she screws the coverlet into tight bunches on either side of the consumed, snarling, black face below her. Salah, sated, rolls off and away from her with a single grunt. Jabir topples her over, going with her, catching his weight on one hand and, poised over her, slides his black beast out of her and directs spurt after spurt of his Arab come from her pubic bush all the way up to her throat, fierce, harsh, guttural monosyllables tumbling from his lips as he does so, ebon eyes reflecting a savage intensity of satisfaction at the result of his massive

110

ejaculation which soaks into the tender, creamy-brown flesh below him.

Shuddering like a great, black bear in its death throes the Bedouin shoots his last with a sound so primitive and aching it might have been an echo snatched from the Atlas mountains, then he keels over and slowly collapses at Frannie's side.

Satiation. An untidy, sweaty mess of sexual repletion. Frannie a discarded doll, arms draped back above her head, torso twisted, legs wantonly splayed. On one side her kasbah guide, on his stomach, gently snoring. On the other the black Bedouin, magnificent in his turbanned nakedness, chest still rising and falling as recovering breath disturbs the air, languid eyes drifting from crotch to belly to breasts of this white tigress from another world whose flesh gleams beneath drying, mini-lakes of his sperm.

The sticky-sweet, pungent aroma of mingled sexual juices and steaming bodies permeates the air in the aftermath of libidinous excess.

Yet Frannie has relaxed into an untroubled slumber and dreams of lying on the grassy bank of a meandering English river and making innocent love with a young and handsome man.

10

BEDOUIN BETRAYAL

'YOUR SUITE'S NOT EXACTLY SOUNDPROOF, you know,'
Matilda remarked casually as she spread marmalade on
a thin sliver of toast before popping it into her mouth.
'Apart from the fact that your bedroom happens to share
my wall.'

Frannie smiled. 'I understood I sent you out for dinner.' She stirred her coffee lazily.

'That was at eight. I was home by ten-thirty.
Your, ah, enter*tain*ment didn't cease until two in the
morning.'

'God, was it *that* late?'

The morning sun slanted obliquely at Frannie from
its perch above the Atlas mountains and she slipped
on a pair of sunglasses against the glare. Clad in
thin cotton bathrobes they were breakfasting on the
terrace. The skin of her ladyship's face, scrupulously
cleansed of make-up, shone soft and flawless. Her
hair, thoroughly brushed and stretched back into a
pony-tail, gleamed like the coat of a seal. Her green
eyes were bright and clear, almost translucent on this
fine morning. There was nothing, not the hint of a
toe of the tiniest crow's-foot to suggest the debauch
of the previous night. She felt wonderfully rested and
perfectly happy to begin the new day with only a

warm, lingering glow in certain well-used parts to remind her of recent hours of unbridled dissipation.

Tucking her bare feet under her, Frannie made herself more comfortable amongst the soft cushions which filled the white cane terrace chair.

'You weren't *half* noisy,' Matilda commented, chewing. 'Both of you.'

Laughing lightly, Frannie examined her nails. 'All *three* of us as a matter of fact.'

'Oh, I *see*.' Swallowing the remains of her toast Matilda began to butter another piece. 'And of what sex did the third happen to be? I'm aware one was our extraordinarily articulate guide – you made that pretty obvious.'

'Did I?' She poured some orange juice over the melting ice cubes in her glass.

'*Male*, actually. The, um, black *giant* from downstairs.'

'You *got* him, did you?' Matilda cast four envious eyes over her mistress. 'You dirty, lucky cow! Talk about Arabian nights!'

'Turkish, more like.'

'*Turkish?*'

'They did to me, and I quote, what the Turks did to the captured soldiers of Lawrence.' A stifled giggle escaped her. 'And did it bloody well, actually!'

Finishing with the butter Matilda dug her knife into the marmalade pat. 'And what exactly *did* . . . .?'

'They sodomised them, of course,' Frannie interrupted. 'Then I suppose they killed them. I . . .' she was about to say she had made a video, stopped as she caught sight of a male figure below them in the garden. ' . . . just one tiny moment. Am I wrong, or could that be . . . ?'

An enormous swimming pool, big as a lake, stretched from patio to lawns. Alone, arranging a towel on a lounger, was a large, grey-haired man. As he began to strip off his robe Frannie went inside and returned seconds later with a small pair of binoculars in one hand and her photo of Clovis Carter-Smith in the other. Focusing the glasses she glanced from the man to the photo and back again. 'Well I'll be damned! It's him all right. That's our fugitive financier.' She handed the binoculars to Matilda. 'Take a look.'

Matilda studied him carefully. He was standing, hands akimbo and back to the water, idly gazing up at the hotel. 'He's got an awfully big whatsit,' she remarked.

'Oh, for *Christ's* sake!' Snatching the glasses back Frannie refocused them on Carter-Smith, then hurriedly lowered them as, looking directly up at her, he frowned. Hastily picking up a floppy straw hat she plonked it on her head. 'Of course,' she said. 'I should have guessed. Didn't give it a thought. The man never once put in an appearance on the "Golden Hind" in almost a week. Ergo he wasn't in Casablanca. Therefore he was probably in Marrakech and, if so, where else but in the most expensive hotel. Right on our doorstep!'

'And so now what?'

'I don't know. Get me the phone out here, there's a darling. See if you can raise Victor for me.'

Lord Ballington's advice was for her to keep her eyes and ears open, but to stay away from Clovis Carter-Smith for the time being. He would give Frannie's next move careful thought. But Morocco, he warned her, was perhaps a dangerous country in which to stage a kidnap attempt. Its internal security, as they had already witnessed twice at airports and once in a routine road check, was notoriously tight.

Frannie and Matilda elected to spend the day by the pool, on the other side of it from Carter-Smith who was shortly joined by his raven-haired hooker. Throughout the morning, until the financier and sex-toy disappeared for lunch, Frannie kept stealing looks at them through her binoculars. She failed to notice, however, that Clovis Carter-Smith, aware of the surveillance, was doing the same thing to her.

Salah drifted by, Matilda watching him with lively interest as he enquired blandly if there was anything he could do for them while Frannie managed to act as if nothing whatever had transpired between them. The essence of polite servility, his mud-pool eyes nevertheless conveyed unspoken remembrances but Frannie pushed sexual stirrings to one side and coolly dismissed him for the day. Perhaps tomorrow, she told herself. Or maybe the Bedouin on his own. Bed the Bedouin. She laughed inwardly. But not today. Such pleasures should be taken like Beluga caviar – in small, well, even *greedy*, portions, but not every day.

After dinner they indulged in the casino, Frannie once again playing her frenetic, game of roulette, magically hauling in a great pile of winning chips, which she carried off in triumph to the blackjack table.

Where she was joined by Clovis Carter-Smith.

Engrossed in dissipating her profits Frannie failed at first to notice the identity of the man who sat by her side with a pile of maximum denomination chips. It was not until he achieved a winning twenty-one twice on split aces after her bust that she glanced at his face. She found herself trapped by walnut eyes which glinted like swords.

'Having so lovely a lady sitting next to me promises to bring me a lucky night,' he said. His voice was deep, a trace of north country creeping into the evident grooming. Instead of 'Lucky', he said 'looky'.

'I always seem to lose at this game,' Frannie managed as, elbowing Matilda in the ribs, she drew her attention from the falling cards.

'No doubt you can afford it.' He threw an obvious glace at her Fabergé diamond brooch.

It needled her. 'You're a bit forthright, aren't you?' she snapped. 'That's hardly your business.'

But he offered her his hand as if she had merely asked his name. 'Digby. Harry Digby,' said Carter-Smith. 'I tend to be blunt. Part of my make-up.'

Returning his grasp cursorily, Frannie failed to respond with her name, turning her attention to tidying her dwindling pile of chips. Jangling nerves made her bet three times what she had intended and, moments later, she watched unemotionally as the ten of clubs landed on her thirteen and sank her bet.

'Let me guess,' Carter-Smith's nutty voice intruded as she slid fresh ammunition to the besieged Matilda and speculated anew. 'Fiona . . . ?'

'I beg your pardon?'

'The brooch. An F. Does it stand for Fiona?'

The Fabergé cluster was in the shape of a scrolled F. A present from Victor. She should probably have said yes, and realised too late. 'Francesca,' she said, then avoided compounding the error. 'Francesca Jones.'

'Pretty.' He hit a blackjack carrying a maximum stake. 'Well, Fran, you're certainly bringing me luck.'

The easy way he said 'Fran' bothered her briefly, but he ventured no more attempts at conversation for the next fifteen minutes and she forgot about it. With Matilda's help her chips soon shrank to zero. Normally, she might have invested in more but she was distinctly ill-at-ease next to the man whom she was somehow intending to bring to justice. Needing Victor's advice she left the table. Carter-Smith made no comment as she did so but his razor-sharp gaze followed her and Matilda all the way out.

A little later, a little richer, on the way to his suite with his hired bimbo for a sodomitic treat, the financier presented the night-duty concierge with a hefty tip in return for sticking his bulky nose into the pages of the registration book. What he discovered there

116

merely confirmed what was already more than simple suspicion.

Late the following morning, the short space of fifteen minutes separated Frannie's brief meeting with Salah in the hotel foyer and the time Carter-Smith's official guide, a greasily subservient man named after the prophet Mohammed, was summoned to his suite.

As she sat with Salah facing the banks of TV sets Frannie felt the collective eye of the Mamounia staff boring into her with undiluted prurience. Her sexual adventure with the two Arabs was clearly now common knowledge, no doubt the sauce of the week, if not the century; far from unnerving her, this intelligence served only to amuse.

Jabir was standing passively near the doors when Salah approached him with Frannie's request and his black eyes, flooding over her as it was delivered, were all she needed as an answer; Jabir would most certainly appear in her suite at shortly after nine that evening, a time that she had set to avoid any clumsy repetition of a call to prayer.

As Frannie strolled through the palatial foyer towards the garden, Mohammed was timidly tapping at Carter-Smith's door.

Some while later Jabir received another, altogether more sinister proposition. He was killing time amongst a group of taxi drivers and guides in the street, beneath some shade trees, adding his voice to a lively argument about the probable outcome of a football match. Salah, hovering on the fringe of this group, was accosted by the perspiring and highly agitated Mohammed. Their voices dropped to whispers but their hands and arms spoke loudly.

Leaving Mohammed, Salah weaved his way through the men to Jabir, hooked a hand on his elbow and drew him to one side. Jabir listened, disagreed vociferously, shook the hand off and stalked several paces down

117

the road. There he stopped, turned and considered, before returning to Salah with grave shakes of the head and dismissive gestures of his arms. They debated further, out of hearing of the group, the sun beating down on them while Mohammed nervously looked on. Finally, elbows were grabbed and shoulders slapped in agreement.

Salah returned to Mohammed to impart the decision and Mohammed took it up to the patiently waiting Clovis Carter-Smith.

Frannie donned no simple, schoolgirlish clothes that evening for her carefully planned fornication. A white sheath dress by Ungaro snuggled her figure to perfection, patent court shoes lifted her six inches off the floor, her hair was elegantly swept back Cleopatra fashion and, beneath the dress, skimpy, creamy-yellow matching silk underwear begged to be revealed to the Bedouin's gaze. At nine fifteen, came a confident rap on her door and Frannie's heart responded with a flutter of excitement.

As usual Jabir was draped in faultless white. He had on a ceremonial, jewel-encrusted dagger and an opal, which surely had to be fake, sat brightly at front centre of his turban. She stood to greet him, the rim of a tulip champagne glass teasing her scarlet rouged lips. Closing the door quietly behind his back, momentarily he appeared as an impassive, noble statue, hand draped over the hilt of his dagger, black, unsmiling eyes drinking in the vision of beauty which confronted him.

The Bedouin had stepped straight from the pages of *The Arabian Nights*, he was Frannie's desert prince and she the queen of his harem. For the evening to come she sought the essence of the mysterious East, something utterly different from a night's dirty-fucking with two of them like before. She wanted to be romantically swept into this unlikely giant's arms, to be carried to the bed, tenderly laid down and undressed, to be possessed by him and in turn to possess him.

In fact what he did to initiate this fairytale had as much to do with romance as a peasant's smock with Frannie's Ungaro dress. Jabir strode heavily to her, dropped his great hands on her bared shoulders and began to push her towards the open door of her bedroom. His eyes, throwing sparks at hers, did as much to push her as his hands. Her arms fell slack, champagne flooded on the carpet, followed by a shattering glass. As she stumbled slightly over the edge of a rug his tightening fingers kept her upright.

In this odd, silent, backwards dance they reached the bed. It caught her calves, he pushed on and she tumbled onto the patchwork silk of the coverlet with its happily clashing threadwork of gold and silver. Her eyes fell on the blue silk canopy above her head, her body tensed, anticipating, as he knelt above her.

Hands invaded her. Crawling, exploring, big, black, gentle creatures with a will and a life of their own they crept from her shoulders down her dress where they lingered, one enclosing each breast, encircling, fondling, squeezing, bringing the hidden nipples up firm and thrusting and then wandering to belly, to hips, fingertips sliding into the tuck of material at her groin to briefly tease the pubic mound beneath, quickly travelling on to thighs, to bare knees, sliding smoothly down shins, hooking off the spiky shoes, cradling feet then slipping, slipping with ease and grace up the length of the slender, aristocratic legs, under the skirt hem, across warm thighs as tense as drawn bowstrings, fingers splaying, thumbs digging into the softness of inner thighs, thumbtips reaching, finding warm, damp silk. Stopping.

Frannie is breathing slowly and deeply through

flared nostrils, luxuriating under the touch of these hands which are flattened against her willing flesh by the tightness of her skirt, sighing at the touch of thumbs which begin circling, probing, questing through the silk of her knickers then sliding beneath them, invading from either side and, nails back to back, centimetre by centimetre they ease into her oozing pussy as the tips of grasping fingers indent the flesh of her upper thighs.

Suddenly impatient, the thumbs withdraw. The hands search for the skirt hem and begin to push the material waistwards. It resists. Frannie opens her eyes, peers down at the top of the turban with its winking red stone, at the white-bundled bearish shoulders. Her own hands awake from their torpor at her sides, reach up to the hem and she pulls with his push, raising her bottom, closing her thighs until Signor Ungaro's expensive creation rests where he had never quite intended in an untidy, stretched pile at her hips. Frannie flings back her head with a strangled intake of breath as the top of the turban mingles in the heap of her dress and the Bedouin's tongue burns its way through damp silk panties. Black hands slide under her backside, claw the panties down over trembling buttocks, the tongue releases their crotch and they are dragged all the way down to her feet and off. Crouching between her knees Jabir hefts Frannie's behind right off the bed and dives his face into her sexual heart.

He gives her head, this Arab, as if his life depends on it, his eager, thirsty tongue busy way up inside her as the tip of one finger steals into her anus and he plays with her buttocks like a potter moulding a lump of clay.

She is limp, boneless, taking no conscious action of her own, letting him do with her what he may, neither helping nor hindering. She is rolled onto her front with the skirt still bunched around her hips; her rear end, rudely exposed, lewdly available, is groped, fingered, tongue-bathed and then teasingly sodomised. Jabir lifts his robe to accommodate this last act, holding its folds against his belly, entering and probing just with his glans, quickly shifting from there to her pussy where he lingers without movement. Frannie is on her face, hands with wide-stretched fingers flat against the bed above her head. The teasing is too much for her and she comes with a smothered shriek. He, pleased by this, at last stands and strips off his dagger and sandals and robes but, as before, leaves the turban in place. Tipping her onto her back he spreads her legs, hooks hands behind the backs of her knees, lifts her legs high until her calves rest on his shoulders where taut muscles ripple and gleam. He pauses, leching eyes ogling a woman as open to man as she can be, takes his cock in a guiding hand and plunges in, the great black club penetrating her to its root. He begins to pump, at first a controlled and steady invasion, but his need soon becomes massive, he heaves and bucks and thrusts and bangs with gritted teeth and straining loins until, wind escaping his lips with a sound like an express train letting off steam, all of his weight supported between rigid hands and tensed toes his sperm gushes and floods into her at the same time as she achieves a climax so consuming she almost throws this huge man off her body.

After the frenetic coupling, something approaching the sought-after Arabian Night. Esoteric love-making with a perfect specimen of black masculinity, Frannie finally naked, her flesh an aesthetic counterpoint to his. She makes love to him, he lays back, perfectly relaxed except for his undemanding erection, content to take his time, to wait, to savour and enjoy as she nibbles and licks and kisses every accessible part of his body.

A little more buggery follows the mutual body-worship, but this is an essential part of this night, exactly what Frannie expects from her Eastern Prince. Once, she swallows his seed, an act which she has long since discovered can be construed as anything from love to perversion. In this case tasting him is a part of the whole, a pleasing way of saying 'I adore your wonderful body', even though his habitual consumption of strong spices have made the sperm so pungent she needs to wash it down with a draft of champagne.

He departs after a long, gentle and infinitely tender kiss which she interprets as an expression of fondness but which he means, quite sincerely, as a token of the deepest, saddest regret.

He closes the bedroom door behind him, crossing the lounge quickly as she happily wanders into the bathroom. As he lets himself out of the suite he makes way for the shadowy, brown-robed figure of a man who slips past him and into the room. A man who wears a dagger which is not merely ceremonial.

11

ALI CAT

THE ARAB FLITTED ACROSS THE ROOM AS SWIFTLY as the passing shadow of a bird of prey. As a naked Frannie stepped into the shower stall he hovered at the bedroom door, turning the handle inch by cautious inch and easing it open carefully enough to see inside.

From the bathroom a shaft of light cut into the dimness of the bedroom and muffled singing could be heard as Frannie adjusted the water mixer. Then came the sound of cascading water. The Arab reached the wall which stretched from the bed to the bathroom door and there he waited, his unsheathed dagger clutched in nicotine-stained fingers.

Frannie luxuriated in the shower taking her time, flushing away the stale sweat and secretions of sex. She shampooed her hair, rinsed it then finished off with a brief burst of water that was needle-cold. Just a few feet from her, hidden behind the wall, the Arab waited. She towel-dried her hair, got rid of most of the dampness with a blow-dryer, brushed it, twisted it into a knot at the back and wrapped it in a dry, white towel. This process took her fifteen minutes; no time at all to the lurking Arab for whom life normally passed by infinitely slowly but who nevertheless had twice dispensed swift and silent death.

Deciding to read a while before finishing her hair and having no need of any clothing except the towel which cosseted it, Frannie padded barefoot from bathroom to bedroom.

The Arab descended ferociously.

She hardly saw him. A flurry of brown, flapping rags. A metallic glint. A cotton-clad arm stifling her mouth bringing with it the earthy smells of the kasbah and a soul-stabbing terror of death.

He dragged her to the bed, she too deep in shock even to struggle, and rolled them both onto it, his arm mashing her lips against her teeth, threatening to split them. Bringing himself into a kneeling position between the backs of her parted thighs he heaved her head back and towards him so that she was tautly arched, the perfect body position for the swallow dive, her neck stretched long and white, the curve of the Arab blade poised beneath, preparing to slice the soft, precious flesh from ear to ear.

There should have ended the story of Frannie and but for the demon sex it surely would have. This alley-cat Arab, son of a desert he had never seen, had never set eyes on a naked white woman, either. Machismo supplanted the instructions to kill. Primitive man had at his mercy a civilised young white woman. His loins responded to this situation with a fierce, hungry need not to be denied and the spoils of plunder fell into their natural, historical order – rape first. Then kill.

He released his dagger, though not his grip on Frannie. A knee found its way into the small of her back, dug painfully there as he produced a grubby piece of cloth and, using the fingers of both hands, stuffed it through her lips until it choked her mouth. Removing the knee he spun her over, rocked back onto his haunches and grabbed her viciously by the ankles. His hungry eyes devoured her nakedness. Spittle dribbled from a corner of his mouth to mingle with grease in his beard. A gap-toothed leer, splitting a face as barren and pock-marked as the Sahara, sent a shiver of mortal fear through her.

Frannie's violent descent into Hell had taken a mere time-stretched twenty-five seconds to the moment when the Arab took hold of her ankles. Horror had left no room in her mind for logical thought but now she remembered the emerald ring. Bringing her hands together over her breasts she reached finger and thumb for the stone.

With a grunt like a pig in rut the Arab let go of her ankles and pulled a length of coarse string from a pocket. Crunching the fingers of both her hands together in one of his, he wrapped the string around her wrists with the other and knotted it tight. On hands and knees between her parted thighs he hoisted his jhalabba high and hooked his chin over the hem. For the first time in her life Frannie found herself staring in fear and revulsion at an erect male organ. Using her ankles he folded her legs back until her knees almost touched her shoulders.

Then he tore his ravishing way into her dry and protesting vagina.

His flesh-and-blood knife ripped into her, and as his weight pressed down on her his foul-smelling breath almost made her vomit into the gagging rag.

Frannie fought for her only chance of survival, convinced that this man was going to kill her. As his demented penile thrusts continued, once again her cramped fingers found their way to the emerald.

Gregory's room was two floors below. He was climbing into bed when the bleeper shrieked. Surprise delayed him perhaps half a second. Then he raced for the door.

The Arab's final convulsions tore through him. Frannie had been savagely raped but had failed to take the oft repeated advice to lie back and enjoy it.

It had been the most disgusting experience of her life, painful and accompanied by a numbing dread of what was to follow.

The business over, with scarcely a pause to recover his breath the Arab reached for his knife.

Frannie began to fight with as much vigour as a tied, slender woman could muster. She thudded her hands at him, kicked, butted, kneed. But he easily smothered her struggles with his heavy body. Ramming her chin back with the heel of his hand he brought the blade down. Seeking the jugular with its razor tip, he nicked the flesh.

Gregory slammed a karate kick at Frannie's door while a gaping chambermaid looked on. The lock splintered through unresisting wood and he charged inside and across the suite to the bedroom. When he caught sight of the Arab crouched over Frannie, the knife poised at her throat, he bellowed like a wounded bull elephant and, even as the killer began to turn his head at the sound, Gregory was on him. Two beefy hands closed around the Arab's head, fingers clawing deep into his face and, with colossal, adrenaline-fed strength Gregory swung the Arab clear off the bed like a giant at some Highland games warming up to throw the hammer.

The pistol-like crack which echoed in the room just before Gregory let go of the Arab's head was the noise of his neck snapping. The body slamming into the carpet was as dead as that of a man who had just been cleanly hanged.

Gregory, aware of this, twisted his hands palms upward, glanced stonily at them for a brief moment, then turned his attention to the bed where Frannie lay in her tethered nakedness.

Blood trickled down the side of her neck, its cause lying near her head. A dirty rag bulged from her stuffed mouth, bluish bruising was appearing on arms, legs and belly. For some reason she closed her legs tight as Gregory's eyes, professionally assessing, unprurient, swept over them.

'Well, your ladyship,' he murmured at last as the chambermaid peered fearfully around the door, then screamed. 'Got yourself in a bit of a pickle, haven't you?'

12

COLD ARAB, HOT WATER

TAKING HOLD OF THE EDGE OF THE COUNTERPANE Gregory carefully folded it over the nakedness of his abused mistress. Immobile, momentarily uncomprehending, Frannie watched. Then, as Gregory straightened up she dragged her tied hands out from under the silk and held them towards him as she grunted protests.

'My future's at stake, Lady Ballington. Yours, too,' he said, as his eyes travelled from her to the body. 'There's a dead Moroccan on your bedroom floor. I want there to be no chance of any mistake why and how he came to end up that way.'

Frannie frowned, she banged her hands twice down on the cover in a demonstration of impatience, then she shrugged, shook her head, grunted no more.

'I take it he *did* try to rape you?' She nodded vigorously.

The waiting is brief. First on the scene is the chambermaid, bringing the manager who, jabbering in French, rushes to Frannie's side and begins to untie her hands. Gregory, firmly, stops him. Police says Gregory, get the bloody police, fast. He takes the telephone from a bedside table and hands it to the man. Fast.

An impatient interlude, riddled with nerves. No

one knows what to do with themselves. They don't want to look at the dead Arab. Frannie throbbing in wrists, arms, thighs, ankles. A soreness at her groin. The corners of her lips taut-stretched by the choking mouthful of foul rag which has been Allah-only-knows-where before. Pulse beating upwards against the cutting string. Head beginning to pound. Having forcibly to breath through her nose giving her the disturbing illusion of shortage of breath. She understands perfectly why Gregory refuses to release her. Damn the man anyway. Not fair, not fair, he has just saved her from death, the lifeless lump of human junk on the floor was about to slit her throat. Damn Gregory for not at least taking this filthy rag from her mouth. *Where the fuck are the fucking police?*

Two men in faded blue uniforms. Underlings. One reaches for Frannie's wrists, Gregory moves his hands away, points from the knife to the dead man to Frannie, says No, get the boss. The manager intervenes, the three argue noisily then one policeman gets on the phone while the other prods the corpse with an unscientific boot.

Finally, an angular man in a crumpled grey suit. Unimpressive. Spare. Perhaps the business of living has eroded him. But he has searching, experienced eyes. Others with him, more arriving. Too many, a circus. Uniforms, suits, guns. A man wrapped in camera equipment. Chaos threatening, the noise loud, like a zoo. The scruffy-suited chief speaks a reasonable variation of English. Gregory patiently explains all with clarity and precision, including the business of the bleeper, is escorted to his room to retrieve this. He puts it between the chief's turkey-claw fingers, turns the emerald on Frannie's ring and the bleeper goes off. Boss man is amused. *Amused!* He wants to have a go himself, does so, examines the bleeper as if it is some instrument from outer space. Frannie sighs, resigned to the cabaret.

Three ambulancemen with a canvas and wood, rolled-up stretcher which they lean against a wall, lean with it. A doctor, summoned urgently from a case. He wears a medical coat which is not nearly as white as it ought to be.

The doctor carries out a rapid examination of the fallen Arab. To nobody's surprise he pronounces him dead. Unintelligible conversation, which might be a buzz were this an English drawing room, grates in the air in guttural monotony. The doctor moves to the bedside and Frannie, her discomfort growing alarmingly, becomes the number one attraction. The doctor leans towards my lady, the chief hovering opposite him, watching him touch her wrists, her face, tilt her head to look at her nicked neck where the blood has already congealed, a dry ditch of it meandering from tiny wound to shoulder. The chief meanwhile picks up the knife carefully in a handkerchief, scrutinising it with a show of intelligence.

The doctor moves to strip back the coverlet, pauses with his hands at its edge above Frannie's breasts, turns his face on the hordes who suddenly become tensely expectant. He lifts an eyebrow questioningly at the chief who raises a finger, twiddles it in the air and, miraculously, all backs are turned except for that of the photographer who is summoned by a curl of the same finger.

Frannie rudely exposed. The humiliation extreme, eclipsing physical discomfort. The doctor's fingers probe and dig at the inside of her thighs, he produces a piece of cotton wool, swabs there, pops the result in a glass phial, stoppers it. The camera flashes, again, again, again from different angles, the photographer darting around the bed. Frannie is the naked star in a real life interest story.

Matilda has materialised, sinks rapidly into shock, no good to anyone. She collapses in a chair, four eyes dancing illogically around the room.

As the doctor examines the bruising the chief watches from behind what is meant to be a veil of disinterested professionalism. But worldly-wise Frannie, an expert reader of the male eye, knows differently. Chiefy is relishing this unexpected, welcome offering of an abused, naked, beautiful white woman in bondage. Sawbones, too, lingers unnecessarily over his intimate contact with her bruised and tortured flesh whilst the photographer, undoubtedly delighted with his good fortune, flashes away and Frannie's incorrigible brain finds time to wonder how much he will make by selling copies of his prints in this land where even *Playboy* is banned.

Finally, regret perhaps showing in his lack of haste in the action, the chief re-covers Lady Ballington. She holds up her hands to him, hoping the grossly informal formalities are at an end, and he frees them, then unstuffs her mouth. She coughs, spits, wipes her lips with the back of a hand. Flicking an imperious finger he says something. Water appears. Sitting up, she pulls the cover tight around her, swallows gratefully.

The chief is finally satisfied with his collection of evidence, the stretcher is let down from the wall and unfurled. At this moment a shock jolts through Frannie as she sees that Jabir has appeared, is almost filling the doorframe. Frannie points. 'He . . . ' she begins, and a warning bell clangs in her head.

The chief picks this up, joins his stare to hers. 'He what, madame?'

She has been about to say, 'He must have let the man in,' stops the words with another sip of water. How to explain this one? Say that the black Bedouin had been in her room earlier, they'd been screwing their brains out? Not exactly a simplification of matters – or an exemplification of her character. Thank God for a survivor's cunning. 'Why is that man here?' she manages instead. 'He's only a hotel employee.'

Her eyes clash with Jabir's for the merest fraction of an instant and an uncanny understanding passes between them. The chief barks something at the Bedouin and he vanishes.

The corpse, decently covered, is rolled onto the stretcher which is lifted and joggled passed Matilda who watches in myopic incomprehension then jumps, a quiver disturbing her plump fold as Frannie, already in charge of herself, snaps loudly. 'Matilda! For *Christ's* sake pull yourself to*gether*!'

The doctor packs his bag, the photographer restrings himself with his. They leave. The other elements of the production drift away, the dust of drama begins to settle. When only the chief and two of his uniformed men are left the chief gives a nod. Gregory, a slight flinch his only visible reaction, is shackled in handcuffs.

Frannie protests. The chief spreads his talons, eagle shoulders shrug regret. 'This is now out of my hands,' he says, mildly. 'A man has been killed, Lady Ballington. The neck of one Moroccan subject has been broken with the hands of this Englishman. The law is needing to take its right and proper course.' His eyes stray over Frannie's silk-wrapped body, irritating her, as he adds, 'You may keep your passport but until I am saying so you will remain within this hotel.'

Suddenly the room is empty, except for Frannie and Matilda who is still cloistered in her blanket of nerves. Hollow.

'Snap out of it, *do*,' Frannie insists. She winces as she lets the cover fall and swings bare legs off the bed. 'I'm going to clean myself up, meanwhile you get hold of Victor.'

But Matilda's recovery is too slow and, for once,

132

Frannie, despite her condition, gets genuinely annoyed. Going to Matilda she shakes her shoulders so hard that her spectacles bounce off the end of her nose and drop into her quivering lap.

'Get Victor,' she grates through clenched teeth. '*Now*, Matilda. *Do* it.'

In London, in the House, the Secretary of State for Foreign Affairs was summoned from a late night parliamentary session by an urgent, and therefore unignorable, call from Lord Ballington. Minutes later the British ambassador in Rabat, capital of Morocco, had his sleep disturbed by the British Secretary of State shortly after which the ambassador was in direct telephone contact with Lady Ballington at the Mamounia.

Amongst the small pile of slips announcing the following morning's business which the king attended to in his study after breakfast was a note detailing the violent death of one of his subjects at the hands of an Englishman in the Mamounia hotel in Marrakech. Having read this, and the attached note about the British ambassador's interest in the affair, he instructed his private secretary to gather detailed information about the Ballington family and Lady Ballington's bodyguard, the killer, Mr Gregory Parks. This done and other pressing matters dealt with, the king went off to his private golf course.

Meanwhile, the chief of the Marrakech police force, having most carefully considered the unusual circumstances surrounding the assassination on his patch the previous evening, dithered. He perceived that the evidence pointed over-whelmingly to the fact that one of his least desirable citizens had raped a highly placed member of British society whom he would surely then have knifed to death had it not been for the timely intervention of this woman's bodyguard. However, aristocracy being involved, not to mention the prestigious Mamounia hotel, he referred the matter upstairs. A detailed dossier was prepared for the commander in chief of police at Rabat.

The king kept an official engagement after lunch, taking him through until six pm when he briefly slept. That evening, hearing that the British ambassador had communicated several times with the palace during the day with reference to the Marrakech slaying, he had his private secretary bring him the data about the Ballingtons and Gregory Parks. He read with interest that Lord Ballington had been part of a small, informal gathering in the palace some six years previously. The French Home Secretary had been one of the guests, as had a British colonel concerned with the internal safety of Dubai. Victor Ballington, the king took favourable note of, was on intimate terms with the British royal family; he was also known to be one of the richest men in England. Vague memories of Victor stirred within the king because at the customary all-male gathering he and the lord had discussed thoroughbred horses together, Victor exhibiting considerable knowledge.

During that same year it seemed that the man Gregory Parks had been a member of the unit of the elite SAS squad which had helped train the king's own security people in certain advanced techniques; one of these had been the swift and silent administration of death.

Finding the Marrakech problem rather more colourful than most of his tedious affairs of state, but acting with the customary Arab lack of haste, King Hassan made it known that he would consent to an audience with reference to the case with the British ambassador at eleven the following morning. The commander in chief of the Moroccan police, he suggested, should also present himself at the palace at the same hour with all the relevant facts. These matters arranged, the king took himself off to evening prayers.

Thus Gregory prepared to spend a second night as a prisoner in a malodorous cell in the odious, Marrakech gaol, with his hands and feet quite unnecessarily manacled. He had received so far one short visit from the British consul who assured him that the ambassador himself was working flat out on the case. Apart from that he was incommunicado. Gregory was uncomfortable, but not unduly worried. The facts of the affair were properly documented and inescapable; besides, the enormous power of privilege was working for him. Well versed in the machinations of the slow-grinding wheels of authority he accepted his lot with typical stoicism whilst frequently revising upwards the size of bonus he could expect from his lordship when all this was over.

Four walls do not a prison make – unless you are Lady Francesca Ballington in which case they most certainly do, even if they are the hedonistic ones of the Mamounia hotel. She was trapped in the circumstances of murder once again and the situation began to stifle her. At least that other time, when Gregory had killed whilst rescuing her from a horrific fate, the police had not been involved, had never connected them with the gruesome events and they had managed to flee Los Angeles unmolested.

She found that not knowing what was happening and being unable to go where she pleased was intolerable, despite Victor's repeated telephoned assertions that all would be fine and that patience was the sole requirement in a country where things fell into place as slowly as a spider weaves its web.

The British ambassador, knowing full well that he would not be received at the appointed hour, was nevertheless obliged to present himself at the palace promptly at eleven, where he found the police commander in chief already waiting. The commander had an audience before twelve; the ambassador was not seen until four in the afternoon.

Barely containing her impatience, no longer caring for the sunny gardens nor even her balcony Frannie became morbidly involved with her inner self, where thoughts of sex, in a new and extraordinary development, became ugly and distasteful. Her physical wounds were slight, her scratches and bruises were already almost healed. But the mental damage was severe, the very idea of being impaled by a male member, until then delightful, became abhorrent. It was crippled by the vivid memory of the pain the smell, the sound, the sight, the horror of rape.

Once, leaving her room to search out magazines in the foyer, she came across Jabir and the look which shot between them sent her scurrying for the lift. Jabir, who was clearly involved, must have let the killer in. But *why*? The why was, indeed, enormous. Carter-Smith? Inconceivable. But who then? What for? What could possibly possess the Bedouin to let a man into her suite to rape and murder her? The ultimate kick? Manson-like destruction of the wealthy? Was that the hidden secret of Jabir whom she had enjoyed with abandoned passion, who had proved that giants really can be gentle? And Salah. Did *he* have a hand in it? He had certainly not appeared since. Yet Clovis Carter-Smith, alias Harry Digby, had most certainly checked out of the hotel early the following morning, that much she had discovered. Why? It was all an improbable, lunatic, mixed-up dream. Life seemed to have dealt her ladyship a crushing blow.

For some reason the heavy weight upon her turned her head to poetry. Unexpectedly, without, it seemed, too much conscious effort, she produced words which, whilst having nothing whatsoever to do with her predicament, somehow mirrored her melancholy. Perplexed by it, yet pleased it had come out of her, she read her poem to Matilda.

'The Clown,' she began, settling herself back in a chair, sheltering her eyes from an intruding sunbeam with one hand.

'Sadness neatly covered with/ a painted smile/ the clown stepped,/ clumsily in boat-sized boots,/ out of his dingy, back-stage world,/ into the trumpeted glare of/ fun-and-laughter.
'The smile smiled, permanent,/ the cracking paint around its edges/ looking like/ laugh lines.
'Through his black-starred,/ happy-funny eyes/ the clown's jelly-dead gaze/ surveyed his/ artificial, canvassed, neatly compact/ world of/ fun-and-laughter.
'They cheered as he/ clumsied around the ring,/ played a cornet,/ fell over,/ lost his trousers,/ as water spurted from his/ plastic-bald head,/ as he/ suffered/ amusing/ indignities.
'They laughed when another clown/ (much like him)/ kicked at his behind,/ once,/ twice,/ three times,/ sending him/ reeling and staggering/ through closed curtains/ to anonymity.
'His soft intake of breath and/ the sound of a single tear/ rolling down his cheek/ could have been drowned by/ a heartbeat.
'They cheered/ and clapped/ so loudly that/ the tears of ten thousand/ crying clowns/ would have rolled away/ unnoticed/ in the Niagara/ of their enthusiasm.
'His happy-sad job done,/ his moment gone,/ he crept back/ to his caravanned/ obscurity.
'The crowd/would laugh/ no more./ Until tomorrow.'

Frannie looked up. 'Am *I* a clown?'

'Hardly. Well, perhaps sometimes.' Matilda, standing close to Frannie, grimaced. 'But then, aren't we all?' Slipping the sheet of paper from Frannie's hands

137

she pushed her glasses firmly into the bridge of her nose and glanced down it.

After a few moments Frannie said, 'Is it any good?'

'God, how should *I* know? It's hardly Shakespeare, but it has a certain feeling – not one I'd usually associate with you.' She shrugged her shoulders, making her breasts tremble. 'Not too jolly, is it?'

'No. But the funny thing is, I *feel* a bit better for having written it. As if some of my misery came out in the ink.' She smiled. 'I suppose it was therapeutic.'

They were interrupted by two firm raps on the door. 'Come.' Frannie called out.

Gregory marched in, on his heels the chief of police. Except that his suit was even more rumpled than that of the policeman, Gregory appeared none the worse for his experience.

'*Oh, thank God!*' Frannie exclaimed.

'It's *you*. Are you quite all right, Gregory?' said Matilda.

'Yes, apart from the pressing need for something stronger than Coca Cola.'

Frannie got to her feet, waving a hand at the bar as the chief quietly closed the door. 'Whatever you like. Help yourself.'

'Your man is altogether free, Lady Ballington,' said the chief. 'He is not to be charged.' He glanced at a chair. 'Perhaps . . . ?'

'Is there something else?'

'Yes.'

'Well then, sit, if you insist.' Frannie's words were icy. With his probing eyes this man had taken advantage of her naked body, in his way he was a rapist himself. Gregory was pouring whisky. She glanced at him. 'Make it a really strong one. God knows you deserve it.' She turned her eyes on the chief. 'Naturally a policeman, particularly a *Moroccan* policeman, doesn't drink?'

He looked straight back at her. 'I confess a weakness for whisky. We are not all devoted Moslems.'

'Oh. Then fix him one, Gregory.' Frannie strolled to the terrace, put her back to it. 'I'd prefer to get this over as quickly as possible.' Her eyes lingered distastefully on the policeman. 'What do you want?'

Her attempts to discomfort the man were having no effect. He smiled. 'You are all free to leave whenever you like. The affair has been attended to at the most highest level.'

'Naturally. What*ever else*?'

Pomposity failed to put him down. Accepting two fingers of neat Glenmorangie he savoured it with undisguised relish. 'However, there are untied ends.'

'*Are* there?'

'Most assuredly. The unspeakable Sidi Ben Dukkala was as a rat which scrabbles around amongst filth in order to feed itself. Such a man does not find his way through the corridors of the Mamounia hotel in search of a woman for appeasing his lust and then to kill. Such a man is going with the filthiest of prostitutes in darkest alleys of the kasbahs. He, please excuse me, takes advantage of the bodies of young boys, do you understand? And for money he will do any thing.' Slowly, he sipped at the malt, his eyes darting around the room but rarely alighting on Frannie.

'Please get *on* with it,' Frannie said.

'There was a great deal of money on Ben Dukkala's wretched body. A body by the way which is now but ashes lying where they belong in the city dump. Spanish money and British money.' He paused. 'Why might you suppose that was, Lady Ballington?'

She shrugged carelessly. 'I'm sure I haven't the faintest idea. He was a rat, your own words. No doubt he was a thief.'

'Of course.' Finishing the scotch he put the glass on the table before him with tangible reluctance. With the barest indication of her chin Frannie had Matilda replenish it. As she was doing so he said, 'A thief. But hardly a man to go raping and murdering in a first class hotel. In fact, consider. Is it possible to conceive of such a man?'

Frannie nodded grudgingly. 'A little unusual.'

'Who is there that would want to see you dead?'

'Why *should* there be anybody?'

'There is.'

'A mistake? Mistaken identity?'

'Oh.' Flat. More whisky-worship. 'How did Ben Dukkala get in?'

'I've no idea. He broke in, I suppose.'

'No. Someone let him in. However, leaving this aside, he was paid to kill you. The money, it tells me this. It speaks to me like a camera. Fresh money, mostly clean, unstained from use. Who paid him this money? You surely must have an idea. It would greatly please me to detain this man. Such crimes are not – encouraged – in Morocco.'

'All right.' Partially overcoming her repugnance for the man, Frannie made up her mind. If it *was* Carter-Smith then he deserved all that would be coming to him. Victor might get a kick out of playing the avenging hero but what had happened to Frannie and the fate she had missed by seconds went beyond the rules of the game. 'There is a man called Clovis Carter-Smith.' She smiled acidly. 'Perhaps you wouldn't *mind* leaving the *whisky* alone and noting this down?'

'My memory is excellent. However.' Unruffled, the chief drained his glass, put it on the table and produced a stub of pencil and someone's visiting card which he read before turning it over for use. Matilda made no further move towards the Glenmorangie bottle. 'Please spell that name?'

Frannie obliged. 'He's staying in this hotel under the name of Harry Digby.' She corrected herself. '*Was*

140

staying that is. He has a yacht in Casablanca called the "Golden Hind". He is wanted in England on massive fraud charges. My husband was one of his victims.'

'*Was* he?' The chief seized on this information with great satisfaction. '*Now* you are telling me something. And, did he recognise you, this man? Did he believe you were about to uncover him?'

'I don't know. I'm not aware that he's ever seen me together with my husband.' This then, *was* it the answer? She remembered how Carter-Smith had parked himself at her side at the blackjack table, the twinges of discomfort his attitude had brought her. And then his checking out of the hotel, perhaps in a hurry. Maybe he *did* know who she was. But *how*? She shrugged. 'Perhaps you're right.'

'It is perhaps doubtful that perhaps is the word,' said the chief, rising. 'Mr. Carter-Smith is of course our man.' Belying his professed excellent memory, he glanced at the back of the visiting card. "The Golden Hind." Then I shall have him within the hour.' He bowed slightly, just enough for Frannie to interpret it as mockingly. 'I thank you so much for your superb whisky.'

But the "Golden Hind" was no longer to be found in Casablanca harbour. She had set sail the previous afternoon en route for Caracas, Venezuela and was by then far out in the Atlantic Ocean.

13

CALIFORNIA CREAMIN'

'BANJUL,' FRANNIE EXCLAIMED, STABBING A FINGER AT THE page of an atlas. Matilda was smoothing sun-cream into the small of her back as Frannie lay naked on her belly on her Mamounia balcony, taking advantage of the morning sunshine to help ease away her aches and pains.

'Beg pardon?' Blinking over the rims of her spectacles, Matilda failed to discern anything but a smudge of colour.

'That's the route we'll take. The first leg. From here to Banjul. Sixteen hundred miles more or less. Three to four hours in the air.'

Matilda groaned. 'Suffer little children. Where on *earth* is Banjul?'

'The Gambia. Down on the west coast of Africa.'

'Let me see.' Adjusting her spectacles Matilda crawled her torso forwards on her elbows until her nose hovered over the atlas. Touching it, she left a grease spot over Marrakech. 'We are here. And Venezuela is . . . here.' Another dab of grease. 'So why do you want to go all that way south? Why not head out over the Atlantic?'

'Good thinking, Matilda. You'd like us to ditch slap in the middle of the ocean, would you? If you study the map a bit more closely you'll observe there's absolutely nowhere to refuel.'

'Oh.' Her shoulders heaved, ponderous breasts shaking beneath the thin bathrobe. 'I really don't see why you don't leave this to the pilot.'

'It might be fun to plan a route myself for a change. Put down for fuel where I've never been before.' Her finger traced its way across the Atlantic towards South America, pausing at the Brazilian island of Sao Paulo. 'This seems to be the only place we can reach which is in roughly the right direction, assuming it's got somewhere to put a Lear down to refuel. From there we'll fly to Cayena in Guyana. That's, oh . . .' stretching finger and thumb over the proposed hop she roughly measured the distance against the scale. '. . . two thousand four, five hundred miles. We can make those two bits comfortably in a day. Then Cayena – Caracas. A mere thousand miles or so.'

'It all sounds positively dreadful.'

Frannie slid the book away from her and rolled onto her back on the towel. 'If we leave tomorrow we'll be there long before them. Give us time to settle in, to think things over properly. It's going to take the "Golden Hind" a good week to get there.'

Easing herself back onto her knees Matilda reached for the pot of cream. 'If you want my opinion you're quite crazy. It *was* Carter-Smith who tried to have you killed, we've agreed there's no room for doubt. That man is a dangerous lunatic who should be left to the police.'

'Hell, Matilda, you don't seriously think the police are going to bother him in South America, do you? Unless it's for a little share in the booty. Besides,' Her eyes slitted, glinting anger. 'I now have every bit as much reason to see the bastard behind bars as Victor. Correction, I have more reason. As long as that, that *madman* stays free, I'll be on his tail.'

'Oh dear.'

'Don't oh dear me, Matilda. Massage me.'

'Right.'

The sun playing over Frannie's bare flesh high-lighted the bruises of violent assault. Reaching for her shoulders Matilda squeezed gently as she began to massage with her thumbs in little circular movements above the collar bones. 'Nice?'

'Mmmm.'

'Calmed down, now?'

'Don't stop.'

In a little while the hands worked their way down to Frannie's breasts, lingering there lovingly. 'Perhaps you could do with some *special* attention?' Matilda breathed hopefully.

'You might try.'

Closing her eyes Frannie awaited arousal, normal response to Matilda's expert ministrations. Less than nothing. Her body exhibited as much sexual sensitivity as a lump of Plasticine, Matilda's well-meant attempts unwelcome, unwanted intrusions.

'To hell and back with that bloody man,' Frannie muttered as she prised the plump fingers away and raised her eyelids. She sighed, long and deeply. 'You'd better just stick to the muscles.' Then she added as an afterthought as she registered Matilda's acute disappointment, 'Sorry.'

Caracas from the air was an enormous industrial and commercial metropolis, surrounded by hills littered with shanty towns. By the time the Lear taxied to a halt Matilda was shattered, her nerves shot to pieces by four take-offs and landings in two days. They had covered almost five thousand miles, taking in just one short night's rest on the Atlantic island of Sao Paulo.

As they checked into the Caracas Hilton, Matilda was at last beginning to pull herself together but her relief was destined to be short-lived. Frannie, only just short of irritable during the entire journey and suffering from a libido which was as flat as stale champagne, was in restless mood. By the time they had paid a visit to the port, where the 'Golden Hind' could not be expected to put in for at least five days, her ladyship had decided that the capital of Venezuela, hit by an exceptional heatwave, was far too uncomfortable to linger in.

She made herself known to the harbour master, slipping him a big enough tip to ensure his cooperation when she rang for information and promising to double it in return for his silence. Then, as she folded her sticky flesh beside Matilda in the back of a taxi, she voiced her intentions for the first time.

'No way I feel like hanging around this sweltering place waiting for a ship which might not even show up. Let's move on.'

They were both thrown suddenly forwards, but Matilda's loud groan was not the result of the taxi-driver's clumsy clutch foot. 'Not *up* again?' she moaned.

'Up, yes.'

'Where to, for *God's sake*?'

'Who cares? Out of *here*. I need some life and somehow I know this place isn't going to provide it.' She frowned in irritation through the open window at the mess of traffic as they turned out of the port. A wild thought occurred to her, a typical Frannie fancy, and she raised an eyebrow at Matilda. 'I've just had an idea. Remember that seedy character Bernard Goldman, the porn producer?'

Matilda grimaced. 'Could I forget?'

'Quite.' Frannie allowed herself a smile, a rarity in recent days. '*Especially* since you got *off* with him sitting bare-assed beside you.'

Matilda feigned indignation. 'There's really no need to be so bloody vulgar.' But then she giggled. 'I did, didn't I?'

'I'll say.' Producing her notebook, Frannie flicked through the pages. 'Here. *Here* it is.'

'What?'

'Somewhere he told us about. Couldn't stop raving about it. Paul's Place at Big River Falls in southern California. Amateur sex shows on Saturday nights.'

Matilda gaped. 'Are you seriously suggesting we go all the way to California, for heaven's sake, for a Saturday night *amateur sex show*? Have you gone quite *batty*?'

'Don't you remember Goldberg insisting how utterly different and wild it is? Considering his experience in the field of sex then it absolutely *must* be. Maybe it'll put some life in me. God knows I need it.'

'Come *on*. There are sex shows all over the world, if you want to look for them. There has to be something appropriately wild right here. After all, this is Caracas, Venezuela.'

'I don't *want* to stay here.' Frannie ran the back of her hand over her perspiring brow. 'Besides, we are in the very north of South America. The south of North America isn't too far away.'

Which expansive statement failed to take into account that Los Angeles is some three thousand miles west of Caracas and that there is a little place called Central America in between. The route selected by the pilot would require two refuelling stops, at Miami and Houston.

Frannie, naturally, pursued her whim and in less time than it took Matilda to recover from it they were in California.

The colourfully named Big River Falls proved to be little more than a collection of one and two storey buildings, mostly pinewood, scattered along either side of a dusty road which stretched, ruler straight, towards the distant Palomar mountains. To reach it you took the coast highway south from Los Angeles, turned inland at Oceanside, halfway to the Mexican border, and then headed towards Indian reservation country.

During the week a sleepy, one horse town, Big River Falls was transformed on Saturday night due entirely to the commercial success of its night club whose infamy had spread throughout California. From the outside Paul's Place was as unassuming as the town. It stood in a dusty, two acre field which, when Frannie and Matilda arrived in their hired Pontiac limo, was fast disappearing beneath chaotically parked cars.

The club was as Goldberg had described it – several tiers of comfortable benches, loose stools and little tables surrounding a circular dance floor. As Frannie and Matilda settled on a bench on the second tier, below them the dance floor was crowded with couples swaying beneath coloured spots to Joe Cocker's rendition of 'A Woman Loves A Man'. Frannie noticed that on the whole the clientele appeared young, respectable and remarkably unboisterous.

Impeccable service speedily produced an ice-cradled bottle of light, dry, Californian white wine. Sipping appreciatively, Frannie, casually comfortable in a cream muslin dress which flowed to mid-calf, settled back to absorb the atmosphere. Despite her apprehension at being back in the same city where, less than two years previously, Gregory had killed on her behalf, Frannie's mood had been steadily improving since their Wednesday arrival. It was warm, the humidity low, refreshing after the wet, stodgy heat of Caracas. She enjoyed the almost boyish charm of the Californian men and found it amusing, whilst amongst so many outstandingly pretty young ladies, to still receive constant male glances of admiration. The freedom, the friendliness, the overt sexuality of Los Angeles were exactly what she needed to restore her battered libido, and it was beginning to take effect. Perhaps Paul's Place would contrive to complete the job.

Sex, the big attraction, was scheduled for eleven, Frannie, by then pleasantly plied with wine, was in anticipatory mood. A tall, lithe young man who had twice danced with her had finally turned the trick of reawakening her interest in males, despite his ponytail and gold earring.

The dancefloor was cleared and an armchair and a bed were manhandled into its centre, a few cushions scattered on them. A sudden hush descended, a tense expectancy hung in the air.

The music faded, the lights were dimmed and a compere appeared by the bed, bathed in the white light from a single spot. Witty, self-assured, the epitome of the clean-cut young American, he announced the proceedings as easily and naturally as if he were introducing an egg and spoon race. 'It's an old-fashioned word,' he concluded. 'And an even more old-fashioned pastime. Couples are coming out here, climbing on to this bed, this chair, and they're going to fuck. Any way they want, anyhow which takes their fancy, anything goes. Screwing their brains out in an attempt to win ten thousand lovely bucks. I will be judging, Paul himself will be judging, but the final decision is really yours, the audience – a thousand people who are here this evening for just one reason, to tune in and switch on to the world's greatest entertainment – S, E, X. Now, let's hear it for our first loving couple.' He raised his hand high, pausing for a brief drum roll. 'The lovely Dinah and her live-in lover, Bradley.'

The spot swung out over the audience where it hovered over two young people who were rising amidst enthusiastic applause. The harsh white light kept track of them as they picked their way down through three tiers and walked hand-in-hand to the bed where they stopped, blinking around into darkness, looking awkward as the applause died. They were both about twenty, unremarkable, casually dressed, certainly shy. In that moment it seemed inconceivable that they intended to make love out there.

The opening strains of George Michael's 'Kissing A Fool' filled the air. For long seconds the couple merely looked uncomfortably at one another then, as the white spot was replaced by overlapping coloured ones, blue red and green, Bradley drew Dinah into his arms. They kissed.

Frannie and Matilda sat in a darkness which, silent but for the music, seemed to be charged with pent-up excitement. The couples' kissing became more fervent, their hands slid downwards, found the mounds of each others' buttocks and Matilda leant forward as far as she could and settled her glasses in place. 'Good Heavens,' she breathed, startled. 'I believe they're actually going to *do* it!'

Frannie, smiling, said nothing. The charged atmosphere was beginning to invade her and her eyes drank in every move as the two Americans began to do to each other what presumably they usually only did in private. She savoured the spectacle with relish. This so far, had little to do with her experiences of commercial sex shows, invariably sordid, tired shams of enthusiasm. It promised to be a truly voyeuristic event, akin to peering through someone's bedroom curtains.

Clumsily, the lovers lay side by side on the bed, knocking two pillows to the floor in the process. Their intimate touches, their kisses, still displayed evidence of nervousness, of an awareness of the blacked out, tense audience. As George Michael's song came to an end and, in the same rhythm, Carly Simon began 'Kept On Lovin', Bradley's hand crept higher up Dinah's knee-length skirt, pulling it above dark brown stocking tops. With a furtive little glance into the blackness, as if daring herself to get on with it, Dinah slid down the zip of his slacks. Her hand slipped inside.

They began to work themselves up like that, their sexual organs still hidden. Frannie found herself reminded of her own preliminary gropings so long ago, before the loss of innocence. Their continuing, though decreasing, hesitancy, had in itself an arousing effect, it made it appear that they were new to the game of sex, were shy about touching one another intimately. Which would come off first, Frannie wondered? His pants or her knickers?

Her prurient musings were rapidly answered. Dinah's skirt was bunched on her waist and, squatting, legs tucked beneath him, Bradley eased off her shoes, hooked thumbs and fingers into her panty waist band and dragged them down over her knees. Her darkly-haired pubic mound was momentarily featured before she rolled onto her belly, fleshy white buttocks quivering and lewdly framed by the heaped green of her dress. With a gesture and a push she had her lover uncurl one leg and put a foot to the floor, the other remaining propped at the knee on the bed. While he balanced like that facing her, looking down on her, she freed the top button of the unzipped trousers, unclipped the leather belt and, almost greedily, as if suddenly forgetting she was being watched, clawed underpants and trousers to mid-thigh.

Bradley's equipment, like himself, was unexceptional but unquestionably male. Coarse exposure under spotlights produced an artless erotic effect. Mere disarrangement of clothes made the nakedness more provocative. Female buttocks and male genitalia, the penis beginning to rise, were highlighted, trapped in the gaze of a thousand pairs of avid eyes. The merest

150

suggestion of a sigh drifted briefly through the audience.

Carly Simon faded into an old but appropriate number, a rise in tempo, the Rolling Stones and 'Star'. Inching forward on her elbows Dinah took Bradley's cock in one hand, flicked a tongue under his balls, then sucked the whole of it deep into her mouth.

At this moment, oblivious of his surroundings, Bradley's erection blossomed. Grasping his girlfriend with one hand around the back of her neck, he began to thrust in little, regular jerks between her lips. His organ grew to full size, unremarkable but too big for all of it to be contained in her mouth as she played with his testicles with one hand and herself with the other.

'Fuck a star. . . Fuck a star. . .' He rolled her over and, kneeling between her splayed and welcoming legs, lowered himself to her. Jerking up to meet him she hooked her feet behind the back of his knees and challenged his initial heave with a powerful one of her own. Then all at once in stark contrast to the bored performance of the professional sex stud, he was banging into her as if his life depended on it, his tight-clenched buttocks beginning to glisten with sweat.

The first Saturday night public screw at Paul's Place, Big River Falls, was off to a rousing start, looking as if it was about to finish almost as soon as it had begun. Locked together, they rolled over until she was astride him, her back to Frannie's table. Her skirt collapsed from her waist, covering her thighs and her lover's legs, obstructing the view. For moments all that Frannie and Matilda could see was the back of one happily riding but seemingly clothed young lady until, perhaps with the prize in mind, Bradley pulled his Dinah down into him and her skirt high up her back so that now the view from Frannie's section was totally explicit – cock and balls, penetrated pussy and a big, white, bouncing bum.

The first of the night's performances was, indeed, about to reach an early climax. After few more orgiastic heaves, his toes curled and he went quite still, any sound he made drowned by the music. Dinah continued to rise and fall, skewering her pussy on Bradley's shining cock, faster, urgently as the male organ started to wilt, faster, bottom furiously pounding, faster, then sharp, sudden, muscle – tensing immobility as 'Fuck A Star' came to a perfectly timed end so that the audience could clearly hear her long, drawn out shout . . . 'I'm cooomminnggg.'

Applause. Loud, yet strangely lethargic, as if the sight of a couple making love to orgasm had drained the onlookers themselves. The coloured spots winked out, leaving only the white one. Dinah uncoupled from Bradley, swung her legs to the floor and the two of them hastily rearranged their clothes. With deflated, sheepish smiles on their glistening faces they left the floor hand in hand, the spot following them until they reached their seats. The overhead lights went on and the club was filled with a rosy glow.

'Incredible!' Frannie enthused.

'I'll say!' Agreed Matilda.

'Short but, uh, *different.*'

'Odd, isn't it? The most practised activity in the world bar none, you've seen it all, *done* it all hundreds, maybe thousands of times. The same old thing, not particularly imaginative, ten minutes watching it, your knickers get wet!'

'Matilda! I'm appalled at you.'

'No you're not. So just how dry are *your* knickers?'

Frannie laughed. At last she was beginning to feel in fine fettle. She was sitting on the physical proof that violent rape had failed to kill her sexuality, had merely anaesthetised it and the anaesthetic was finally wearing off. Relieved, she settled comfortably back on the bench, replenishing both her own and Matilda's glass as the compere, announced the next couple.

Jojo and Bro went into their performance with a zeal and enthusiasm quite lacking in their predecessors. Described as an actor and actress they seemed out to prove this, dancing suggestively around the chair and the bed to heavy rock as they helped each other to strip naked, but showing enough lack of polish to dispel any ideas that they may have been professionals in the field of sex. Lean and fit, their bodies perfectly tanned all over, the exposure of their flesh provided a very different titillation from the crude display of Bradley and Dinah. That they had practised this act became evident as they moved from scene to scene, wasting little time on preliminaries once they were out of their clothes.

As he stood, blatantly displayed to all, she brought him quickly to full erection with a practised, experienced blow job. His organ was thick and strong. When she slid her lips off it and stood back in hammy adoration it stood solidly with gorged glands pointing above the forty-five degree angle. Insolently, as the music changed to Queen, Bro grabbed his cock and waved it at the rapt audience so that all should have a good look. Then Jojo arranged herself on hands and knees on the bed. Bending down to her, he briefly tongued her pussy. Then, his action illiciting such a gasp from the crowd it momentarily stifled Queen, he grabbed her breasts from behind and penetrated her with one massive lunge which, but for his grip on her breasts, would have knocked her sprawling across the bed.

They kept changing positions, these two, controlled in their coupling after that first violent stab, seemingly determined to demonstrate every trick in the Kamasutra before reaching their climaxes.

Frannie found herself wholly fascinated but nevertheless not as keenly turned on as she had been by the inexpertise of Bradley and Dinah. That is until Bro finally allowed himself his orgasm. Having no doubt learned from porn material the value of not wasting the visual effect of a climax in its intended place, he climbed off Jojo, knelt between her legs and sprayed her from mouth to pubis with his sperm. While this was happening Frannie's hand insisted its way up and under her skirt.

As the applause went through its birth and death, no more enthusiastic than for Bradley and Dinah, Matilda, distracted from the dance-floor by Frannie's movements, remarked, 'Well, well. I'd say my lady must be on the road to a cure.'

Unhurriedly, as if she had merely been scratching an itch, Frannie removed her hand from beneath her dress and wrapped her fingers, warm from their travels, around the bowl of her wine glass. She smiled blandly, lifting the glass to her lips but wickedly licking at the side of a damp finger before taking a sip at the wine. 'Your lady is . . . all *but* cured,' she murmured.

A fat pair came next. They were not quite grotesque. They fumbled and tore at one anothers' clothes with an eagerness which was infectious – naked mountains of flesh wobbling like jellies under lights which striped them in different colours, groping, poking, sucking and screwing. It was obscene, but obscenity, close cousin of eroticism, has a certain fascination and no one looked away as Billy Bunter gave it to Miss Piggy. Even the music went fat, with great, swelling chords from Vangelis. There was disappointing orgasm, for the crowd at least, buried in carnal folds and lardy heaps, and reflexive tightening of thigh and buttock muscles disguised by rolls of meat, any ecstatic vocal outpouring drowned by thunderous chords.

The level in the wine bottle was once again low. Frannie, her head just beginning to float a little, ordered a fourth as Matilda cleaned the lenses of her spectacles on the hem of her mauve velvet dress, on her face a smile of beatific contentment.

Two more unashamed and hopeful couples took the stage with variations on a theme as old as Adam and Eve, but these were different bodies, fresh personalities with changed approaches and responses, guaranteed to produce renewed audience arousal.

Then came a change. Bondage, spanking. The girl petite and pretty, no more than eighteen. The man big, black and muscular, the sight of him bringing a shudder to Frannie as he all too clearly reminded her of her Bedouin. Clothed at first, they embraced and kissed, the girl as diminutive in the man's arms as Frannie had been in those of Jabir. She wore a brief gymslip and tennis shoes, schoolgirlish, no doubt intentionally so. Releasing her he perched on the edge of the bed where, swiftly and unexpectedly, he doubled her over his knees, yanked her skirt up with one enormous black hand, downed her knickers with the other, then brought a heavy palm down across her very white behind with a thwack which echoed through the club like a pistol shot. He began laying into her buttocks with serious intent, and a thin white spotlight settled on the offended area as it rapidly turned blotchy red. But no screams accompanied this castigation. With each blow the girl's short, shapely legs jerked, her back arched and her head jumped up, her mouth opening wide. But there was no question of suffering; this little girl was relishing the stinging pain of having her backside thoroughly tanned by that big, black hand.

Punishment over, bottom very red indeed and unquestionably sore, it was the lady's turn to take disciplinary action. The negro, wearing T-shirt and jeans, lay back and she secured his ankles and wrists to the legs of the bed. This act was clearly as planned as that of Jojo and Bro, but amateur nevertheless, a couple doing things in public which they enjoyed in private. As the last knot was tied Frannie's gaze momentarily shifted to Matilda who, hands clenched on thighs, neck stretched forward, was positively goggling.

Grinning briefly at her maid, Frannie returned her attention to the bed where Delilah was pulling down Samson's pants to reveal the largest hard-on seen so far that evening. Delilah stripped naked, leaving her clothes where they fell. She had small, fine breasts, a downy pubic thatch, a body to delight, her red-splodged behind in startling erotic contrast to the white of the rest of her. Slowly, seductively, she sinewed around the bed, offering her body to her man from every angle, not touching him, he unable to reach out and touch her. The torture was prolonged and delicious, becoming progressively more exquisite. From jiggling those lovely little tits over his head she climbed onto the bed and straddled him, squatting over his face, her crotch inches from his mouth but unreachable by his tongue, her weight on hands resting either side of his hips, lips close to his erection but never brushing it. For what seemed an eternity she remained like that, quite still except for a rhythmic side to side movement of her hips in time to the music. Appropriately, Frank Zappa was singing an old number of his about a girl called Dinamoe Hum and her bet that her man couldn't make her come. The teasing went on, all the way through that song and the next, until Frannie, Matilda and the rest of the audience were willing the girl to bring the black stud's suffering to an end.

At last she spread her legs a little wider and lowered her head and there was another of those collective sighs as mouths made hungry contact with genitals and the two sixty-nined voraciously. Carried away on a wave of lust by this performance, almost savouring the taste of the black cock between her own lips, Frannie was busy with her hand between her legs. No longer was there any sort of barrier in her psyche. Lady Ballington positively craved a man.

This salacious pair achieved climax with Samson still secured to the bed. Delilah knelt astride him, hands resting on his knees, facing his feet, his huge organ impaling her as she rode it faster and faster, squealing an orgasm fractionally before his, their mutual schooling in pornographic arts sufficient for her to know how to hoist her pussy off him at the crucial moment so that his gushing sperm splashed all the way up her back.

Frannie gratefully came along with them. The little whimper which escaped her lips was drowned by the loudest applause of the evening.

The most popular act of the night returned to their seats, the compere took the floor. They had watched all the scheduled couples, he announced, amateur evening was over unless there happened to be any other two lovebirds out there who were sufficiently aroused to come on down and put on a show of their own. If not, the judges decision would shortly be announced.

The crowd stirred and buzzed, the compere, a boyish smile splitting his face, waited patiently.

'Well? Shall we do it?' The voice, close to Frannie's ear, startled her. She looked up into a questioning, earringed face. Big blue eyes surveyed her in cool amusement. 'We already danced twice,' the young man with the pony tail went on. 'Fancy jiving with me right now?'

Shock was surmounted by instant temptation. A single, tiny, masturbatory orgasm had whetted Frannie's appetite as well as her pussy. She caught the blue eyes mockingly as the compere repeated his invitation, carnal thoughts tripping over each other as they rushed her brain. 'You really have the balls?' she found herself saying. Frannie was back to pure Frannie.

'Do I have . . . ?' the man exclaimed, only slightly fazed. 'Heh, heh, lady, them's fighting words!' He grabbed her hand but she was already halfway to her feet. 'You . . . are about to find *out* about my balls. Let's *go!*'

A ripple of excitement ran through the audience as the white spot highlighted Frannie making her way to the compere – not led by the young man but leading him, stepping with assured, ladylike elegance, Valentino cream muslin hem swaying confidently at her knees. Welcoming them with arms raised on high as if to say that here, finally, were the stars of the show, the compere huddled them on either side of him like long lost friends.

'A truly *gorgeous* couple, ladies and gentlemen,' he crooned. 'Truly gorgeous. What's your name, lovely lady?'

The microphone was shoved under Frannie's nose. 'Francesca Ballington,' she announced, loud and clear, eyes sweeping the tiers of people, nerves tingling with anticipation.

'Do I detect a *British* accent?' The compere seemed genuinely startled.

'*English*, *ec*tually,' said Frannie.

He stood back a pace, admiring. 'And a *rose*, ladies and gentlemen. An English rose right here at Big River Falls.' He pounced on the young man. 'And you, sir, lucky guy. What's *your* name?'

'Lee.' Lee's eyes swept over Frannie, undressing her, frank, unconcerned about the audience. His jeans, Frannie noticed, had a designer cut about them, they fell neatly on expensive, shiny black leather boots. And his open-necked white shirt was silk. Suddenly she did not mind the ponytail and earring at all; they suited him.

'And you handsome pair have enjoyed a relationship for just how long?'

The mike was back under Frannie's nose. She smiled disarmingly. 'We don't *have* a relationship,' she said. 'We just met. Right here, this evening.'

The compere blinked several times, eyebrows high, fine dramatic pause. 'You just . . . ' He spun through three hundred and sixty degrees, one hand aloft.

'How does *that* grab you, friends? *They just met!*' Once more, he hugged them into him. 'And you are *sincerely* going to *make love* for the first time right *here*, in front of one thousand people?'

'You bet,' said Lee.

'Well, I'm not exactly a virgin,' Frannie found herself saying.

'You are not exactly a *virgin!* You hear *that*, folks? The lady ain't no virgin! Well, *good* for *you!*' He stood back from them, his free hand lightly resting on Frannie's elbow. 'Okay you guys. The *bed* is all yours. *Music, please.*'

Bon Jovi's 'I'll Be There For You' filled the air as the compere faded away and Frannie and Lee were bathed in coloured spots. Frannie, acutely aware of the audience but no longer able to see them, stepped forward into arms which enveloped her with rippling strength. She pressed her groin into him and they swayed together to the soft number.

'That was a relief,' Lee said into her ear.

'What was?'

'To hear that you're not a virgin!'

She put a finger to his lips, smiling. 'That *would* complicate matters, would it not?'

'I'll say.' He tasted her mouth. 'Jesus, you're beautiful.'

Frannie felt utterly strange, the enormity of the position she found herself in almost overwhelming. There was no turning back. She tried to imagine that she was alone in a bedroom with this stranger but the crowd, invisible as they might be, pressed in from all sides. 'You've, er, you've done this sort of thing before?'

'No. You?'

'No.'

He danced her close to the bed where he stopped them, kissing her lips long and hard. 'Listen,' he said, breaking off the kiss. 'I usually like to take my time, the first time, a new chick, know what I mean? But we're kind of expected to get on with it.'

Frannie rotated her groin against him. Dirty words spilling from her lips brought a lecherous surge. 'To *fuck*, don't you mean? So let's *get* on with it. What did you say about your balls?'

'Jeeesus. Okay . . .' He sank to his knees, hands trailing down from her shoulders and across her breasts as he did so, then reaching for her buttocks, clutching. Pulling her tightly to him he buried his face in the muslin folds at her crotch, the heat of his breath searing its way through them.

Frannie suddenly sags at the knees, only dimly aware now of an audience. Perversely, the knowledge serves at this moment, to encourage, rather than daunt her. Hands on the top of the ponytailed head, she stares down as those big blue eyes, the only part of the face she can see above the swell of muslin, look up into hers and hold them. Still holding her gaze, he leans back, rides the dress up her bare, smooth thighs until her pantied crotch is exposed and then, breaking eye contact, he fixes his eyes on Frannie's well-travelled pussy and commands, 'Hold your skirt right there.'

Bon Jovi waxing lyrical as Frannie watches her fine mesh knickers peeled to her knees and his tongue trailing, hot and wet, inside each of her thighs before finding its way between. Fingers gently spread the lips of her vagina, the tongue tip explores, vibrating. Ecstacy drains Frannie of muscle power as the tongue thrusts deep, retreats. She lets her weight rest through her hands on his shoulders and he catches her eyes once more. 'Sit.' he says.

She folds back thankfully onto the edge of the bed while he removes her shoes and strips off her knickers, throwing them to the chair which they miss, hitting the floor. Then he climbs to his feet, stands between her splayed knees, unzips himself. 'My turn. Take it out.'

Fires Frannie had feared may have been quenched forever begin to rage within her as she reaches inside with both hands and, finding the top of his briefs, works them down over the solid bulge within. She eases her right hand over the warm, rigid flesh and frees a hard, strong pole of a cock from his jeans. Letting go, she stares at it for long moments of fascination. It's the first since her rape, but this one she *wants*. It's another cock, not unlike most of the rest, but new, different, challenging. As she draws it into her mouth she feels his tremor of excitement transmit itself to the thousand people watching. As she cups his balls, bulging over the lowered waistband of his briefs, and looks up into his feasting eyes with her mouth full of his penis, for one, incongruous, moment she wonders how Matilda is reacting.

That lady, for whom there can be few surprises left as far as her ladyship's headstrong actions are concerned is rapt. Her initial shock has long dissolved. In Matilda's book of delights, watching her mistress making love is second only to actually making love to her and she is on the edge of her seat, eyes boring through pebble lenses. Her Frannie is once again her old, wicked, daring self, the days of rape-induced misery are behind them and Matilda, fingers busy beneath her dress, laps up every erotic second.

The music changes, faster but cool, Deacon Blue and 'Real Gone Kid'. In their blatant dishabille Frannie and Lee fall back on the bed where they thrash around carnally. He rolls on her, tongue sliding far into her mouth, then he turns them over until she lies on top of him, his cock poking through the still-belted jeans tightly nestling between the tops of her thighs, the glans in the cleft of her buttocks as she grinds her hips in time to the music. Frannie is game and ready for anything, thoroughly abandoned, wanton, gripped by a raging sexual fever, her lust fed by the knowledge that she is watched by an audience of ogling people, this alone is at least as arousing as acting in a porno film.

She turns voracious. She wants her man naked. She kneels on the bed, unbelts him, drags off boots and jeans and briefs, impatient, clumsy about it, fingers trembling. She lets the items fall to the floor as, unbuttoning his silk shirt he mutters, 'You, too. Everything,' swings off the bed, collects his clothes and drapes them, with his shirt, carefully over the chair. He holds out his hand, his swaying, proudly erect tool washed first in green light then in blue as he takes Frannie's dress from her and folds it next to his jeans. Naked, Frannie stands, goes to him. There is a collective intake of breath as the voyeurs appreciate just how sensational her body is.

Lee dances Frannie backwards to the bed, topples her onto it, falls with her, taking his weight on his elbows on either side of her. Where he *rests*, smiling down at her, unmoving, the side of his cock lying flat against her thigh. Each second of delay is pure torture and Frannie gasps, 'Do it. Please?' But he lies there quite motionless with that irritating, self-confident smirk on his face, the dominant macho in full control and she grits her teeth, hissing through them, 'Do it, *bastard*. *Do* me.' Angrily she watches the smirk change into a grin as his cock slides slowly up her thigh, then stops. Grinding her hips up at him, lifting her legs and wrapping her calves around his, she heaves uncontrollably as if in the throes of screwing. Desperate for penetration, an imperative cry comes from deep within her, 'Fuck me. *Fuck* me. *Fuck me!*' and his grin broadens as he answers, incredibly, 'Only if you promise me tomorrow,' she gabbles, 'Yes, *tomorrow*. Whenever you *want*. For fuck's sake, *fuck* me!' Finally, finally, he obliges, and she feels the wonderful heat of his cock scorching its way inside her, plunging and filling as she clings as tightly to him as a limpet and sobs her thanks into his shoulder.

Some of Frannie's favourite sex music hits the air, Rod Stewart's, 'Angel', the timing a miracle of perfection as Lee rocks his big and competent tool in and out of her grateful vagina in long thrusts which pick up Mr Stewart's sensuous rhythms. Meanwhile, hidden in the darkness, Matilda has two fingers buried inside her to the hilt and the constant sounds of sexual exhilaration all around her are more highly charged than at any other time that evening.

Lee's rhythm is unchanging, he has hit a solid sexual groove and Frannie settles into this fuck with the knowledge that she is whole again. Relaxing her arms and legs she lies back happily, eyes barely open, hands palm upwards on the bed above her head and experiences the delight of a string of preliminary orgasms.

Lee is a stayer. Powerful, lithe, in command, he begins to move her around. From having her straddle him, his big blue eyes drinking in the full view of her bare body as he bounces her on his cock, he lifts her and makes her kneel, her hands grasping the headboard, and impales her from behind. As he stabs her and she goes with it easily, inevitably her perverse streak shows itself. She turns her head to him, he can just make out her half-strangled words above 'Maggie May'. 'Bugger me,' she mutters. 'Go on, *bugger* me.'

He grunts assent, thoroughly wets two fingers with his spittle and eases their tips into her anus, preparing the passage as she moans and wriggles. His weight on the headboard, his hands either side of hers, legs splayed so that at least half the audience can clearly see the action, he guides the end of his cock inch by inch up Frannie's sweet bum. She gasps with the initial pain which combines with the pleasure of this penetration as the audience, witnessing sodomy for the first time this evening, appears to hold its breath.

Frannie's head rolls around, her eyes opening and closing, hair bouncing around her neck and shoulders as Lee's thrusts go deeper. He's good, this boy, knowing how easily this invasion can cause real pain he takes care to control it so that there is only exquisite pleasure.

Frannie is overwhelmed by a cocktail of delights, with the unique feeling of being stretched to the limit in this way, knowing that it's a male organ up there being gripped tight and hot, and experiencing ecstasy of its own. Even the mind is involved because it is profligate, this act she is indulging in, she enjoys the idea that in many places it is considered an unspeakable degeneracy, and she revels in the knowledge that there is an audience of breathless, unseen people intently watching this vigorous performance of forbidden pleasure.

Enough. My lady is unplugged, laid on her back once more and re-entered in the favourite, old-fashioned missionary position. Lee's buttock-clenching heaves get faster, reaching a speed which denote the point of no return. Beneath him, Frannie is right there too. The primordial power in him is close to explosion and when he groans, 'Can I come in your mouth?' her wailed and moaned fifteen second 'yeeesss' accompanies a frenzied orgasm, his words the final touch on her trigger.

Replete, in the clouds, barely aware, she dimly watches as he slides out of her quickly, brings himself to his knees over her face, his engorged penis in one hand as, sliding the other beneath the damp hair at the back of her neck, he pulls up her head. Wicked lady that she is, Frannie opens her mouth wide and closes her lips over two inches of pulsing flesh. Sperm erupts. Her favourite liquid. She swallows hungrily. He withdraws, still spurting. With teeth clenched, head back, muscles bulging and twitching on sweaty thighs, he bathes her lips and chin and throat with three long jets. Suddenly he stops. For moments they are frozen together like an erotic statue, then Lee slowly keels over and collapses on the bed beside Frannie as a joyous tumult of applause thunders around the auditorium.

Opening her eyes, rolling her tongue over sperm-wet lips, Frannie raises a throaty giggle. 'They *adored* us,' she says.

Then there is just the cold, white spot, as the rosy lights flicker out over the crowd. Exposed in this harsh light, glistening with the sweat and excretions of sex, Frannie feels soiled. She hurriedly wipes her face and neck with the corner of a sheet and the two of them scramble into their clothes amidst unending applause. Still tucking in an errant shirt-tail with one hand, Lee grabs Frannie with the other and leads her off the floor.

The applause only began to die as they reached Frannie's table. Frannie sat down next to an unusually red-faced Matilda and Lee squeezed up to her on the end of the bench. All the dance floor lights went on as the compere reappeared to announce that it appeared there was no doubt which loving twosome the audience felt deserved the prize, it only remained for this to be confirmed in a couple of minutes by Paul himself.

'Matilda, this is Lee. Lee, Matilda,' Frannie muttered lamely.

Matilda raised an eyebrow. '*Friend* of yours, is he?'

'You might say that.' Frannie was bursting with contradictory emotion. The heavy sexual afterglow she felt could not be enjoyed in these circumstances. All around, curious eyes roved over her and tongues wagged busily. Curiously, she felt a touch of embarrassment at the situation, the absurdity of which was about to be heightened.

'*Hi* there, Frannie,' enthused a vaguely familiar voice. 'I see you've kinda *met* Lee,' It chuckled. '*Great* performance.'

Looming above them, stood the gold-draped figure of Bernard Goldberg, the porn producer, his mean mouth clamped around a half-smoked cigar.

Frannie gaped. 'Bernard,' she managed. 'What a surprise.'

'Hello, Mr Goldberg.' Lee produced a weak grin.

'You two know each other, then?' said Frannie.

'We do, we do.' Goldberg waved a hand towards the floor where Paul himself, a cadaverous man dressed in a smoking jacket and a cynical smile, had joined the compere. 'Of course, you two babies have scooped the prize.'

Indeed, Paul was already declaring them the unquestioned winners of the competition. In a daze Frannie found herself led a little reluctantly back to the bed, which was still rumpled from their performance, and there she received a cheque for ten thousand dollars and a statuette on a marble base of two naked people coupled together in sexual ecstasy. Applause thundered once more, there were even several delighted whoops.

'Congratulations,' mouthed Goldberg as they returned and sat down. He had appropriated a stool from somewhere and, uninvited, joined them.

'Congratulations indeed,' echoed Matilda.

Frannie slid the cheque to centre table and plonked the statuette on top of it. 'I suppose one should be fearfully embarrassed,' she muttered.

Goldberg guffawed. 'Not the Lady Ballington I know.'

Frannie flashed him a look of annoyance as she drained her glass and replenished it. 'Never mind the innuendo.'

'Innu*endo*?' The Goldberg paw briefly dared to rest on her knee, found itself rudely brushed away. 'Hardly.'

'*Lady* Ballington? Did you say *Lady* Ballington?' Lee said to Goldberg.

Frannie covered Lee's hand with hers on the table. It already seemed inconceivable that what they had finished doing to one another not more than fifteen minutes ago had been other than an unbelievably erotic dream. 'Yes, he did. It's really not that important.'

Goldberg produced another irritating guffaw, with words to match. 'You can say that again.' He emptied the remains of Frannie's bottle into his glass. 'Some lady!'

An indignant Matilda rose to the defense. 'Don't you dare!' she exclaimed. 'Don't you *dare* be so bloody rude!'

The Goldberg eyes went beady. Still smarting from their last encounter when Frannie and Matilda had left him with barely a goodbye, he was more than ready to bandy words. 'All right. She's a fucking *Mother Superior!*' he grated.

Frannie's hackles rose. She had no desire to bump into Goldberg again and here he was, being thoroughly disagreeable, at her table. 'I don't recall inviting you to join us, Bernard,' she said coldly. 'Neither did I ask you to drink my wine. But since you're here, *do* stay – just as long as you manage to behave yourself.'

Goldberg pushed a calming palm at her. 'Yeah. Well, I'll get some more wine.' But, seconds later, he was needling again. 'Enjoy yourself, Lee? Great lay, ain't she?'

Frannie had had enough. Unhappily, she had no defense for behaviour which had been thoroughly outrageous. So she launched a scathing attack. 'As a matter of fact I *am* a *superb* lay, Bernard,' she said. 'How are *you* in that department these days?'

'What . . .?' He looked quickly at the startled Lee, then back to Frannie, scratching his nose, hesitant, as if waiting a knockout punch he couldn't avoid.

'How many years is it since you could get it *up*, Mr Porn? Seven, isn't it? Wasn't *that* what you were whining about that night? Seven years without raising a hard-on? Bet it didn't even stir tonight.'

Goldberg's expression went stony. 'This is not very nice,' was all he managed in reply.

The waiter was hovering, Goldberg ignored him. 'We'll have some champagne, please,' said Frannie. 'Your very best, on Mr Goldberg's bill.' She returned her attention to the fray, producing for the movie-maker her most saccharine smile. 'No, it's not very nice, Bernard. But then I'm afraid *you* are not very nice.'

Lee intervened. 'Maybe that's enough, huh?'

Frannie appraised him. 'Have you by any chance worked for him?'

'One film, yeah.'

'Porn?'

Goldberg sneered. 'Naturally, porn. I don't make kids' stories.'

Frannie ignored this. 'Well, sorry to create a scene,' she said to Lee. 'But the man is *truly asking* for it.'

Goldberg appeared to be on the verge of apoplexy. Rage boiled behind his eyes, a vein bulged in his forehead. 'In all innocence, in all *fucking innocence* I make a couple of remarks which, considering your performance here tonight, were more than justified, and you insult me. Just because you're some snobby, snotty, English bitch with a fucking title, you think you can get away with murder around here. You're no more than some jumped up whore!'

Frannie's grin was pure steel. She wanted to tear the man apart limb from limb. 'My husband would see you in hell for that.' She picked her next words slowly, with malevolent care. 'Except that you're too contemptuous a man to be worth that sort of trouble. But, that aside, let me tell Lee what *happened* on that famous night.' She turned to Lee. 'He took us to his flat and showed us a porno film . . .'

'Which you were the star of,' interrupted Goldberg, as the waiter invited him to taste the champagne. He did, like a man swallowing a mouthful of medicine. 'It's terrible. Serve it!' he snapped.

'Which, indeed, I *was* the star of.' Frannie warmed to her attack. 'However, I have no recollection of either myself *or* Matilda inviting you to remove your clothes, Bernard. Am I right, Matilda?'

'Heaven forbid.' Matilda was fascinated by this rare appearance of Frannie the vixen.

Goldberg scowled, furious. 'Enough of this *shit*. Just lay off, bitch!'

'When I've finished. As I was saying Lee, he took off his clothes. All of them, except for his socks. Fine, Bernard, but you might then at least have exhibited some *fibre*. I mean, strip off by all means, but at least let it be because you can't contain yourself any more. Don't then sit there like some baby playing with yourself and moaning you can't get it up. What a miserable, pathetic performance – you should have put *that* on film!'

Goldberg stood with such violence he knocked the stool flying. His hands, fingers hooked like talons, trembled in front of his gold-chained chest, saliva oozed from one corner of his mouth. 'Nobody, *no-fucking-body* talks to me this way. You are some fucking *pig*!'

'*Pig* now is it? Well.' She raised an eyebrow, kept her voice deadly calm. 'And you, Bernard Goldberg, are nothing but a miserable little half-man. A failure in every respect.' She offered him a casually mocking smile, sipped from her glass. 'Delicious champagne. I really wish you would now permanently leave my table.'

'You pay for it.' His final words, he was lost for anything more. Trying to exit with dignity he merely managed to skulk away.

Matilda was all admiration. 'By God you really handed it to him,' she said. 'Cured in all departments then, including that of the bitch.'

Frannie sighed heavily. 'Not forgetting the pig. I don't believe *anybody* has *ever* got so far up my nose.'

'I'm impressed,' said Lee, watching the slumped, departing back of Goldberg. 'Even if you *have* cost me my next part.'

'*You* didn't say anything to upset him. Even so, you can do without the Goldbergs of this world.' Frannie was beginning to feel a little pleased with herself as the anger drained away.

'But not their money.'

'*Are* you an actor? I mean, apart from that one porn thing with our friend?'

'Yes.'

'Any good?'

'I hope so.'

'Then do yourself a favour. Don't get involved in porn work. It's fun once or twice, agreed. I suppose it's useful for paying bills. But as far as I understand it's a one-way street. You can get stuck in it, the other opportunites elude you.'

Lee sipped a little champagne. 'I'm surprised you should know that. But you're right, I've seen it happen.'

'Are you broke?'

'More or less.' He shook his head. 'What am I *say*ing? – I almost forgot.' He nodded at the cheque still pinned under the statuette. 'At this moment I have five thousand dollars.'

'No.' Frannie freed the cheque, slid it to him. 'Ten. You have ten thousand dollars.'

He looked puzzled. 'But half of this is for you.'

She picked up the statuette, revolving it in her hands. It really was rather tawdry. 'Half of *this* is for *you*. I'll buy it from you with my half of the cheque.'

'But that thing can't be worth more than a few bucks. You're crazy.'

'No I'm not. I just happen not to need money, Lee. If you must know, I'm one very rich lady. You keep the money, I want you to.'

'Rich, uh?' He grinned, neatly folded the cheque, then shrugged. 'Well, if you insist, I guess I'm grateful.' He slipped it into a shirt pocket. 'Rich. And titled. They're just about the only things I know about you.'

'You're forgetting what we did down there.' Frannie relaxed enough after her Goldberg encounter to let her body do some remembering. It felt remarkably good. 'And that's more than *most* people know about me.'

Matilda giggled. 'I wouldn't say *that*!'

'So now *you're* looking for trouble?'

'Whoops! I take it, take it . . . *back*. In its en*ti*rety.' Matilda was clearly getting the worse for el vino.

'I'd like to know everything about you,' said Lee. 'We have a date, tomorrow.'

Frannie frowned surprise at him. 'We *do*?'

'Short memory, huh?' Leaning forward, he put his lips to her ear.

'You were *begging* for it, remember?' he whispered. '*Pleading*. Fuck me. *Fuck* me. And I wouldn't, not until you promised. You most *certainly* promised.' The tip of his tongue found its wet way into her ear, making her squirm with delight. 'I want you all to myself tomorrow,' he went on. 'There is something,' the tongue dipped again, ' . . . very *special* I would like to do to you.'

He was making her feel weak again. She clashed her lips with his as Matilda looked on with a satisfied but enigmatic and woozy smile. Their tongues mingled then Frannie broke away. 'And what *is* this special thing?' Husky.

'Surprise. Very, very horny, I promise. You may just have indulged before, a woman of your undoubted experience. But I doubt it.' He darted a kiss on her lips. 'I very much doubt it.'

Little tremors of delight skipped through Frannie's belly. 'So tell me.'

'Tomorrow.' He kissed her again, this time on the tip of her nose. 'We'll do it tomorrow. You can spend the rest of the night wondering.'

She pouted. 'Not even one, tiny clue?'

'No.'

'Okay, Mr Teaser.' She searched the deep blue of his eyes. 'I bet I know what *your* hobby is.'

'Sex.'

'Naturally.' She chuckled throatily, snuggled up closer to him. 'I'll be awake all night wondering. And I have one hell of an imagination.'

'Well, I'll feed it. Mind if I dictate one part of your tomorrow's clothing?'

'Within reason.'

'I'd like you to wear a short skirt, above the knees. And it shouldn't be too tight, have some give in it if you know what I mean.'

'The mind boggles. I have an idea you're a very, *very* bad boy. I know *what* you mean, but not *why*.' Someone else, once, had come up with a similar request. He had been an actor, too, but world famous. He had asked for a loose skirt so they could make love at one of his favourite places, which had turned out to be a volcano. The memory sent a shudder down her spine. Touching Lee's nose with the tip of her finger, she traced down its side. A good nose, she considered. Rather Roman. 'All right. I believe I have the very skirt.' She paused. 'Anything else?'

'Yes. Yes, there is. Something you *shouldn't* wear. But you don't have to take *those* off until the time is right!'

She smiled crookedly, wetted her lips. 'You have a dirty mind, my boy.'

'Don't you?'

'*Me*?' Frannie produced one of her rare but wonderful looks of pure sin.

'Oh, *yes*! I have an *exceptionally* dirty mind!'

14

ON BRUNO

'YOU'RE QUITE SURE THIS IS THE RIGHT PLACE, Lady Ballington?' Gregory had stopped the Pontiac on a small beach road flanking a caravan site. Stretching from the edge of the road to the undulating sand dunes of a long, sweeping bay was a large, confused collection of mobile homes. By the side of the Pontiac a crudely hand-painted sign proclaimed 'Coral Beach – Caravans for Sale or Hire.'

'Unless there are two Coral Beaches.' Frannie's eyes wandered, not entirely amused, over the scene. 'He didn't say anything about *caravans*.'

Gregory coughed. 'Shall we go on?'

Frannie was too keyed up for whatever was to happen to her on this balmy day to let mild distaste intrude. 'No.'

And there he was, not far away, emerging from an unassuming blue caravan which sat on a lawn behind a tiny white picket fence. He was waving. He wore a T-shirt, loose white cotton Bermuda shorts and sneakers. He seemed browner than Frannie remembered and his blond hair, streaked from the sun, was out of its ponytail, straggling over his shoulders. '*Hi* there,' he bellowed.

Noisily, Gregory cleared his throat. 'I assume *that* is

the gentleman in question, madam?'

'Indeed it is, Gregory. Yes indeed.' She waved through the open window. 'You may let me out.'

Releasing the electric doors, Gregory then made an elaborate show of stepping smartly from the car and opening Frannie's door for her. He even offered a brief salute.

'Do *not* take the *piss*, please Gregory,' Frannie hissed as she climbed neatly out.

'I beg your *pardon*, Lady Ballington?'

'You know damn well what I mean.'

'Do I, madam?' Gregory's face remained unreadable as his inscrutable eyes followed her progress between the caravans. She was wearing a red crepe cotton dress which reached to mid-thigh, white tennis shoes and socks and a red halter top. The sexy simplicity entirely suited her, but the video bag hanging over her shoulder was rather out of place in the ensemble.

Taking her by the finger tips Lee surveyed her with approval, his eyes lingering on the skirt. 'Perfect,' he said. 'Stunning.'

'Pleased you still like me.'

'I'll say.' He planted a kiss on her forehead. 'You didn't say anything about having to hire a driver. I'd have picked you up. Can't you drive?'

'Of course I can, but I don't. That's Gregory, my chauffeur.'

'Oh.' He glanced towards the road where Gregory was leaning against the Pontiac, lighting a cigarette, watching them frankly. 'You did mention you were rich. I didn't realise . . .' He swept a hand around, taking in the site, shrugging. 'Sorry about the surroundings. It just happens to be cheap convenient and on a wonderful beach.'

She smiled. '*I* don't mind.' And suddenly she didn't. 'My chauffeur disapproves, of course. Staff can be such dreadful snobs at times.'

'I wouldn't know.' He looked down her, inspecting the skirt once more, then touched her thigh, feeling the material. '*Exactly* what I had in mind,' he murmured.

A catch in Frannie's throat. 'Is it? I'm delighted.'

He took her hand. 'Come. Time you met Bruno.'

'*Bruno?*'

Bruno was parked on the other side of the caravan. A motorcycle – 1000cc of potent monster. BMW's latest model in gleaming black enamel and shining chrome, every line suggesting awesome power. Lovingly, Lee ran a hand along the length of the double leather seat. 'Beautiful, uh? How does it grab you?'

Motorcycles not being a part of Frannie's life experience, with the exception of the 49cc runabout she occasionally used around the grounds of Stratton Castle, she surveyed Bruno, on which she was clearly expected to ride, with very mixed emotions. 'It's, it's . . . *inter*esting.'

'You *can* ride one?'

'I can balance, if that's what you mean. But I've never been on anything quite *this* big. I'm not at all sure that I . . .'

'There's nothing to it.' Taking her in his arms he kissed her deeply, pulling her close to him and she forgot the bike as the taste and smell of him brought memories of last night flooding back. Breaking the kiss he searched her eyes, hands slipping to the rise of her buttocks. She could feel him hardening in the region of her belly button. 'Wait until you feel the power as Bruno throbs between your legs.'

'Oh.'

He kissed her again then swung himself onto the bike, kicked it off its stand and started the engine. A deep, hushed, throaty roar. 'Climb up behind me.'

'I'm just a little scared,' Frannie confessed.

'Don't be.'

Reluctant, she hitched her skirt and clambered on.

'Just hold me tight around the waist and sit there. Don't try to do anything.' He looked around at her. 'I'd leave that bag behind, if I were you.'

'I'll leave it with Gregory.'

Gregory was behind the wheel of the Pontiac, reading, as the bike drew alongside him and Frannie dropped her bag through the open rear window. He inspected his mistress, the bike and Lee, with a disbelief bordering on comedy. 'Are you *quite* sure you know what you're *doing*, Lady Ballington?' he said.

'I usually *do*, Gregory.'

'With respect, I can think of some notable exceptions. This appears to be one of them.'

'That's quite enough.'

'Are you ready?' from Lee.

'Let's go.' She found herself staring at Gregory in defiance as she said it.

'Hold very tight.'

The acceleration was smooth but enormous. One second Gregory was challenging Frannie's stare, the next she was half a mile away, rapidly disappearing down the road in a haze of dust. Cursing, Gregory started the Pontiac, slammed it into drive and put his foot down.

The thrust was such that Frannie was holding onto Lee for her life, her cheek pressed into his T-shirt, her hair streaming and flapping behind. There was no time for fear. She felt overwhelmed and exhilarated, as if she had left herself miles behind. At a hundred Lee levelled off and she caught up with herself, but stayed glued to Lee's back.

'Okay?' He yelled back at her.

'Fine.'

She found that she was revelling in this new experience. There was little traffic on the road and Lee was clearly in perfect control. Frannie found that the powerful emotion aroused at a hundred on a motorcycle was akin to that she experienced when galloping on her thoroughbred stallion at thirty. The horse, of course, had to be a finer feeling, but this was a new experience.

Glancing in a mirror, Lee frowned. The wind snatched his words back to Frannie. 'What's *he* want?'

Frannie glanced around. Fast gaining on them was Gregory.

'Stop a moment,' Frannie shouted.

They did, and Gregory pulled up beside them.

'Why are you *following* us Gregory?' Frannie queried.

'Bit of a funny question, isn't it?' Gregory responded. 'That's my brief.'

'Well, it's all *right*. We're just going for a little ride.'

'Oh. I see. At a hundred, with no helmets. And if you 'appen to fall off, what then? And what if Sir Galahad here turns out to be another freak?'

'What the hell do you mean by *that*?' exclaimed Lee.

'Skip it. I'm paid to protect Lady Ballington, and protect her I shall. Unhappily I can't force her to get off that contraption, but I'll do my duty as best I can.'

'She's perfectly safe with me,' said Lee.

'Not as safe as with both of us.'

'The guy's nuts,' Lee breathed. 'Let's go.'

A hundred, a hundred and ten – and twenty, Gregory still kept on their tail. But then they throttled back slowly to thirty, with Gregory keeping his distance until they turned into a narrow, winding track through corn fields where Gregory could not possibly negotiate the Pontiac.

'Do you mind?' asked Lee.

'Not really,' said Frannie. 'Gregory's going to be hopping mad.'

'Tough on him.' The track was becoming rutted, bumpy, Lee slowed down to little more than a walking pace. 'In any case, I can't do what I had planned with your chauffeur sitting on our asses.'

'Ah.' Sweet tension. 'And what *do* you want to do?'

'What you have that skirt on for.'

177

'I imagined it was for bike riding.'

'In that case shorts or jeans would have done.' He grinned over his shoulder.

'But it *is* for Bruno.'

'Explain?'

They stopped. He propped the bike on its stand and swung himself around so that, still straddling the saddle, he faced her. On either side of them the corn was almost to their shoulders, bending to a gentle breeze. Watching her eyes Lee put both palms forwards and covered her breasts with them. Gently, he squeezed. Keeping hold of her like that he leant forward and and licked her lips with the tip of his tongue. Quietly, he asked, inducing a tremble in her, 'Do you want to fuck today?'

She swallowed. The leather seat suddenly felt sticky between her thighs. She nodded.

'Then, we'll do it my way. You're about to become a member of the *original* ton-up club.'

'How is that?' Excitement mounting as those strong, practised hands kneeded her breasts and his breath played over her mouth.

He gestured ahead. 'Through there, couple of miles. There's a deserted airstrip. We're going to screw there. On Bruno.'

She did not think he meant any more than variations of her bending over the standing bike, the anticipation of which quickened her pulse as they arrived at the ruined remains of a hangar, where he propped Bruno on its stand. Dismounting, he had her swing her legs over the saddle so that she was sitting side-saddle. He knelt at her knees. 'I'll remove that little article I mentioned we wouldn't be needing,' he said, putting his hands on her bare lower thighs.

Frannie, collapsing inside, raised her bottom with her hands to help him as he slid cool fingers under the little dress, hooked them beneath the elastic top of her skimpy Bonni Keller knickers and yanked them down her legs, over her feet and off. For long moments his eyes rested longingly on her pubic thatch and she watched him, not daring to move, waiting for what ever was about to happen.

She felt the briefest touch between her legs, which caused her toes to curl, then he handed her her panties and stood up. Having no pocket, she tucked them into the waistband of her skirt. 'Sit where I was sitting,' he commanded. 'In the driver's seat.' She brought a leg up and over the petrol tank, settled onto leather still warm from his contact. 'This foot, here,' he said, placing it on a bar. He walked around the machine. 'And this one, here.' Taking hold of her hands, he positioned them on the handlebars, close together at the centre. He walked some more, appraising her, then stopped, a hand on her bottom through the skirt. 'You're going to have to stand a bit, and crouch down into the tank. Try it.' She did, his hand pushing her behind up, her breasts flattening into the cool of the petrol tank. In that position he hiked her skirt a few inches, exposing her bare buttocks. The tips of two fingers indented her already damp vagina, then slid to the knuckles. 'You like?'

Stupid question. This is infinitely delicious. His fingers are motionless but she moves up and down twice, riding them.

'Are you going to be comfortable like that' He whispers in her ear which he teases with a wet lick, his fingers tight up her.

'Christ, let's *do* it,' escapes from Frannie.

'Okay. Take a look at this.' His fingers glide out of her, she turns her head as he lowers his Bermudas, just to the top of his thighs. A rigid hard-on points towards her. He swings onto the bike behind her, starts the engine. *Starts the engine*! Then he is leaning over her, hands at the controls, telling her to stay just as she is, he will do the rest. He kicks down the stand, they roll forward, slowly beginning to accelerate, and when they reach twenty miles an hour, as Frannie watches the edge of the airstrip roll forward under the bike, she sees that one of Lee's hands has left the handlebars. She feels the head of his cock being manoeuvred behind her and, as they approach twenty-five, it slips swiftly and smoothly up inside her, so deep she feels Lee's balls nestling amongs the back of her inner thighs.

Frannie is impaled on a moving motorcycle! She cannot believe this. The wind tugs at her hair as, now out in the middle of the ancient runway, turning towards one end, Lee staying hard up there, they gather speed. As they reach seventy he begins to rock, riding Frannie and Bruno almost as if doing a post-trot on horseback, bumping regularly, lightly, up and down on his saddle, his tool humping steadily within her bringing paroxysms of delight as the wind washes over her.

With the end of the runway approaching, he slows down. They reach it and wheel slowly around. Lee is out of her for a moment as he props the bike up, then is just as quickly back inside her, pumping. 'Look ahead,' he mutters. She sees the entire length of the crumbling asphalt stretching away into the distance. 'When you're ready, we go.'

'Ready?' she pants, vagina contracting on him. '*How* ready?'

He heaves in and out of her, good, strong thrusts which send her nose-diving close to her hands. 'I'm going to *come* at a hundred. I don't want *you* missing out.'

'Are you *kidding*?' A gasp. 'Go, Lee. *Go!*'

They are away. Careful with their balance he builds speed cautiously, humping her as they hit sixty, seventy, eighty, ninety miles an hour, and finally the ton with the wind tearing at her hair as he *slams* into her and *slams* into her, Frannie close to swooning with the extraordinary sensations of this high-speed coupling.

It's still a long ride to the end of the runway. They hit a pothole, wobble precariously, an instant's fear, he pulls them out of it, then he is *shouting* into the wind, and his voice is instantly snatched away as she feels him flooding into her, her vagina tightening on him in a series of little spasms and, at one hundred and seven miles an hour, impaled to the depths of her pussy on a motorcycle called Bruno, Frannie comes, and comes, and *comes*.

Back at the hangar Frannie slides off the bike to find that her knees are so cramped from the unusual strain of half standing and being screwed like that – something she was unaware of during the event – that she almost collapses.

'Bloody hell,' she exclaims, laughing. 'Oh, bloody, bloody hell!'

Lee sits there looking a little drained, his Bermudas still undone, stretched across the tops of his thighs, his penis once again flaccid. Reaching out, Frannie cradles it in the palm of her hand and strokes the back of it with loving attention as if petting a hamster while he grins sheepishly. 'Good *boy*!' Frannie coos.

'Beats flying,' says Lee. 'We made it. Me, you, Bruno and . . .' he touches the backs of Frannie's caressing fingers. '. . . him. Welcome to the club.'

Wrapping her fingers warmly around Lee's tool, Frannie tugs playfully. She feels elated and very, very happy. 'Didn't we, though? That may just have been the biggest wow of my life.' Squeezing, she adds, 'Do you do this often?' There are renewed stirrings of life in her palm.

'Often as I can.'

'Sensational.' Frannie drops to her punished knees.

'You want another run?'

'What do *you* think?' She touches the end of his growing organ with her tongue.

Lee suddenly goes tense. 'Shit!' he exclaims.

'What?'

'Your fucking chauffeur.' Pushing her hand off him he swings off the bike and hauls up his Bermudas. Frannie sees the Pontiac approaching along one side of the hangar. She is facing it, her anger growing as the car whispers to a stop by their side.

'What in hell's name do *you* want?' Frannie exclaimed, aware, as the words spilt out hastily, that she was being cattishly unreasonable.

Sighing, Gregory opened his door and got out. 'I am *trying* to do my job, Lady Ballington.'

'You're being a damned nuisance, Gregory. Snooping around.'

Folding his huge arms stubbornly across his chest, Gregory leant back on the dusty coachwork. 'Casablanca, less than two weeks ago, I saved your life. Los Angeles, a couple of years back, I saved your life.' None of them said anything for seconds as Lee studied Gregory with renewed curiosity and Gregory looked Lee up and down with outright disapproval. Then Gregory added, 'This *is* Charles Manson country.'

Lee flared up, his fists clenched. 'Thanks a million, buster!'

'Have a care boy. Have a care.'

'Good God, that's quite *enough*, Gregory,' Frannie broke in. 'That you're paid to protect me, of course I agree. But not to start squalid rows with my friends.'

'Your *friends*? Of course, your *friends*.' He was still regarding Lee as if the Californian was some sort of leper.

Frannie, sexual hunger evaporating, suddenly felt awkward. She shrugged. 'Well, do as you want, Gregory.'

'As *Lord* Ballington would *expect*, my lady.'

'I don't believe so, in this case. Lee happens to be a very nice, harmless young man. However . . .'

'He probably is.' Gregory spotted something at his

feet. Skimpy pink lace by Bonni Keller. Frannie's knicker's had slipped from her waistband. Crouching, Gregory picked them up in his finger and thumb, dangled them at her. 'You seem to have dropped something, Lady Ballington,' he intoned as she snatched them from him. He climbed back into the car, slammed the door and started the engine. 'I'll be just over there, on the road.' The Pontiac slid away, both of them watching until it went out of sight around the hangar.

Slowly, Lee shook his head. 'There seems to be something I don't get, here. Not quite real. A little crazy.'

'Don't let it worry you.' She laid a hand on his arm. 'Gregory can be a terrible nuisance at times. But he's fiercely loyal.'

'Is that true what he said? He's saved your life twice?'

'It's true.'

'That's incredible. How do you get yourself in situations like that?'

'Oh, I do. Don't ask me how, but I *do*.' Stooping, she stepped into her knickers, pulled them up tight.

'You don't fancy making it again?'

'With Gregory sitting with his damned binoculars?'

'I can give him the slip. I know another place, almost as good.'

Frannie pursed her lips, thinking. 'No, Let's *not* give him the slip again. He's been tiresome enough already.' She climbed onto the back seat of the bike. 'I'll tell you *what*. I'd be very interested in seeing the inside of your caravan.'

'It's on wheels. That's about all I can say for it.'

'It seems that I *like* it on wheels.' She treated him to her sexiest smile. 'Gregory, as you have gathered, will wait just as long as I want him to.'

Frannie was in gay and carefree mood. Engrossed in her Lee, day after day, night after night, drunk on more orgiastic delights at a hundred plus; making it on the beach, in the Pacific Ocean; creaking the caravan springs. Healed. Glowing with health which blossomed from constant sexual indulgence with one very fit, and extremely imaginative young man.

'Gregory's been very sulky lately,' Matilda mentioned one afternoon during lunch. 'What have you been doing to upset him?'

Frannie was admiring a clean-limbed diver as he turned two and a half somersaults before neatly cutting into the water of the hotel pool. She popped lettuce into her mouth before she said, 'Nothing, apart from keeping him more than usually occupied hanging around waiting for me. Which happens to be his job.'

'That seems to be the point. He's complaining you're *not* letting him do his job. That you and Lee keep giving him the slip on Lee's motorcycle.'

'I did tell you what we *do* on that machine, Matilda?' The diver was climbing from the pool, unaware of Frannie's prurient gaze at his bulging briefs.

Matilda grinned. 'You know damn well you did. Several times.'

'I somehow doubt that the good Gregory on our tail would be conducive to comfortable sex.'

'*Comfortable*?'

Frannie wriggled, a faraway smile hovering around the edges of misty eyes. 'Extremely, actually, once your knees get used to it. You should try it.'

'If you'd give me half the chance.' Matilda followed Frannie's eyes as she watched the diver who was bouncing on the springboard. Then, as he hit the water, she said, 'Gregory's making noises about chucking it in.'

'He's *what*? My God, he can be so difficult at times.'

'You wouldn't want to *lose* him?'

'Sometimes. But no, you're right. I don't seriously imagine he's about to walk away from the sort of money Victor pays him. Still . . .' She raised a hand. Within seconds a waiter was at their table and was then remarkably quick about producing a telephone. As she punched a number, reading it from her little book, Frannie said, 'In any case the "Golden Hind" ought to be in Caracas. If so it's time to move.'

Matilda pulled a woeful face. 'We've just settled in.'

'And I'm having fun. But there's a certain job to be done, remember?'

Clovis Carter–Smith's yacht had already been in Caracas for five days. Frannie made up her mind to indulge in one final fling on Bruno with Lee and then head back to Venezuela to see what could be done about getting her revenge on the murderous financier.

15

SOMEBODY HATES ME . . .

'YES. VERY NICE. *VERY* NICE INDEED. What's your name, girl?' Clovis Carter-Smith positively drooled.

'Lisa.' No more than sixteen, the girl who had just been brought into the stateroom of the 'Golden Hind' by Christian da Silva stood, precociously confident, a pout on her fleshy young lips, in front of the white leather sofa upon which the financier was taking his ease.

Carter-Smith's eyes roved salaciously over the fetching curves in front of him, lingered on the black leather mini-skirt. 'Lisa,' he murmured. 'Pretty. Stand a little closer, Lisa.' Swinging his bare legs to the beige carpeted floor, he sat up ponderously. 'Turn around, there's a good girl.'

It was exactly the kind of bottom which heated his blood, the buttocks curved like peaches, straining at the fine leather. He touched himself fleetingly through his multi-coloured swim shorts. 'Excellent choice Christian. Goodbye.'

As da Silva retreated and closed the door behind him, Carter-Smith clutched at the hem of the mini-skirt, attempting to tug it up the girl's thighs. As it resisted his efforts the girl glanced over her shoulder. 'Is too tight,' she said. 'I take off, no?'

'Do, my pet. Please *do*.' Carter-Smith's voice was as thick as her Spanish accent.

The snap of a press stud and the crisp slither of a zip were accompanied by the soft buzz of a telephone. Silently swearing as he watched the skirt being eased down over snaking hips, Carter-Smith snatched at the receiver. 'It had bloody well better be urgent,' he rasped.

In his cramped office within the ancient customs buildings at one corner of Caracas Port, the harbour-master absent-mindedly chewed the soggy end of a pencil as he waited to be put through. Hearing Carter-Smith's words he jammed the telephone between ear and shoulder as he calmly announced himself. 'The young woman who was asking for information about the arrival of your ship?' He picked a loose piece of wood from the pencil. 'Mrs. Jones?'

'Yes?' Carter-Smith watched as the girl's slim feet, poised on six inch heels, were neatly lifted one by one out of the skirt, but his mind had been rudely jerked elsewhere. He sat back. 'What *about* her?'

'We have of course an under*stand*ing in this matter?' The harbour-master rolled the little piece of wood between finger and thumb and dropped it in an ashtray as he congratulated himself for recognising the promise of plenty more cash to be made after Frannie had left a hundred dollars American on his desk.

'An agreement, yes. For Christ's sake get on with it.' In flesh-coloured, satiny knickers the girl hovered in front of him, clutching her bit of leather skirt. A delectable promise.

'She just called. I told her the "Golden Hind" was in port.'

'You *told* her . . .?'

'I cannot concern myself with lying about the affairs of this port.'

'Great. Just great.' Carter-Smith's eyes rested impatiently on the teenage hooker's legs. 'All right. Where was she phoning from?'

'Not here. She will arrive, she say, tomorrow. She has promised me an extra reward.'

'I'll double it. Call me the moment you've seen her.'

Hanging up, Carter-Smith buzzed for da Silva who rejoined them with a preen of his bushy moustache as he ogled the skirtless girl.

'Fix us something to drink, Christian.' The financier said, thoughtfully. As da Silva reached for the phone he stopped his hand. 'No, *you* do it. I want a very private word with you. Open some champagne.' He waved a hand across the stateroom. 'Lisa, there's a bathroom through there. Fix your face or something. I'll call you when we're through.'

'*Como?*' Her English was clearly not up to this.

Getting to his feet Carter-Smith took her elbow and steered her across the room, opening the bathroom door. 'In there and *wait*. Close the door. *Comprende?*'

'Wait. Dig it.' Lisa shut herself in as the champagne cork popped feebly.

As his aide filled two glasses Carter-Smith said, eyes gleaming malevolence, 'That, *prat* we've been having trouble with? It seems she's on our tail again.'

Da Silva handed him a glass. 'Lady Ballington?'

'Lady fucking Ballington, yes. I'm expecting her to come snooping around very shortly.'

'Marrakech wasn't enough to dissuade her then. I'm amazed.' He tried the champagne. 'Lifeless. That mid-Atlantic storm, probably.'

'She would have been *permanently* dissuaded if that incompetent bloody wog had done the job right. However . . .'

'The situation's decidedly naughty. The bitch could cause you plenty of trouble.'

'*Fuck* it. Here am I, supposedly quietly incognito, boat untraceable to me, *me* untraceable to me according to my papers, and she's shooting her mouth off to God knows who. Already we can't go back to Morocco.' The way in which he swallowed his flat champagne bordered on the savage. A fury was building within him, as compelling as his craving for a well-shaped *derrière* it generated the touch of madness which was a driving part of his misplaced genius. 'We, Christian, you and I, are going to *punish* Frannie Blueblood. I want to *hurt* her. *Badly*. She has to *suffer*. I'm going to get her off my back for *ever*.' His eyes were spitting venom into every corner of the room as they danced around agitatedly. 'Ideas, Christian. *Ideas*.' He snapped his fingers.

'Jesus. I'm an accountant, Clovis. Not the fucking Marquis de Sade.'

'And, unlike the good Marquis, sadly lacking ingenuity. Never mind.' He calmed as rapidly as he had flared up. Holding out his hand he sank onto the sofa. 'Give me my telephone book.'

As he picked slowly through the pages, he muttered, 'I know who, but I can't remember the bloody name. Sex party, Amsterdam, couple of years back. Some *very* weird people, most *interesting* tastes. Two women in particular, I'm almost certain they were from Caracas. What the hell was the name of the party-giver?'

'I don't see what this has got to do with Lady Ballington.'

Carter-Smith didn't look up. 'Just about everything, if I can get it together. She'll wish she'd never been born!'

A few minutes later, he had it. He shoved the book under da Silva's ample nose, finger stabbing an inked address in triumph. '*These* people. I'll leave it with you. Make contact. You can mention my name without problems. I want friends of theirs who were at that party. Two South American women. Kinky as you can get. One was certainly called Dolores.' He paused, an evil grin creasing his big features. 'Known to their friends as the vampires.'

'*Vamp*ires?' echoed da Silva.

'With some justification.' He thrust the book into da Silva's hands. 'Go to work. Track them down.' His eyes fell on the bathroom door. 'Now leave me until I call you.'

Carter-Smith opened the door on Lisa who, perched on the edge of the toilet, was tweezering her eyebrows. He licked his dry lips, his inner fires stoked by anticipation of what he had in mind for Frannie.

'Come on out, my pretty,' he mouthed quietly. Obediently, silently, the half-dressed whore left her toilet and ambled past him. Meaty fingers roughly pinched a buttock cheek, but she barely flinched. 'Go to that chair. Over there.'

The white leather armchair matched the sofa. 'Bend down. Rest your hands on the arms.' As she obeyed, Carter-Smith dropped to his knees behind her and grabbed her satin-covered backside like a drowning man clutching a life belt. His face fell forward and he buried his nose, mouth and chin in the fleshy mounds, slobbering there, saliva dribbling from both corners of his mouth. For more than a minute he remained like that, snuffling, sniffing, licking, a great, overgrown puppy, his paws dipping into the front of her pants, pushing under her blouse and roughly squeezing and pinching her tits as her big, black eyes rested in blank resignation on a copy of Van Gogh's Sunflowers. Then, rocking back onto his heels he peeled the satin knickers, patchy with his saliva, down her thighs, eyes droopy and bloodshot with lust.

'I'm going to have your bum, my pretty,' he drooled. 'Oh, am I going to *have* your bum!'

16

BAITED TRAPS

'I RATHER THINK THIS WILL *DO*, MATILDA. What do you think?' Frannie was leaning on the wooden verandah of a small house overlooking Lago de Valencia, thirty kilometres west of Caracas. Less than a half hour's drive away was a small airport at Puerto Cabello – close enough and, she hoped, with lax enough security to suit her purpose. Before her the blue of the lake rippled away to the horizon.

'Think? Since when was I paid to think?' Matilda brushed a stray hair from in front of her nose and tucked it under the ribbon which held the rest of her greying coiffure in an untidy bun.

'Will you stop being so damned irritable?'

'Christ. We're hardly on terra firma again for five minutes and you drag me around with estate agents on tours of the countryside. I'm not well!'

'You're being silly. There's nothing on earth wrong with you.' Frannie looked around. 'Not a neighbour in miles. Perfect!'

'*Is* it?' Matilda stared through open french windows into the sparsely furnished lounge. 'What a dump!'

'As I remarked, perfect.' She raised her voice. 'Senor Martinez!'

A portly figure detached itself from shadows in a

corner of the room and strolled onto the verandah.

'We'll take it.' said Frannie. 'Three months cash in advance.'

'You *will*?' Martinez appeared mightily surprised.

'One condition. Get it properly cleaned up within the week. Make sure everything functions. Get new curtains and cushions.' She paused. 'The telephone works?'

'Yes.'

'Fine.' She fished in her bag. 'Here. A couple of hundred bolivars advance. I'll settle the rest in your office.'

On the way back to the Caracas Hilton, sitting behind Martinez as he drove them in his fifteen-year-old Mercedes, Frannie scanned the small ads of a Caracas newspaper. Every so often she ringed one in pencil. 'This promises to be a super job for you, Matilda,' she said, encircling the words – Club Venus, *chicas jovenes y guapas, hotel o domicilio.* 'Get a short list of the very youngest girls and I'll decide on the final two. And no flabby rear ends – I think I know *exactly* what will tempt him.'

Close by the hotel reception desk, a woman who was looking the other way barged into Frannie. She staggered and dropped her bag, but the woman got the worst of it, tripping over backwards and hitting the floor heavily.

While Matilda retrieved her mistress's bag, Frannie took hold of the woman's elbow as she struggled to her feet saying loudly, in educated but accented English, '*Sorry.* Entirely my fault.'

'Are you all right?' Frannie asked, noting that she was expensively dressed in a silk suit, designer cut to show off a slim, well-moulded figure.

The woman brushed herself down. 'It's nothing serious. Totally stupid of me. Are *you* all right?'

'Absolutely.' Frannie smiled into slanting eyes of a

192

much deeper green than her own. They were set in a dark-skinned, thirty-year-old face with high Oriental cheekbones. An extremely attractive lady, Frannie decided at once. Just short of beautiful. She offered her hand. 'Francesca Ballington. Friends call me Frannie.'

The woman insisted on buying them both a drink. She told them she was a temporary resident of the hotel whilst her Caracas apartment was being decorated. There was something compelling about those large eyes which lingered on Frannie's, expressing a frank interest which Frannie was not sure whether to take as natural friendliness or something rather more.

Almost an hour later they parted on good terms.

'What did you think of her?' asked Frannie shortly afterwards.

'Dunno. Rather nice, of course. But something odd somewhere. Hard to put your finger on.' Matilda began to compile a list of hostess telephone numbers from the newspaper.

'Very sexy,' Frannie decided. 'Is she lessie, do you think?'

'Possibly. Why – are you interested?'

'Maybe, we'll see. But you're right. There *was* something funny about her. Did you notice how high on her neck she wore that chiffon scarf? Kept fiddling with it, too, as if afraid it might fall down.'

'I noticed, yes. Probably just an affectation. Nerves, maybe.'

'Or love bites,' said Frannie. Then she added, 'Pretty name, Dolores, don't you think?'

Standing at the kerb of the uneven, flagstone pavement, Carter-Smith looked up and down the street. The road was long, and straight, rising from the plaza at one end to the main thoroughfare at the other. It was lined with ancient, terraced houses, many of them divided into flats, or shops with office premises above.

The building from which Carter-Smith had just emerged was forelorn and unoccupied and sadly in need of a coat of paint. The windows were sealed tight with flaking green wooden shutters. It was a house which presented a grimmer face to the dusty street than most of its neighbours.

'That one will do nicely,' said Carter-Smith in satisfaction to, ironically, the very same Juan Martinez, estate agent, with whom Frannie had dealt the previous day. His eyes fixed on da Silva. 'Have a couple of the boys fix it up appropriately.' As Martinez walked off in the direction of his car he repeated his promise of yesterday. 'Lady Ballington is going to wish she'd never been born!'

Lord Ballington had just returned from the hunt when Frannie rang from Caracas. He was still wearing his mud-caked boots, had not even removed the spurs, and as he sat in the entrance hall to take the call he scraped the veneer off the leg of a Louise Quinze chair.

Frannie explained in detail how she was laying her trap, telling him about the isolated house she had rented not far from the airport at Puerto Cabello and the delectable pair of teenage whores she had employed as her lure.

Victor Ballington's scepticism spanned the Atlantic Ocean and the breadth of North America. 'You seriously think those girls are going to wiggle their bottoms and Carter-Smith will come running?'

'*Absolutely!*' In the bedroom of her suite Frannie was lying naked on her belly with Matilda busily soothing skin lotion into her shoulders. 'They are going to play demure young girls, hardly out of school, and be dressed in that innocently revealing way that is guaranteed to drive men insane. Mini-skirts, ankle socks, barest touch of make-up, simple blouses, you

194

know the sort of thing. Irresistible bums will do the rest. Lower down, Matilda.'

'I beg your pardon?'

'Matilda's giving me a massage.'

'Wish I were there. So, okay, he chats up the girls.' Lord Ballington slipped his riding crop out of his right boot. 'Then what?'

'They tease him like mad, give him the distinct idea that perhaps they're nowhere near as demure and innocent as they seem, knickers flash a bit, make sure their blouses have that crucial button undone. Then they invite him to a small private party out of town.'

'And you believe a couple of South American whores can handle that? They won't seem suspicious, give the game away?'

'Oh, they're brilliant, these two. It took Matilda and I a lot of work to find them. Consummate liars. Been at it since they were about eleven, I should think. Bloody expensive, too. There's a carnival coming up in a few days, prime earning time, so I've had to employ them at what they say is double their rate for most of the rest of the year. Without doubt they've even cheated me on that, but who cares?' She turned over, wriggled herself comfortable on her back on the crisp sheet. 'Around the shoulder blades, Matilda. Then work your hands down – all the way down. You *know* the way I like it.' Husky.

Lord Ballington cracked his crop against the side of his boot; lumps of mud fell to the carpet. 'Are you attempting to turn me on, or explaining your plans?'

Frannie giggled. 'Why not both?'

'Because you happen to be several thousand miles away.' He frowned. 'Please get on with it.'

'All right. I doubt that Gregory, capable though he is, can handle this on his own.'

'Two more equipped with his special sort of talents will do nicely.'

'Exactly. Between them they kidnap Carter–Smith when he's *in flagrante delicto* so to speak with the bimbos, sneak him aboard the jet and we haul him home to Blighty and his just deserts.'

'As simple as that.' Ballington grunted. 'I sincerely hope so. Well, okay, I approve. There will of course be a number of details to take care of.' His eyes shone as they did when hunting a fox at full gallop. 'Get me Gregory on the phone.'

'I'll have to get you transferred. 'Bye darling.' Frannie dangled the receiver at Matilda. 'Get this put through to Gregory's room, there's a dear.'

That done, Frannie stretched luxuriously. 'Carry on then. Be firm, but gentle.'

It was the first time that Matilda had properly massaged her mistress since their first trip to Caracas, over three weeks ago. Then there had been a negative sexual response from Frannie, her libido deadened by the Arab rape. Now, Frannie was clearly experiencing pleasure from Matilda's confident fingers beyond that of simple muscle relief. Plump, soft hands encircled and manipulated her breasts until the nipples stood hard and firm, then they inched their way down across her belly. As they closed in on the outpost of pubic hair Matilda, like Frannie, was beginning to take her breath in deep, slow inhalations. Frannie suddenly sighed, 'Strip yourself off, Matilda. *Ages* since we've had a friendly cuddle.'

Frannie wallowed in Matilda's generous, Rubens-like flesh. Breasts crushed against breasts, hips busily ground together as they rolled around, feeling, squeezing, panting, Matilda grunting in her pleasure as they manoeuvred themselves on their sides. At last she had Frannie all to herself. Faces to pussies, tongues flickering, savouring, licking, dipping, nosetips damp with female juices, mouths shiny with saliva, Frannie's face cushioned in Matilda's crotch as Matilda's teeth nipped Frannie's bud and her darting tongue swept across it, dived into the aristocratic pussy, swept back to the clitoris, swept, dived, swept, dived, until Frannie's thighs locked rigid around Matilda's ears and she reached her climax with a long, drawn-out hiss as Matilda whimpered hers into her mistress's dewy crotch.

Minutes later, on their backs, side by side, Frannie murmured, 'Dolores's hand was on my knee during dinner last night.'

Matilda, spectacleless, squinted into the fog above her head. 'It's obvious she fancies you like mad. Been obvious for days. Can't think why you haven't done something about it already.'

'She's waiting for me to react and I'm waiting for the right moment. Amusing situation. I confess, there's something *very* intriguing about Dolores. A special, mysterious something and I can't imagine what it is.' She paused, a thoughtful smile on her face. 'It's going to happen with her, that's for sure.'

'Funny how she's always wearing some sort of scarf high on her neck. I mean, it's not as if it's cold or anything.'

'I daren't ask her about it. *Very* rude. She'll tell us when she wants to. Some sort of disfigurement, I expect. A scar, something of the sort.'

'Can't be just love bites, surely?'

Frannie bit her bottom lip, shook her head. 'No. Can't be just love bites.'

17

DANSE MACABRE

IN PREPARATION FOR THE PLANNED Abduction of Clovis Carter-Smith, two massive, singularly capable, excommando buddies of the good Gregory were rapidly installed in the house on Lago de Valencia. Meanwhile, the succulent bait for Frannie's trap lingered around the port day after day, as Caracas assumed carnival mood. The financier, however, stubbornly refused to put in an appearance.

Their chance came at last on the opening day of the carnival when, for the first time in a week, Carter-Smith decided to sun himself on deck. He was in buoyant mood; his plan had progressed perfectly, all being well tonight was to be his night of triumph.

His attention was attracted by shouts and giggles. Two extremely pretty, fresh-faced young girls were clambering on the harbour wall close to the 'Golden Hind' taking it in turns to take snapshots of one another. They both wore short, pleated skirts, one white, one dark blue, unfussy blouses and brightly coloured sneakers and ankle socks. As they posed for each other gusts of wind kept catching their skirts and flicking them around the tops of their shapely thighs, occasionally offering a glimpse of panty.

As he ogled the firmness of their rear ends and large,

jiggling breasts, Carter-Smith experienced a familiar urge in his loins.

He stood and hailed them. Adopting what he imagined to be his most charming smile, he invited them aboard his yacht for a drink.

Almost to his surprise, they accepted.

During the next hour Frannie's hired hookers did a wonderful job of raising Carter-Smith's blood pressure very nearly to critical level. Not for a second did he suspect that they were acting.

When one of them told him they were giving a little party that evening and asked him to join them, he was sorely tempted. But certain plans were already too firmly laid. 'I can't,' he said. 'Any other night, I'd love to.'

One of them was sitting on the deck facing him, her knees to her chin, seemingly unaware that she was offering him a blatant view of her crotch with black pubic hairs curling around the edge of her tightly-stretched white panties.

'We can have a party every night if we want,' she warbled. 'Her parents are away, we stay at her house.'

'Tomorrow then,' the financier breathed. 'I'll bring some of the best champagne.'

If only these two gifts from Heaven could be taken advantage of tonight, he thought. But no. That was impossible. Tonight held out promise of the most special of all delights. This was a night he would not postpone for a dozen little treasures like these.

Frannie, splendidly boyish in shiny topper and tails trailing Matilda dressed as a ginger tom on a golden lead caused only the barest stir of amusement in the foyer of the Caracas Hilton. It was the first night of the carnival and the city thronged with people in fancy dress. Gregory, a pace behind them, was wearing his full chauffeur's uniform, his cap under his arm.

Frannie did not recognise Dolores until she spoke. Her green eyes were surrounded by heavy red, green and blue make-up drawn into points high up on her forehead. Frannie gasped weakly, then she chuckled in delight – Dolores was dressed as one of Count Dracula's daughters with fangs protruding downwards on either side of her blood red lips, the carefully applied stage make-up transforming her face into a mask of evil. She was wearing her raven hair loose over the shoulders of a crimson cloak whose upturned collar cradled her chin. Beneath the cloak she wore a tight black pants suit of the finest leather and patent leather boots whose heels were so high she must have been standing on the points of her toes.

Taking Dolores's hands, with their three-inch, green nails in hers, Frannie stood back and admired her. 'My dear, you look absolutely breath-taking,' she enthused.

'My surprise – just for *you*,' said the horror mask, the lips barely moving. 'If I don't smile it's because I'll crack my face.'

Gregory escorted the unlikely trio down to the basement car-park and watched without expression as they arranged themselves carefully in the back of Frannie's hired Merc. They all had their little problems; Matilda, carrying her cat's head with its eyeholes big enough to accommodate her bi-focals had to coil her long tail over her lap; Frannie arranged her coat-tails over her thighs and Dolores, whose boots creaked eerily, was most concerned not to crease her cloak.

Approaching the heart of the carnival driving became increasingly difficult. It was not just the traffic – people were everywhere, singing, dancing, drinking, at least a half of them in some sort of fancy dress. As the roads began to snarl up Frannie and Dolores sat hand in hand. Tonight, Matilda observed silently, Frannie the gentleman swell was most certainly going to indulge herself with Dolores the daughter of Dracula.

200

Miraculously Gregory found somewhere to park in a small side-street. As Frannie got out she said, 'No need to wait, Gregory. It's going to be quite a long night. We'll get a taxi when we want one.'

'Never mind not waiting. I don't intend to let you out of my sight, Lady Ballington,' he replied, flatly.

She froze. 'I said you may *go*, Gregory.'

Taking her by the elbow he led her a few yards away from the others. 'I'm afraid I may *not* go,' he said and, cutting off another protest, went on, 'Consider the situation. Somewhere in this city lurks a villain who we've laid careful plans to capture. But we 'aven't got him yet. This gentleman tried to get you bumped off in Marrakech. If he's out on those streets tonight, if 'e should spot you . . . ' he shrugged. 'I'm *staying around*. No buts, my lady.'

Frannie examined his determined face for several silent seconds as she thawed out. Then she said, 'You're right, of course. But you know we're invited to a party later and it's fancy dress only.'

Allowing himself a grin, Gregory plucked at his uniform jacket. 'What do you think this is?' But then he added, 'I'll be, as always, somewhere close by.' He paused. 'All night if necessary, at the receiving end of the bleeper.'

Frannie laid a hand on his arm. 'Sorry I was touchy.'

'It's nothing new, madam.'

Arm in arm, with the cat in the middle and Gregory close behind, the three ladies swept themselves into the epicentre of the carnival storm, a riot of sound and colour where wildly dressed figures jostled, capered and danced as they joyously awaited the main attraction, the procession of floats. On three sides of the huge plaza, bands blared in competition each trying to outdo the other. In the middle the noise was appalling yet it carried with it such exuberance that no-one, not even Gregory, could fail to be carried away by the atmosphere.

Drinking was rife and the sweet smell of marijuana drifted on the evening breeze. Frannie and Matilda shared a strong mixture of vodka orange which Matilda carried in a flask in her catsuit; Dolores was certainly in gayer spirits than usual but it was not quite clear if she was indulging in anything.

As the dancing got wilder and the noise even louder, the first float entered the square. The whole of Caracas, it seemed, was swept along on an unstoppable tide of revelry.

Suddenly, as the huge, colourful floats spread across the square amidst a blaze of fireworks, Frannie and company were no longer three, but five. Their party was joined by the macabre addition of a green-faced, wild-haired, female Zombie in a torn nightdress, and a lurching Hunchback of Notre Dame who wore a mask fashioned in imitation of Charles Laughton. Bawling above the cacophony of sound, Dolores explained that these were the friends who would lead them to the party and Frannie, wondering why they were bothering with a party at all, found herself being danced through the crowds with one arm linked to Dolores and the other to the Hunchback: the Cat and the Zombie followed with Gregory warily bringing up the rear.

They were soon away from the square and on the fringe of the carnival, in a long, narrow street where the music from busy bars was louder than the muffled background noise of the bands. They stopped in front of a terraced house with flaking green wooden shutters and the Hunchback rang the bell. A tall, warped, wooden door instantly swung inwards and a shaft of light hit the street as the oddly assorted group filed inside.

From across the street Gregory watched balefully as the door closed, running his eyes over the front of the house. With the shutters closed there was little indication of the party going on within. Behind him was a convenient bar, Gregory elbowed his way through the crowd within and prepared himself for a lengthy wait.

As soon as the front door shut behind her, Frannie sensed that something was amiss. They were in a dreary, ill-lit corridor, the faint sound of music above them almost drowned by that from the street. The man who let them in could hardly be said to be in fancy dress. Big and muscular, he wore tatty jeans and a sweatshirt.

For the moment, however, Frannie felt no danger. It was weird in here but only in contrast to the gaiety of the carnival.

'I'm desperate for a pee,' Matilda complained tipsily as they all trooped along the corridor and the Hunchback began leading the way upstairs.

Frannie giggled. 'I wish you luck in that outfit,' she said.

Behind Frannie, Dolores spoke briefly in Spanish to the man in the sweatshirt who opened a door in the corridor and beckoned to Matilda. 'Here. Toilet,' he said, and he went through the door with Matilda on his heels.

Dismay began to swamp Frannie as she followed Dolores through a door off a passage at the top of the stairs, the Zombie and the Hunchback hard on her heels. She entered a high-ceilinged room with peeling paint and time-worn, nondescript furniture. In one corner, stood a metal-framed bed with a bare, striped mattress. Music, crackled from an ancient radio and was interrupted by a DJ gabbling in Spanish as the Zombie closed the door.

There were no other people.

Taking in these dreary, unnerving details in a handful of seconds, Frannie sank nervously onto the arm of a chair. The other three were all staring at her. 'Just what sort of a party *is* this?' she queried, fearful of the reply.

The Hunchback loomed over her, his Charles Laughton mask suddenly anything but amusing. In the yellow light and under the nerve-racking circumstances, the warted face was threatening. No longer carnival fun figures, Dolores and the Zombie became chillingly grotesque.

'What *sort* of a party?' Mocked the muffled voice of the Hunchback. The intonation, the bulk of this man, plucked a frightful memory chord in Frannie's brain. 'A *surprise* party,' he went on. 'Just for *you*, my dear Lady Ballington.'

The memory chord twanged, reverberating terror through her from head to toe.

The instinct for self-preservation sent Frannie's trembling thumb and index finger twitching for the emerald.

'No, you *don't*!' Carter-Smith grabbed her wrist, jerking the hand with the emerald ring high above her head and dragging her to her feet, her forehead brushing the rubbery chin of his mask. In shock she felt the ring being savagely pulled from her finger. Then she was shoved violently backwards into the chair, shoulders thumping into it, topper tumbling forward into her lap as the Hunchback held the ring to the feeble light of a lantern, admiring it. 'Very pretty. Very pretty indeed. You see, I *know* about the ring, Frannie my love!'

Clovis Carter-Smith peeled off his mask. Grey hair was streaked across a perspiring forehead. 'Hot as hell, but worth the effort,' he gloated.

As Frannie opened her mouth to scream he produced a gun from the inside pocket of his shapeless, baggy jacket. Pointing at her, he said, 'I doubt if anyone would hear you with all that racket outside, but keep quiet anyway. If you scream now I'll cut it short with a bullet.' He placed the ring carefully on a stained plastic coffee table, grinning. 'But it would be such a shame to spoil the fun, don't you agree?'

Shivering with fright, Frannie shrank back into the chair as Carter-Smith put the gun next to the ring and removed his jacket. He released the two pairs of straps which, buckled over his chest, secured the hump on his back. 'That's better,' grunted the financier as the contraption hit the floor. Dolores and the Zombie sat down, and Dolores began to roll a particularly fat joint.

'What – what have you done with Matilda?' Frannie managed.

At that moment, below them, Matilda was emerging from a bathroom into a bedroom much darker than when she had left it. As she made to put back her cat's head, a heavy hand with a butterfly tattoo latched onto her forearm. She started to scream and the back of the other hand was cracked around her face, splitting her lip at the corner. A wave of dizziness engulfed her.

'No sound, please,' hissed the sweatshirted man. He snatched away her glasses. 'Take off the suit.'

Gooseflesh rising all over her arms and back, whimpering in fear, Matilda fumbled off the cat suit. Totally blind in the near darkness, she licked the blood which ran from her split lip, her head reeling but not allowing her the mercy of unconsciousness.

As she stood trembling in her bra and knickers, her assailant wrapped a strip of heavy rag around her mouth, pulled it tight and knotted it behind her head. Without speaking he began winding wide, sticky tape around and around her quivering flesh, the ripping sound it made as he tore it from the roll as loud as the music from the bar, across the street where Gregory was at that moment sipping iced lager.

Ignoring Frannie's question, Carter-Smith took a long toke from Dolores' joint and perched on the arm of Frannie's chair. He let the smoke dribble slowly through his hairy nostrils. 'Defenseless and at my mercy at last, your ladyship,' he said, immensely satisfied. 'I wondered how it was that your demise in Marrakech was so opportunely thwarted by your chauffeur. I wondered a lot about that. My man was a practised killer, he would hardly have allowed you the grace of a telephone call. Money, Frannie, and who should know better than you, is at least as important a tool in Morocco as it is in the rest of the world. A simple call to your one-time guide, Salah, via the Mamounia, a telex transfer of funds with the promise of more when he found out what I wanted to know . . . Gregory – that *is* his name, isn't it? – *Gregory* deemed it necessary as a part of his defense to demonstrate your ingenious little system to the Marrakech policemen. Salah, naturally, had little difficulty in getting hold of this information.' 'He smiled triumphantly at the ring where it glinted in the yellow light on the table, next to the gun. 'Pretty. Very pretty. But now quite useless.'

'Look – I abso*lute*ly won't chase after you any more. You have my word.' Frannie tried vainly.

'What – let you *go*?' Carter-Smith laughed. 'After all my trouble? And spoil what promises to be a fantastically amusing night? You must be *joking*, my dear.' Dolores, by his side, was holding out two fingers. He slipped the joint between them and, taking the Zombie by the hand, she led her across to the bed. 'My gorgeous *vampires* are about to warm up, Frannie,' the financier went on. 'By the way, the dead one's known as Sangria.' He fiddled with the radio until strains of Bach filled the room. Through her fear Frannie saw the two women lie down on the bed and fill their lungs with smoke from the joint before mashing their painted lips together.

Vampires? Fright crept icily over Frannie's heart. It was only fancy dress. *Wasn't* it?

There is no time for further morbid speculation as Carter-Smith yanks her to her feet. 'Strip off,' he sneers. 'We will all appreciate your naked charms.' He jerks a finger at the pins which have been holding her hair up under the topper. 'Let this down.'

She shakes her head vigorously. 'No, no. I won't. I refuse.' Sighing, Carter-Smith takes her little finger in both hands and bends it back.

'I'll break it. And the rest, if need be.'

As she observes this scene, Dolores removes her plastic fangs. Then she reaches for Sangria and the two women embrace, their hands groping beneath each other's clothes. Frannie intakes her breath sharply in pain as Carter-Smith increases the pressure and her finger threatens to snap. 'All *right* for God's sake.'

Slowly, she removes her evening wear then, in just her knickers, lets down her hair. From the corner of her eye she judges the distance to the table. Clovis Carter-Smith's bulky frame blocks the way to the gun. And the ring.

'The panties. *Off*.' His eyes gleam as she drops them and kicks her feet free. 'Go and show yourself properly to the ladies. And forget about any heroics.'

Her whole being brimming with fear, Frannie approaches the bed, the financier's rapacious stare abusing her perfectly moulded bottom. Sangria, her nightdress unbuttoned all the way down, has green rouged nipples. She offers the joint, now three-quarters consumed, Frannie shakes her head in mute refusal. Fighting off panic, sweat beading her upper lip although the room is cool, she notices that Sangria's throat is covered with a wisp of silk. Following Frannie's eyes, Dolores grins, not afraid to crack her make-up now, her painted features twisting horribly. She reaches out and touches Frannie's thigh with the backs of her fingers, caresses them upwards as the flesh shrinks.

'You've been wondering, as everyone does, about my neck.' Dolores's grin is fixed as she speaks. 'Look.' Undoing a tiny bow which holds together the points of her cloak collar, she unhooks the collar at the throat. Frannie starts back in horror.

All over both sides of Dolores's neck are a mass of swollen, purple welts. She gazes into Frannie's wide-staring eyes. 'Teeth,' she says. 'Bites which nip and open the veins. *Real* love bites.'

'And me.' Zombie Sangria strips the silk from her neck. There is the same awful revelation, a pathetic, dreadful sight. 'Blood,' she says casually, a marrow – chilling smile on her green lips. 'We drink each other's blood. Those who know call us the Vampires.' Her pale grey eyes sweep Frannie's curves voraciously and come to loving rest on her neck. Frannie's hands leap protectively around it as a shudder runs through her and the tiny blond hairs down her spine stand on end.

'Occasionally,' says Dolores. 'Unfortunately it's only on terribly rare occasions that we get the chance for a variation in our diet.' She licks her lips. 'I've been saving you up!'

Numbed with shock, hands wrapped around her slender neck, Frannie sways above these two freaks as Dolores, curving her body over Sangria, searches the bruised and puffy flesh with the tips of her nails then dips her head and nips. Taking a long, deep toke Sangria finishes the joint, her eyes glazing completely as Dolores draws blood with a sound like a sucking kiss.

Vaguely aware that Carter-Smith is in the process of removing his trousers, Frannie summons enough courage to attempt an escape from this nightmare but Carter-Smith is too quick for her. As she turns and rushes for the coffee table he grabs her around the waist, tripping in his half-mast trousers and bringing them both crashing to the floorboards.

His bulk rolling on top of her knocks all the wind from Frannie's body. She can only lie still under him, gasping, close to vomiting as he kicks free his trousers. 'Not very bright of you,' he pants. 'I'm afraid you'll have to be restrained.'

Clambering to his feet he pulls Frannie, still fighting for oxygen, to hers. His eyes dart over the room and alight on the bed where the two women are locked in their vampiric embrace unaware of this little drama. Hauling Frannie effortlessly over to them he slides the satin cord of Sangria's nightdress out from under her.

Barely a minute later Frannie, her hands securely tied behind her to the iron bedhead, is squatting helplessly next to Sangria.

'So, Lady Ballington,' Carter-Smith rasps, his great, slack belly drooping over the top of outsized Y-fronts. 'No more stupidity.' His eyes eagerly assault her. 'Nicely accessible . . . to all of us!'

Dolores lifts her face from Sangria's throat, blood smeared into the smudged paint on either side of her mouth, her grin exposing stained red teeth. 'Look, darling,' she breathes, a hand brushing Sangria's emerald eyelids which flicker open drowsily. 'How stunningly beautiful our bedmate is.'

'So lovely and clean. Not a mark, no blemish,' sighs Sangria, reaching for Frannie's neck. '*Virginal!*' Frannie shrinks away, unable to escape Sangria's oh-so-gentle and admiring touch with its fearful implication.

'Clovis first.' Dolores' hand finds the top of Frannie's thigh as Sangria's steals to her breast. Defeated, waves of nausea surging through her, Frannie closes her eyes tight. 'A little *show* for us, perhaps, Clovis . . . ?' Dolores' hand dives deep between Frannie's warm, shut thighs, nails scratching, the side of the index finger digging up at her pussy lips. 'An *appetiser* before the main meal. A little *sodomy*, perhaps? She has the most fantastic *bottom*.'

Frannie's eyes stay as firmly closed as her legs, saving her the sight of Carter-Smith's lips beginning to drool and insanity surfacing in his expression as he steps out of his Y-fronts. Under the sagging belly his big penis is already half-erect. He makes a fist around it and jerks. 'Open your *eyes*, Frannie,' he insists. With his free hand he grasps her little finger. '*Watch* me, or so help me I'll break it.' The finger bending backwards under pressure brings a twitch of pain and her eyes open reluctantly.

'That's *better*. You do everything you're told to, Frannie. *Everything*, without question or struggle, from now on.' He jerks on. 'Snapping fingers is not one of my particular pleasures, but I *might* grow to like it.' Dropping the hand he moves a pace closer, masturbating steadily, almost at full erection. 'You *like* it, mmm? You like my *dick*, my lady?'

'For Christ's sake!' Frannie mutters.

'Let me tell you what's in store for you. Unhappily for *you*, I've decided not to kill you. I failed once and it's perhaps unnecessary. You're going to get a lesson you will *never* forget. A terrible lesson. They'll drink a pint, maybe two, of your blood. Perhaps more. *Is* it really blue, by the way? Soon, we'll find out. When you've recovered you will never, ever, *dare* to get on my BACK again.' He leers at Dolores, takes a step closer, lets go of his nearly erect organ. 'Why not suck it a bit, Dolores? Get it good and hard for Frannie's bum? I'd have her do it, but she might well bite!'

Spared the disgust of having Carter-Smith's cock thrust in her mouth, Frannie, so scared that she can hardly draw breath, watches dully as Dolores kneels on all fours across her and fellates with gusto, bringing him quickly to a full hard-on. The radio incongruously crackles out a Viennese Waltz. Sangria, a fresh joint between her lips and a misty, enrapt expression in her grey eyes looks on, playing with herself with one hand, the fingers, working lazily amidst green-dyed pubic hair, and mauling Frannie's breasts with the other.

'Turn sideways, Frannie.' Carter-Smith's voice has plunged an octave.

Frannie does nothing, the financier's hand lashes out, cracks across her cheek. 'Turn *around*, *cunt*. *Do* it.' She does so, awkwardly, hands tugging against the knotted satin, until she is doubled on her side on the bed.

'Ahhh!' He fondles her rump with both hands. 'Indeed a superb piece of arse!'

'Wait.' From Dolores, who unmouths him, climbs off the bed and goes to her bag. 'Here.' She unstoppers a bottle of baby oil. 'Let me. No sense ripping her with that mammoth dong of yours. Save the blood for later.' She drops to her knees by the side of the bed, pours oil onto her fingers and smothers Frannie's tiny hole with it, working two fingers up there as Frannie wriggles and squirms. 'Now. Just a *little* foretaste of *this* before your buggering,' Frannie hears and, with the Blue Danube lilting loudly from the radio, she screeches and tries to roll away as Dolores' teeth nip into her buttock flesh.

Again, Carter-Smith seizes that little finger. 'Keep *still*, bitch!' And she does, tensing as the teeth painfully break through and Dolores greedily sucks as if extracting a splinter.

Not more than fifty yards away as the crow flies, Gregory slumps on a bar stool surrounded by boisterous drunks. He is close to the open doors, his eyes on the house across the street as he steadily sips his cold San Miguel lager. Gregory is just a little puzzled because within those walls there is supposed to be a carnival night party in full swing, yet nobody has entered or left since the arrival of Frannie and company. Also, except for a first floor window, its shutters fractionally ajar, there is no evidence of light in the house. He is not particularly suspicious, closed shutters disguise everything inside, but he is on his guard. Gregory is ready to spring into action at the very first note of a bleep.

He finishes his beer, orders another.

Dolores has indulged herself in just a little of Frannie's buttock blood. It has perhaps not the richness of direct vein blood, she mutters. But as a *hors d'oeuvres* it is delicious. She lubricates Carter-Smith's impatient member with baby oil and stretches apart the cheeks of Frannie's rear end as the salivating, grunting financier eases it in.

She feels little pain, not to be compared with the smarting from Dolores' bite. There is no pleasure in an act which, on other occasions, has made her almost swoon with enjoyment. Rape again. The awesome fear of what is to follow. Frannie lies unprotesting, achingly uncomfortable, hopeless to prevent this forceful sodomy, pained eyes on Sangria. Above her the green-faced, green-nippled, stoned Zombie kneels, the better to watch this violent act, rubbing her green-bushed clitoris with tireless devotion.

Carter-Smith is mercifully, quick. He comes with a great, shouted heave, his shuddering belly enveloping Frannie's behind as his seed floods into it and his hands wrench so hard at her shoulders that they threaten to break them.

Sangria comes too, with the tiniest, whimpered moan. As Carter-Smith's convulsions, Frannie still fully impaled, begin to lessen, Sangria takes a lung-filling drag at her joint, holds it in for seconds, lets it out slowly. The Blue Danube changes to the Emperor Waltz and she begins to hum along with the music. Getting off the bed she sways dizzily to the radio, turns up the volume.

Clovis Carter-Smith slides to his knees on the floor. Dolores, scrambling back on the bed, helps Frannie into a sitting position. 'Did you *like* that, Frannie?' she coos. 'Did you *like it*? *I* thought it was fantastic.' Her eyes alive with green fire, make-up smeared around her lips and cheeks and mingled with blood, her contorted face is a horror story. She focuses on Frannie's neck, closing in, leering, licking her lips. As Carter-Smith pulls himself heavily to his feet she spreads her fingers on either side of Frannie's neck and begins to dip her head.

Frannie is frantic. 'No,no, no, no, *no*!' she cries jerking her head from side to side, hair flinging across her shoulders as the utterly stoned Sangria begins to waltz around the room, singing.

On his feet, now slowly recovering from his orgasm, Carter-Smith entwines thick strands of Frannie's hair around his meaty fists and drags her head backwards over the bedrail until she is unable to move it. Her neck is stretched taut, white and vulnerable. 'Drink, Dolores,' he hisses.

Frannie, immobile except for her kicking legs which Dolores promptly kneels on, feels vampire breath at her throat.

The teeth close in.

Whirling past the coffee table, open nightdress floating around her naked body, the glassy-eyed Sangria fuzzily snatches the emerald ring. Holding it between thumb and finger of either hand she sings to it to the rhythm of the waltz. '*Pretty* ring, *pretty* ring, *pretty* ring, *pretty* ring . . . .'

Dolores' teeth find a fat little vein and sink in as Carter-Smith notices Sangria and, seconds later, realises exactly what she is doing. With a bellow he lets go of Frannie's hair and Frannie, neck dripping blood, wrenches away from Dolores' mouth. Bounding at Sangria he makes a grab at the ring and, finding this great fun, Sangria swings it, still in both hands, up above her head.

And in doing so, twists the emerald.

Having wrested the ring away from Sangria, Carter-Smith could not be certain, whether it had been activated or not. Seconds later, hearing a crash from below as Gregory burst through the front doors, he was no longer in doubt. Dismayed, he picked up the gun.

In trying to stop the adrenaline-charged mountain which was Gregory, the man in the sweatshirt was smashed to the ground, his face mashed into the wooden floor as Gregory used the back of his head as a springboard for the stairs.

Carter-Smith heard the crash of the door downstairs. His hand trembled perceptibly as he pointed the gun.

As the door splintered inwards beneath Gregory's furious assault Carter-Smith's first bullet missed. The second hit Gregory full in the shoulder. But in such a mood, summoned to protect his master's wife, the bodyguard was unstoppable. He swarmed over the naked financier, knocking the gun from his fist, cracking his forearm in the act, kneed him in the groin with enough power to sexually disable him for life and felled him with a knockout rabbit punch.

Clutching his shoulder, Gregory spun away from the pole-axed Carter-Smith. His eyes swept over the weird, frozen scene, missing nothing. The grotesque freaks, Dolores and Sangria, were huddled together on the bed, Sangria hysterically laughing. Frannie, with blood streaming from the severed vein in her neck, was shaking with relief.

Tearing a strip of material from Sangria's nightdress Gregory bunched it into Frannie's wound and, pressing tight, threw a threatening glance at Dolores. 'Untie her.'

With Frannie now free, decently covered and her throat roughly bound, Dolores morosely silent, Sangria's laughter reduced to intermittent giggles and Carter-Smith coming around with a groan, Gregory muttered. 'Odd sort of party, this, was it not?'

Frannie blinked at him. 'Rather,' she said.

Gregory hooked a boot under the financier's belly and heaved him over onto his back. 'Let me guess,' he said. 'Carter-Smith?'

Frannie nodded.

'Well, we've got 'im then, haven't we?' He shook his head in disbelief, once more looking around the room as the financier stared up at him in loathing. 'Not *quite* according to plan, though, was it? Funny old world, when you stop to think about it.'

18

AFTER THE BALL . . .

IT WAS A DELICATE OPERATION, BUT PROVIDENCE was on the side of my Gregory and his macho boys. Clovis Carter-Smith is six three and around seventeen stone, not a lump to be easily hidden and secretly hauled almost a third of the way around the globe. Sedated, he was taken from the house of horrors in Caracas to the one I had rented on Lago Valencia. My hookers were not needed after all. A pity, it would have saved me unbelievable terror had my plan worked out, but that's life, I suppose. They insisted on full payment nevertheless.

From Lago Valencia Carter-Smith was man-handled onto the Lear at Puerto Cabello, a success achieved not without considerable bribery. And there he remained, through the several refuelling stops until his presence, and the fact that there was a warrant for his arrest, was revealed at Heathrow Airport.

Matilda and I stayed on in Caracas for a few days to give us both time to recover from our ordeal. If anything, Matilda was worse off than me. Her nerves were in tatters from the experience of being left tightly trussed, so tightly that the circulation in her arms and legs had been cut off, in the dark on a rough wooden floor, a corner of her mouth badly cut and all that side of her face swollen. She was in such a state, poor love, that even four days later the prospect of yet another flight made her almost speechless with fright. Electing to be unusually kind to her I booked her passage to England on a cruise ship whilst I flew scheduled airlines – one of the rare occasions I have done so since my marriage to Victor.

Incredibly, human vampires *do* exist. They don't turn into bats and fly in and out of bedroom windows at night to suck their victims' blood, neither do they sleep all day in coffins, but they do take a perverse sexual satisfaction from drinking life's most precious liquid.

I solemnly swear I did not dream up the account of vampirism you have just been reading, neither did I invent it to provide a sensational end to this story of my travels. As Shakespeare had Hamlet say, 'There are more things in heaven and earth, Horatio, Than are dreamt of in your philosophy.'

Vampires exist all right, I had the bite marks to prove it, albeit the scars have now faded. Whilst confessing a more than usually healthy appetite for most of the delights sex has to offer, including a little bondage and mild castigation, I detest anything which violently oversteps those limits; I cannot remember ever being more nauseated than when that vile creature's teeth cut into my neck.

It was an eventful odyssey. Describing it in writing has proved, as on the first occasion when I produced *Frannie*, almost as arousing as when it was taking place. It was as if I were living through it all over again – and that includes the nasty as well as the wonderful. My flesh has crawled a lot, but in consolation I have found myself turned on time after time whilst working here at my typewriter. I am not ashamed to admit to having paused many times during the past four months work, so enflamed

that I have found the need to masturbate irresistible.

There is little more to record. Victor and I have
together thoroughly enjoyed those videos I succeeded
in shooting, limited as they were to the Welsh stud in
Spain, the Arab sandwich in Marrakech, and a rather
super little sequence of Californian Lee and myself
going through remarkably athletic sexual contortions
in his caravan. His lordship is mightily pleased with
these unique additions to his Blue Room collection.

Naturally, I kept him to his promise of my special reward should I be instrumental in the capture of Clovis
Carter-Smith. He hired me two lithe, black studs for a
night and joined in the fun and games himself with
consummate enthusiasm – but that's another story.

Why do I bother, you may ask, to commit my experiences to paper when patently I have no need of the
money? It's a silly thing, really. I have discovered
within myself a deep-rooted desire to turn on the
entire world. Whilst, of course I do realise the utter
impossibility of this endeavour I am determined to do
what I can, to bring to as many people as possible the
harmless pleasures of vicarious sex.

Did it work for you? I sincerely hope so.

Au revoir.